MIDNIGHT VISITORS

I was just too sleepy to think. I was beginning to get ready for bed when I heard a knock on my door. I looked at my watch. It was late. I shouted through the door, cane in hand.

"Who is it?"

"Oralia and Vick!" came the return shout.

I grabbed my cane in my right hand, holding it securely aloft, in preparation for mayhem. And with my left hand, I opened the door. I just couldn't think of a plausible reason not to open it, besides "I don't open my door late at night to people I think might be murderers." I wondered if there were statistics on the number of people who had died for the sake of politeness. But by then my door was open, and I saw Vick and Oralia. They didn't look like murderers—they looked scared.

"You have to find out what happened to Seeger Snell," she pronounced.

Her voice was firm and clear, but lacking the serenity it had in the group. I almost laughed. *Right. Someone else who thought I held the answer to Seeger Snell's death.*

"Oralia has me convinced that if we don't put Seeger Snell's death to rest, no one will come to our future seminars," Vick murmured.

He sounded embarrassed. Was he ashamed to be at my door again? Or ashamed of Seeger's death?

$\mathcal{B}$ODY *of* $\mathcal{I}$NTUITION

CLAIRE DANIELS

BERKLEY PRIME CRIME, NEW YORK

BODY OF INTUITION

A Berkley Prime Crime Book / published by arrangement with the author

PRINTING HISTORY
Berkley Prime Crime mass-market edition / December 2002

Copyright © 2002 by Jaqueline Girdner.
Cover art by One By Two.
Cover design by Erika Fusari.
Text design by Julie Rogers.

Visit our website at
www.penguinputnam.com

ISBN: 0-425-18740-3

Berkley Prime Crime Books are published by The Berkley Publishing Group, a division of Penguin Putnam Inc., 375 Hudson Street, New York, New York 10014.
The name BERKLEY PRIME CRIME and the BERKLEY PRIME CRIME design are trademarks belonging to Penguin Putnam Inc.

PRINTED IN THE UNITED STATES OF AMERICA

10 9 8 7 6 5 4 3 2 1

To Greg Booi,
With love from the center of my energy field
to its farthest reaches.

ACKNOWLEDGMENTS

My eternal gratitude to Marilyn King for sharing her expertise on tantra groups, Dr. Anna Vertkin for giving me murderous ideas (any medical errors are strictly my own), and Lynne Murray for listening to it all.

CAST OF CHARACTERS

Cally Lazar: A medical intuitive and recovering attorney whose intuition screams murder. She's the youngest sister of the Lazar clan.

Geneva, Melinda, Arnot, and York Lazar: Cally's over-protective siblings in order of age, though not necessarily in order of maturity.

Warren Kapp: Cally's octogenarian cane-fu sparring partner, attorney, and know-it-all-in-chief.

Dee-Dee Lee: Cally's comrade in intuition, a hypnotherapist.

Ben Remington: Dee-Dee's honey, a body movement repatterner.

Oscar Suiza: Cally's fellow energy worker, he can talk to your body directly, really!

Joan Hussein: Cally's attorney friend, prerecovery vintage.

Roy Beaumont: The man Cally loves, only he's afraid of the "dark forces" . . . and afraid of a relationship with Cally.

Trica (Patricia) Snell: A grieving widow and Cally's client.

Seeger Snell: Trica's deceased husband, former entrepreneur and lady's-man-about-town.

Don and Mary Snell: Seeger's strangely discordant parents.

Oralia Quennelle: One of the leaders of the "Love Workshop," where Trica was widowed.

Vick (Victor) Usher: The other workshop leader.

Linda Frey: Grieving workshop member, though not a widow.

Eddy Hilton: Linda's escort, a whiner—not a winner.

Aileen Meyer: Seeger's business partner and workshop reveler.

Harley Isaacs: Aileen's sullen, bagpiping workshop squire.

Rhoda Neruda: Keeper of The Inn at Fiebre, where the fatal workshops are held.

Wiz (William) Neruda: Rhoda's precocious son.

Phyllys Nesbitt: Rhoda's partner in life and in work.

Dulcie Le Fevre: The inn's punk kitchen help.

Chief Deborah Dahl: Chief of the Fiebre Police Department and aunt to Dulcie.

Sergeant Zoffany: Chief Dahl's dangerously loyal sergeant.

Officers Yukawa, Walras, and Xavier of the Fiebre Police Department.

ONE

"Like tantra, you know?" the lush blond woman on my massage table said, her voice high and girlish. Too girlish for thirty. I'm thirty-five myself, so I figured I ought to know.

I shook my head without speaking. I was running my hands lightly around the edges of her body, trying to get a sense of her energy field—and reminding myself not to be so critical. There was value in this woman, sweetness in her lusty innocence.

"You know, tantra is sacred sexuality," she insisted.

I nodded, a light clicking on in my brain somewhere. Tantra, right. The Tibetan Buddhists might have a problem with her definition, but here in Glasse County, California, tantra was sacred sexuality.

"So the people that are, you know, really into tantra, are tantricas."

"Uh-huh," I muttered. This woman had come to me because her husband had committed suicide at an intimacy workshop a couple of weeks before. But her aura wasn't the color I'd expect from a grieving widow. No blue or green of mourning or loss. Not that everyone's auras are the same, mind you. But she didn't feel sad either. She felt afraid. And the color I saw radiating from her center was a sickly yellow.

"So instead of Patricia, I go by Trica," she finished up,

blinking blue eyes in an animated face. "Trica like tantrica, get it?"

"Got it," I answered. Criminy, she liked to talk.

"So why are you Cally?" she asked.

"Cally's short for Calypso," I answered and placed my hand on the top of her head, feeling the surprising softness of her blond curls. "Calypso Lazar."

"Your parents named you Calypso?" she asked in surprise. I recognized the surprise in her voice easily. I've heard it almost every time I've introduced myself formally from my first-grade teacher on.

"They named me after the sea nymph who kept Odysseus captive, not Harry Belafonte or Jacques Cousteau's boat," I explained briefly. The Lazars are a little different. We even have our own curse words. I'd tried to conform to more common standards at one time, but the Lazar in me always won out. So here I was, seeking auric clues, with a talkative tantrica on my massage table.

"Cool!" she squeaked.

This was not going the way my sessions usually went. I'm an energy worker, and I don't mean for a utilities company. Some people call me a medical intuitive, but I try to keep the word *medical* out of my own description. It's too close to *legal,* and I'm a recovering attorney. I even go to a twelve-step program to ensure I never practice law again. Once I quit law, I started doing massage for a living full time, your basic Swedish/Esalen massage. And as I was doing massage, I began to see things, auras mostly. And I began to feel the energy flows in the body. Some of the auras seemed wrong to me, some of the energy flows seemed blocked, and it bugged me. So I started playing around, maybe taking a massive red blob of color around the liver and imagining it transforming into crystalline light, or imagining energy flowing through the arms and out the fingertips where it had been blocked.

And my clients started feeling better. It was wonderful, but it was scary, too. In fact, it scared me into learning more about what I was doing. I ended up taking as many classes on alternative healing as I could absorb. And I kept seeing, and feeling, and people kept getting better. At least most people. Metaphysics doesn't work for everyone.

And Trica was just a tiny bit difficult. Keerups, she was more than a tiny bit difficult. First off, she had no real presenting issue. She just told me that her husband had committed suicide, and she needed some help. She wasn't sick physically. She wasn't even crying. And she wouldn't stop talking. She was a five-year-old in a thirty-year-old's body. And with that thought, even the glimpse of yellow in her aura disappeared from my perception. I tried to breathe in light and get my center back.

"Why did you use a cane to walk in here?" Trica demanded. I stroked her hair impulsively. Maybe I was right about her inner age, despite all the evident femininity rolled into her size-eighteen body.

"I have a weak leg," I told her. "Sometimes it buckles."

"But you're not using the cane now," she accused.

"No, I don't seem to need it when I'm focused on my clients," I told her.

I didn't tell her that my leg had been weak since my parents had been killed in an explosion when I was fifteen. Actually, my leg had buckled *before* I heard about the explosion, which was even stranger. Healer, heal thyself, right? But my fellow healers had convinced me that it was okay to have an occasionally weak leg, a memorial to my parents' death, and besides, it was getting stronger all the time. And, best of all, the weak leg allowed me to use a cane. Not very many people understand that a cane is a great weapon, but my brother York is a creative martial artist who has taught me the delights of what we chris-

tened "cane-fu." With cane in hand, I was Jackie Chan.
As long as I had my glasses on, too.

"The guys at the intimacy workshop are always going
on about focus," Trica told me. "But I have a hard time
focusing, do you believe it?"

I kept the smile off my face. Yep, I believed it. "Anyway, all that intimacy stuff is really tantra. They're just
afraid people will think they're into orgies or something,
like some of the other tantra groups."

"But they aren't?" I asked, not really sure for all of
Trica's verbiage just what had gone on when her husband
had committed suicide. Orgies? Intimacy with illegal
drugs? Listening too long to Trica?

"Oh, no, the group wasn't into orgies," Trica assured
me, shaking her head sadly. "Seeger, you know, my husband, or um . . . whatever he is now, he just wanted to
have fun, you know. He always complained that he
worked too hard at The Sensual Body, you know, the shop
that he and Aileen owned. But Aileen did most of the
work anyway. Seeger was thinking of opening a winery.
I guess he won't now, huh?"

"No, I guess not," I said seriously. I put my hands on
Trica's temples. There was something endearing about
Trica. I can find a core of goodness in most people I work
on, and I was finding hers now.

"You've got a nice house," Trica offered. "It's like . . .
um . . ."

"Little," I helped her, smiling.

"No, not just little." Trica's eyes widened. "It's so cute,
you know, like a dollhouse. I love the latticed deck and
all the flowers. And your goats are so cool. What were
their names again?"

"Moscow, Persia, and Ohio," I answered. I saw the yellow field again, now emanating from Trica's feet, and felt

a strange tension in Trica's temples, almost as if it wasn't hers.

"Where's your cat?" she asked suddenly.

I looked around. Leona was gone, which was strange. It was usually all I could do to keep her claws off the massage table.

"Maybe she's playing with the goats," I whispered.

Trica giggled, and the yellow dimmed.

I was beginning to get a handle on Trica's energy. She was frightened. The girlishness was part of it. But still, there was something else at odds with the rest of her energy field.

Then I saw it. An orange blob hovering at her shoulder. I yanked my hands back, startled.

"Seeger would have liked you," Trica went on. She sighed softly. "You're skinny."

I breathed in again and didn't argue. Size acceptance is a two-way street. I loved the beauty of queen-sized women, like my friend Joan, and the grace of my 300-plus-pound friend, Ben. And I wasn't really skinny. Like all Lazars, I was small, dark-haired, and fair-skinned, with features sharp enough to cut paper. It's those gaunt features that make people think we Lazars are skinny. They're in our genes. I guess the silly curse words are, too.

"I like your braid," Trica kept on in a small voice. Was she afraid she'd offended me? "It's really long."

I looked down at Trica and wondered if Seeger had made her feel unlovely as a large woman. Of course he had.

"Trica, you know skinny ain't all it's cracked up to be," I told her. She grabbed *my* hand now. "You are really beautiful," I told her honestly. At exactly five feet tall, Trica was a pint-sized goddess, bursting with beauty. Anyone would be crazy not to see it.

"Thanks, Cally," she whispered. Then she laughed. "Is your braid like a goat's tail?" she asked. I laughed with her, even though my goat's short little tails couldn't have competed with my braid.

I put my hand on Trica's shoulder and saw the yellow field shimmering. I sensed cold somewhere nearby and felt a wash of new understanding. Trica needed protection. I was sure of it. But what did she need protection from?

"Trica—" I began.

"You know, Seeger just smiled at me that day from the balcony, then he climbed on the railing, waved, and dived, like it was a pool or something."

I squeezed her shoulder a little tighter as the hairs went up on the back of my neck.

And suddenly, I felt myself falling. For a moment, I thought my leg had buckled, but, no, I was hurtling head-first toward nonexistent terra-cotta tile. Endlessly. I wanted to scream . . . and then I heard the voice.

"Tell her I didn't commit suicide," it said. "I was murdered."

TWO

"Murdered?" I asked, and suddenly I wasn't falling anymore. I steadied myself on the edge of the massage table, still trembling. "Son of a lizard, murdered," I repeated, oblivious to everything but the fact that I'd heard a voice I shouldn't have. I didn't hear voices in my head. I was clairvoyant, not clairaudient.

But before I could wrap my mind around what had happened, there was an earthquake on the massage table. Trica jumped up and threw her damp arms around my neck, almost taking me down in the process.

"Murdered! I knew it!" she screamed full blast into my stunned face. Criminy, I wanted my cane, but I wasn't going to find it with Trica dangling off of me.

"I knew Seeger couldn't kill himself. I knew it! But that lady in charge of the police convinced me—"

"Trica," I choked out as calmingly as possible. "Can you let go of me and get back on the table?"

"Oh, yeah, right," she mumbled, pausing midrant to take her arms from my neck and sit back on the massage table. I panted and pictured a centering line running from the end of my spine down to the core of the earth. I could stand again. And of course, Trica didn't need any help speaking again.

"Cally, they lied to me, those cops," she told me. She looked down at her dangling feet. "They said he committed suicide. They said I oughta get the funeral over real quick like and spare myself . . . um . . . something or other." She raised her head suddenly. "Damn, I had him cremated, Cally! Cremated. There's nothing left of him and—"

"Shhhh," I whispered and stroked her hair.

I needed to calm Trica down. Her aura was yellow and pulsating now. Even her skin was yellow. And she was hyperventilating. She was terrified. At least now, I knew my energetic task.

"Lie back down, and we'll talk," I suggested, imagining the yellow turning into a fountain of flowing clear light, draining away from her. Once she was lying down again, I touched the outside base of the cuticles of her two smallest toes, drawing the fear down and feeling it dissipate. Slowly, Trica relaxed. When she spoke again, her voice was quiet but determined.

"Cally, my husband wasn't so cool all the time, but nobody should have murdered him," she declared.

I nodded and finished my work. And I wasn't just nodding to comfort her. Nobody *should* have murdered her husband. She was right. It was time for a heart-to-heart talk.

Two hours later, Trica had told me everything she remembered about her husband's death, *and* she had talked me into infiltrating the ongoing intimacy workshop where Seeger Snell had died. Because she was still afraid. And as far as I was concerned, she had reason to be. I'd heard the voice. Don't get me wrong. I don't believe in evil. Desperation, self-absorption, confusion. Those are things that I believe in. And much as I didn't hear voices, I believed I might have heard Seeger Snell's voice. And if I had, he'd been murdered. I didn't want Trica to be next. Besides, heal her, and then let her be killed? No way. So the third time Trica begged me to come to the group's next workshop and find out who had killed her husband, I agreed.

It wasn't until she was gone that I thought about the implications of my promise. And then I thought about something else. Seeger was as weird a first name as Calypso.

The following Thursday evening, I was driving my Honda down to The Inn at Fiebre with my friend Warren Kapp in the passenger's seat. Yes, *the* Warren Kapp, the attorney who made Glasse County famous with his courtroom shenanigans, *the* Warren "call me Kapp" who was connected to everyone from city hall to the White House. He'd even been in *Newsweek*. At eighty, he was still a vital man, his hair combed over his balding spot and steel-rimmed glasses pulled over his bulldog face. A bulldog complete with jowls, petulant lips, and a Roman nose. And a heavy dose of aftershave.

I rotated my head, easing the soreness in my shoulders. It had been a long drive. We were skirting the ocean now, and the waves shimmered with colors of rolling chaos beneath seagulls and pelicans in perfect formation. We passed farms, too: Brussels sprouts, squash, and flowers.

"Got the names of all the people who were at the last workshop," Kapp rapped out. "Leaders: Oralia Quennelle and Vick Usher. Participants: Seeger Snell—"

"The dead guy."

"Trica Snell—"

"His wife."

He glared at me. This was a one-man show, Kapp's show. When he wasn't jabbing me with his cane (he carried one, too), he was bossing me around, but I still liked him. Actually, Kapp risked becoming a stereotype—a little like a hooker with a heart of gold. Only in his case, he was a ruthless attorney in the courtroom who was a soft touch outside of the boundaries of his practice of law. He was a good man as far as I was concerned. Of course, I'd never been up against him in court.

"Then there was Seeger's ex-business partner, Aileen Meyer; her loverboy, Harley Isaacs; and a couple of others, Linda Frey and Eddy Hilton," he continued once he was sure he had his audience back.

"How do you know all that?" I asked. I didn't mention that I'd already gleaned the same information from Trica.

He grinned.

"Private informants," he bragged. "I got 'em in government, law enforcement, computer hackers, you name it. I can find out anything."

"Right," I challenged. "Betcha you can't tell me the color of my aura."

He laughed, loud and hearty.

"You got me there," he admitted. But someday, maybe . . ." His eyes went out of focus.

"Maybe?" I prodded.

"Never mind," he said gruffly, focus back in his eyes.

"Owners of The Inn at Fiebre are a couple of . . ."

"Lesbians," I helped him out.

"That word still okay?" he asked me. Kapp hated to be behind on anything politically correct.

I nodded. It seemed fine to me.

"So, two lesbians own the inn where the incident took place: Rhoda Neruda and Phyllys Nesbitt. Also present were the kitchen help, Dulcie Le Fevre, and Ms. Neruda's ten-year-old son William, usually called Wiz."

He was one up on me there. I hadn't known about the kitchen help. But that wasn't the kind of thing Trica would notice. Kapp, however, didn't miss anything.

I'd first met Kapp when sneaking some cuttings of roses from his yard. He streaked out of his house, waving his cane, and roared, "Do you know who I am?" And I did. He was Warren Kapp of civil and criminal litigation fame. He'd sued just about anyone on two legs, and it looked like it was my turn next. He brought up his cane to point at me. I knocked it out of his hand with my own cane and explained that the cuttings would actually help his roses since they were overgrown and needed dead-heading anyway. We'd been friends ever since. Now I called him Kapp, at least when I could get a word in edgewise.

"Chief of police is a woman, Dahl. Calling it a suicide."

"What if it is?" I wondered aloud, uncertain now that a few days had passed since I'd heard the voice.

"Nah, I don't buy it. Lots of police just don't like murders in their jurisdictions. Takes too much money to investigate and gives the town a bad name. They always cover up if they can."

My jaw fell open.

"I could tell you stories," he said and proceeded to demonstrate for the next half hour.

I listened, glancing at the shimmering blues and grays and greens of the ocean as Kapp filled me in on corruption in the specific. I had hoped Kapp might be my Watson on this case, but it was looking like he might be my Holmes instead.

Of course, that's why I'd invited him. And then, there was my friend, Dee-Dee Lee, the hypnotherapist. She'd insisted on coming to the weekend workshop, too. It's hard to resist when a hypnotherapist wants something, let me tell you. And Dee-Dee was a dynamo of a woman, a mixture of Asian, Irish, and tornado ancestry with a will of iron. She was meeting us at the inn. She'd insisted she'd bring her own date. I was curious who he'd be. She swore it wasn't her sweetie, Ben. And Trica had agreed to hide out in a nearby hotel while I investigated. This was gonna be one midgin party, as the Lazars might say.

The prospect of murder seemed more interesting than frightening to my friends Kapp and Dee-Dee. I wasn't so sure, myself.

"Intimacy workshop." Kapp leered. "Don't suppose you'd overlook our minuscule age difference."

"Forty-five years is nothing," I teased, knowing Kapp was teasing himself. Kapp never tried to seduce me. He found a lot more pleasure fighting me with his cane. "Have a another sandwich," I added.

Kapp sighed melodramatically, then grabbed an egg salad sandwich. He took a bite and mumbled, "Still got the hots for your boyfriend, Roy, I suppose."

"Ex-boyfriend," I corrected dispiritedly, though the rest of his statement was all too correct.

I took a breath and got my mind back on the subject at hand.

"So any of your informants tell you who did it?" I asked. It was worth a try.

"You're assuming it's a murder," he pointed out.

"But you just said—" I protested.

"Never assume—" he cut in.

"But I heard it, Kapp!" I cut back in, the memory of the voice suddenly clear in my mind again.

"I guess I believe you," he growled softly. I knew my peculiar skills worried Kapp. If they weren't real, he would feel defrauded. And if they were real, he wanted to know why *he* didn't have them. We sat in quiet as we drove down the ocean highway. I let my mind drift and scarfed the last of the cookies from our picnic dinner.

"So what's this business that Seeger and Aileen owned about, anyway?" Kapp asked after a time.

"You mean The Sensual Body?"

"Yeah," he said. "Is it some kind of sex shop or what?"

"It's a what," I told him. "According to Trica, it's a

sensory pleasures 'R' us store. They sell massage oils, lotions, aromatic oils, candles—"

"Sex toys?" Kapp inquired hopefully.

"Probably."

"Hmm," he murmured and then lapsed into silence again.

I wondered if the inn had a weight room. I lifted weights—obsessively, my friend Joan said. But it helped strengthen my body, especially my bum leg. And my leg was tired from driving now. We'd driven a long way, out of Glasse, through Marin County, over the Golden Gate Bridge, and down the coast for the extended weekend at the "Love Workshop." The "Love Workshop, Exploring Sacred and Intimate Connections," to be complete. Dack! I felt my face flushing as I took a curve. Exploring "intimate" connections with strangers?

I turned to my traveling companion, but Kapp was still quietly mulling. And in the moment that I glanced at him, we reached Fiebre. I almost missed the tiny town. Highway 1 was its main street, comprised of a gas station, a mini-mart, a hairdresser's, a low-slung building with a neon sign announcing Marge's Restaurant, as well as a decrepit stone edifice that I figured might have been the city hall. A block past, I saw the sign for The Inn at Fiebre amid cypress trees. It was lucky I'd spotted it, or I would have kept on driving.

Instead, I stomped on the brakes and swung my car into the circular driveway. It took me a moment to actually take in what was beyond that driveway: a magnificent old Victorian building, or maybe it was Gothic. It was three stories high, with turrets, stained glass windows, and two long balconies spanning the second and third stories. Gargoyles peered out from the top tiers as if trying to catch a glimpse of the redwood hot tubs below.

I brought my Honda to a stop, glad we were finally here . . . and afraid.

"Are we getting out of the car or what?" Kapp demanded. I wiggled my shoulders in answer. The place was spooky. And that isn't a technical term.

But I didn't want to embarrass myself in front of Kapp, so I dragged myself out of the car into the ocean wind, and we strode—well, hobbled—into the lobby to register. And suddenly, the place wasn't spooky. It was beautiful. Marble floors intersected plush rose-colored carpets. The walls, made of stucco with a hint of the rose color of the carpet, were covered in Renaissance paintings in brass frames. A jungle of plants, along with a guest library of real books, gave the room character. It smelled of peaches. I wanted to live in the lobby. I could sleep on one of the velvet couches, though the love seats might be a problem.

"May I help you?" a deep, warm voice asked.

I turned to see a bronze-skinned, black-haired woman with a rosebud mouth and dark almond eyes looking my way. She smiled, and I felt welcome. I stepped closer and saw the name on her badge: Rhoda. Rhoda Neruda, I presumed.

"We're here for the . . . um . . ." Keerups, I couldn't even spit it out.

"The love seminar," Kapp finished for me. His jowls pinkened. "Separate rooms, of course," he added brusquely.

"You're just in time," Rhoda assured us. "The evening workshop starts in twenty minutes. Just enough time to put your things away."

Then she gave us a five-minute summary of the amenities. The inn provided a buffet breakfast and lunch. Most people ate dinner at Marge's, the restaurant we'd passed on the way in. And they did have a weight room. Rhoda pointed to the left. And the workshops were held in the ballroom to our right.

"Have you eaten?" she asked.

"Dinner in the car," Kapp growled.

Rhoda smiled, and then she was gone through a door behind the desk.

When I carried my bags into my room, I was greeted with the same decorating scheme used in the lobby. Delicate rose and plenty of greenery and bronze. I paused to breathe it in, thinking how lovely it would be to spend time with Roy here. And the quilt—

Kapp banged on my door. We were going to miss the "Love Workshop" if we didn't hurry.

We hurried. When we got there, we barged through the ballroom doors and stopped. Somehow I didn't think the ballroom was designed for the Indian silk hangings glittering on the walls and covering the windows. But they kept the room dark, except for the flicker of candlelight and the light coming through the now open door.

"Welcome to the realm of intimacy," a female voice called out as we closed the doors behind us and joined the circle of standing people. Now the room was really dark. I smelled incense and thought for some reason of my sister Geneva.

Slowly, my vision adjusted to the darkness, and I saw the woman who belonged to the voice standing next to the largest and brightest candle in the room. She was a tall, square woman with long, dark hair. I could see that much. And she was clothed in a flowing gown that might have been made from the Indian draperies. The shimmering material looked odd on her though. She would have looked more appropriate in a prison guard's uniform, I decided, her substantial bosom notwithstanding.

"We hope you will enjoy this evening's experience of the pleasures of the body, the heart, and the spirit," a male voice interrupted my thoughts. I looked at the man standing next to the first speaker. He was gorgeous, with mul-

tiracial features that might have been Brazilian or
Caribbean or any number of mixtures. Large, dark eyes
and cheekbones to die for dominated his face . . . and
something else, an evident crush on the square woman
standing next to him in Indian draperies. Not that the
woman seemed to notice.

I rotated my head ever so slightly to survey the others
in the room, but so far, even the closest were just shapes
in the flickering dark. And the woman was speaking again
anyway. I turned dutifully back.

"My name is Oralia," she told us, her voice clear and
firm. "And we will be cohosting tonight's workshop."

"And I'm Vick," the gorgeous man beside her chimed
in as if on cue, his voice as soft and sweetly musical as
Oralia's was firm. "We will be concentrating on the experience of intimacy this evening. Some might call our
work tantra, but it is more."

"Many of you may have heard of or been to workshops
that concentrate on the sensuality and pleasure of sexuality only," Oralia said. This was definitely scripted,
Vick's and Oralia's voices intertwining hypnotically.

"Those groups go no further than the body." Vick
spread out his hands.

"But there is heart, too." Oralia put her hand over her
heart solemnly.

"And where there is heart, true intimacy and commu-
nication are possible." Vick smiled and brought his hands
together.

"And there is spirit." Now, Oralia lifted her eyes. I
looked up, wondering if Seeger Snell was watching us
from the rafters.

"Spirit is the most important to us of all," Vick intoned.
"This evening, let's see if our energies can reach up to
our spirits."

"We hope to guide you there," Oralia stated with finality.

There was a short silence, and then the leaders got practical. "We'll begin by introducing ourselves. I'm Oralia, and I'm a nutritional counselor in my other life. I come here to lead these groups so that my soul can be nourished, too."

I smiled in the dark, thinking that having one's soul nourished couldn't be all bad. My shoulders relaxed a little.

"And I'm Vick." His eyes slid toward Oralia. "I come to this group in hopes of achieving communion." I was pretty sure who he wanted communion with, but she didn't seem to notice.

"Many of us were here last month," Oralia went on briskly. "But we have newcomers, so, please, everyone introduce yourselves and say something about your reason for being here."

"My name's Eddy," the man on Oralia's other side announced. He was a man who might have been handsome with intense blue eyes and unruly black curls, but frown lines were already carved into his symmetrical features, spoiling the effect. I turned away from him and saw Dee-Dee beyond Kapp. Someone was behind her, too, but it certainly wasn't her giant of a man, Ben. "I'm writing a new novel," Eddy plowed on. I thought I heard a sigh somewhere. "The tragedy of Seeger's death will be my subject."

I stopped worrying about Dee-Dee and whipped my head back toward Eddy.

But Eddy was done speaking.

The woman next to him began, her voice trembling. "I'm Linda. I . . . I need some understanding . . . some love, maybe." She was tall and sinewy with cartoon round eyes in a sweet face. Her hands were spread, palm out, to the group as if grasping for something. "I . . . my sister . . . I . . ."

Vick mumbled something consoling that I couldn't hear as the woman's hands flew to her throat and came back again.

"Aileen here," the next woman in the circle cut in. Seeger's business partner, I remembered. Aileen was a good-sized woman with steel-rimmed glasses and curly red hair. Or maybe it just looked red in the light. "I'm here for some fun. And don't forget to shop at The Sensual Body. We've got everything you need to enhance your sensual experience. Our newest product is Chi-Breeze. All hedonists welcome." She laughed, and the group seemed to lighten up. Literally. I could see a wisp of multicolored light floating toward the ceiling. And I had no idea what it meant. "Also, I wanted to say that if Seeger was here, he'd be having fun, too, groping the ladies, most likely. So let's have some fun for him."

So much for the spiritual realms. The laughter from the group sent a chill through me. I was glad Trica wasn't present for the eulogy.

Someone cleared a throat by my side. I turned. The man between Aileen and me was big in height and girth with dark hair and a white beard over an unhandsome but attractive face. He radiated tension.

"Harley," he spat out. "Aileen's here, so am I."

There was silence, and I realized it was my turn. Criminy. I didn't have a speech planned.

"Cally, I'm Cally," I tried as my brain searched for a follow-up. "Spiritual nourishment sounds fine to me."

A couple of people chuckled, including Kapp next to me. Then he realized he was on deck.

"Kapp, on behalf of the defense," he began, then smiled to show he was joking. "I'm just an old dog looking for new tricks."

I thought the word *tricks* might be unfortunate under the circumstances, but murmurs of laughter circled the room.

"I'm Dee-Dee," a familiar voice told us. Dee-Dee grinned, her tiny heart-shaped face an elf's in the flickering light. "I'm very interested in your workshop."

Not very creative, but at least she didn't lie, I thought, suppressing a chuckle myself.

Then the man behind Dee-Dee stepped out from behind her, and my heart stopped.

"Hi . . . um . . . I'm Roy." he began. Then he turned his so-well-remembered golden eyes in my direction and spoke softly. "I'm sorry, darlin'. I had to come. I've been so worried about you. I'm afraid the dark forces brought you to this group. And it's all my fault."

THREE

Silence flickered in the candlelight of the darkened room. I took a big breath, then coughed, choking on the incense.

"Roy!" I objected when I got my voice back.

Someone whispered nearby. Were they whispering about us? Did it matter? I felt the dampness of nervous perspiration on my forehead. Roy.

I looked at Oralia, thinking to explain, but she was smiling benignly, her square jaw softened by the expression.

"Very good," she summed up. "Now, we've all introduced ourselves."

Maybe "dark forces" wasn't a weird introduction for her group. Maybe I was overreacting. But Roy—

I guess I haven't explained about Roy. He's kinda hard to explain. I looked at him, seeing more of him in my memory than in the dim light.

Roy's my size, surprisingly muscular in a weedy kind of way. He's got reddish brown hair and the telltale freckles of a childhood spent as a carrottop, with sharp features in a bony face that could have come from the Lazar family, and intense golden eyes. He's a sweet man, an accountant who was originally from Kentucky. A man with an endearing drawl when his guard is down. A man eager to please. A soft touch.

We'd been lovers since my lawyering days, some seven

years, when he'd started talking about "the dark forces." He read a lot of science fiction, and that's all I thought it was at first, but then he asked me to take a look at his aura. There really was something dark hovering around him, and worse, it seemed to be moving in my direction. That's what really scared Roy. I asked his permission to remove the darkness, and he agreed verbally, but something nonverbal in him wasn't a party to that agreement. No matter what technique I used, the darkness remained. Did I tell you that the hardest person for a healer to work on is her own self? And the second hardest, someone she loves.

Well, I loved Roy, and I was afraid he was going a little crazy. I'd taken him to a psychotherapist. She'd suggested drugs. But Roy didn't want drugs. I couldn't blame him. Except for the dark forces, Roy was functioning just fine. He was still sweet, worked hard, pleased me in his loving, slept at night, but he obsessed and theorized about the dark forces constantly. We went to my healer friends after the psychotherapist. Opinions varied, but essentially everyone agreed. There *was* something dark hovering around Roy, something swirling my way. Whether it was of his own making or someone else's, no one was sure. We were all playing Stump the Psychic.

And then I began to get stomachaches, bad ones. Criminy, I could have swallowed barbed wire. Roy told me it was his fault, or at least the fault of the dark forces. Then I went back to my healer friends myself, the ones who'd helped me come to terms with my weak leg. They said my frustration in failing to help Roy was making me sick. And it was. Unfortunately, once Roy heard that diagnosis, he told me that our relationship had to end. He'd moved away from my little house more than three months ago. It might as well have been three years. I'd seen him for lunch once, but that was it.

My stomach got better. The darkness was a mystery I could have untangled in someone else's energy body, but not in either of ours. And no amount of pleading could bring Roy back. He believed he was acting for my sake. He was afraid something truly terrible would happen to me if we stayed locked in love together, that his darkness was attracted to me. And yet neither of us dated anyone else. We couldn't. So I waited out the dark forces and tried not to cry too much.

"I had to come . . . to protect you," Roy whispered.

"Oh, Roy," I whispered back and put out my hand. Roy reached my way.

Oralia's voice broke the spell.

"Boundaries," she announced.

Roy and I both dropped our outstretched hands as if smacked, then dutifully turned to our leaders.

"We always start our workshops with an exercise on boundaries," Vick informed us. "Without a sense of your own boundaries, none of the other exercises would have integrity.

"But with your boundaries in place, you'll be free to really experience your partner without fear or discomfort," Oralia went on. "What are *your* personal boundaries? For instance, how close can you stand to someone and still feel comfortable?"

"Or is there somewhere you don't like to be touched?" Vick took it up.

"My liver," Aileen snickered.

Oralia shot her a look that could have lit the incense.

"My throat," Linda squeaked. "I don't like people's hands near my throat."

"Very good," Oralia praised as if Linda was a puppy. She nodded and smiled. "Anyone else?"

Wasn't anyone going to mention their personal parts? I certainly hoped carnal touching was verboten, because

I wasn't about to enumerate all the erogenous zones on my body that were off limits. Except, of course, for Roy. I looked his way again—

"And it goes without saying that no one is to touch anyone sexually unless invited," Vick said, his musical voice stern. I was glad Vick said it, even if it went without saying. And I suddenly realized that despite Vick's gentle demeanor, he was tall and well-built. He'd make a fine bouncer if we needed one. For that matter, so would Oralia.

Within minutes of that stern statement, Vick and Oralia had us all standing across the room from our designated partners, male to female. My partner was Harley, the big, quiet man who'd come with Aileen. I was first, along with all the women on my side of the room. My task was to ask Harley to walk toward me until I felt comfortable, asking him to step back if I didn't, and telling him what to do to make me feel safe in his presence. I felt silly at first, but when Harley was within a few yards of me, I began to feel squeamish. He was too close.

"Stop walking," I demanded.

"What can I do to make you feel more comfortable?" he asked in a mechanical voice. Somehow, his face didn't match his voice. He was glaring at me.

I had a feeling he'd done this exercise before. I didn't tell him to dim his aura, which flickered with a red that I thought had more to do with sexual power than anger. I didn't ask him to switch with Roy either.

"Talk to me," I suggested.

"About what?" he replied sullenly.

"Take a step back," I told him.

He sighed and stepped back. Simon says. Yes, he'd played this game before.

"I like music," he muttered finally.

"Can you smile?" I asked, really curious.

He smiled. Dack! He looked like a wolf, a very large wolf. His hair was dark, but his beard was white. And his teeth were whiter than his beard. And suddenly bigger, too.

I took in a big breath. I wanted to tell him to walk out of the room. "What else do you like?" I asked instead.

The lines in his rough face softened ever so slightly. "Water," he tried. "Trees. Nature stuff."

"Take a step closer," I said. So this was how you trained a man.

"And hot women like you," he added, smiling again.

"Back to the wall!" I ordered.

When it was Harley's turn to tell me how close I could step to him, I told him all about cane-fu as I walked forward. I even demonstrated a few strikes in the air. He never asked me to get closer than the length of my cane. That was fun. Maybe he was trainable, after all.

As Harley and I sparred, part of my mind listened to the voices around me. Kapp and Aileen were boisterous, bordering on bawdy, Aileen moaning orgasmically every few steps. Eddy's snerky complaints were matched with Linda's soft, wounded words. And Dee-Dee and Roy were inaudible. Of course. The one conversation I would have liked to have heard was the only one I couldn't.

Finally, as I was staring at Harley, and Harley was staring at my cane, neither of us going anywhere, Oralia called the exercise to an end. We all sat down in a circle. I, for one, was glad. Not only was I tired of Harley, but my bum leg was trembling.

"Would anyone like to share what they learned?" Oralia asked, surveying us with her eyes. Eddy's hand popped up like a kid's in class.

"I really learned something about my own boundaries," he began. "As a novelist, I'm acutely sensitive to space. My parents never gave me enough space. Always touching me. They didn't understand my needs—"

"Uh-huh," Oralia interjected. It wasn't a nice therapeu-tic uh-huh. It was more like an I've-heard-this-before-thank-you kind of uh-huh.

"Well, I, for one, could go all night," Aileen put in. "Kapp is a real gentleman. Whooee, him I could get to like! Seeger needed a choke collar."

The room went silent. Had Aileen forgotten her former business partner was dead? Had she forgotten the circum-stances of his death? Or did she just not care enough to keep her mouth shut?

"Let's keep our comments to tonight's experience," Or-alia suggested brusquely. Even sitting, Oralia exuded a prison guard's authority. At least to me. But apparently not to Aileen.

"Hey, get real," Aileen challenged. She thrust her head forward. "We all had feelings about Seeger, good and bad. I know you hated it when he called you Lalie."

"Don't call me that!" Oralia snapped.

"I didn't call you that," Aileen pointed out smugly. "Seeger called you that. I just wonder why it pulls your chain."

I tried not to stare at Oralia. Because our "Love Work-shop" leader seemed to be in the hate mode now. The dirty orange and brown swirls in her aura were not at-tractive. The colors could mean a lot of things. But I was guessing fury. And if it was fury, was that fury directed at the now dead Seeger Snell? Or at Aileen Meyer? Or both?

I glanced quickly at Aileen but didn't see a wisp of anything that might be an aura on her. Was she just having fun, baiting Oralia? Or did she think Oralia had something to do with Seeger's death? Or was she manip-ulating her for some other reason? I just couldn't seem to get a reading on her.

A soft, melodic voice brought the fun to a stop.

"I feel a lot of grief in this room," Vick told us. I looked at the handsome man's big, dark eyes and wondered if he'd really missed the anger. "Perhaps the heart exercise could help?"

At least we had multiple partners for the heart exercise. We were still arranged male to female, but this time in a circle, so that we could experience the "heart message" of one member of the opposite sex at a time. We stood with each and put our hands on their manly chests, as they touched our feminine ones (strictly above the personal bits), and then moved on to the next.

Harley's heart message was still the same, simultaneously hostile and sexual. Keerups, he was nasty. But oddly enough, there was grief underneath the hostility. Maybe Vick was more intuitive than I gave him credit for. Before I had time to really study Harley though, it was time to move on.

I put my hand on Eddy's heart and he put his on mine. Then he began to talk.

"It's hard with all the despair . . ." he began, and his words dissolved into colors of green and blue and yellow.

It wasn't as if I was really trying to see his aura, but I just couldn't seem to help it. I even saw auras when I was a child, though my parents were unfazed by my revelations. They told me I had a unique tool of perception, but not to tell anyone outside of the family because others might not understand. Good advice that it took me years to fully comprehend. Ratsafratz, I missed them.

Kapp was next. He was in full swing now, leering and winking. I laughed as he touched the tip of his cane to my heart, and I touched my own cane to his. This man had a big heart. Maybe we both needed the lightning rods.

And then I was standing across from Roy. I held my breath for a moment. We put out our hands hesitantly, touching each other gently enough that a bird could have lighted on either hand and not flown away. And we closed our eyes. Crystalline light filled my mind, and memories: smiles, making love, eating breakfast, laughing, holding each other. I felt the warmth of tears on my cheeks and leaned forward, touching Roy's face with my own, feeling his tears mingle with mine.

"Don't think about the darkness, Roy," I whispered. "No darkness."

"Cally, I have to think about it," he insisted. "I believe you're in danger here. I'm afraid the darkness drew you into this situation—"

Then someone clapped their hands. The exercise was over.

Once again, we were asked to share our experiences. I couldn't. I could barely look at Roy.

But Eddy was ready, as usual.

"I felt such a longing—" he began.

"In your partner or yourself?" Oralia asked.

"In myself!" he answered, as if insulted by the idea that he might have felt empathy with anyone else.

"It was really moving," Linda interjected softly, her voice thick with sorrow. "I've had a hard time opening up since my sister was killed in an accident—"

"Car?" Kapp questioned. He couldn't help it. Just the facts, ma'am.

"No, weights. She was weight-lifting." Linda mimed lifting a barbell to her throat and losing it, her hands fluttering. Then her cartoon eyes filled and spilled over like a waterfall.

Vick moved nearer to her and put his hand on her shoulder. "Linda, this is the place to experience your sadness," he said quietly. "After my father died, I felt I had nowhere to go, but this group really helped. Let it all go."

"My wife passed away more than ten years ago," Har-

ley put in. I whipped my head around. I couldn't have
been more surprised if a dog had spoken those words.
Was that the grief I'd felt when I'd touched his heart?

Then Eddy started up again. "I know Seeger's dead,
but Aileen's right. We all have our tragedies, and he
didn't help any, pawing Linda. He was a real jerk. He
didn't understand that some people have sensitive natures.
He haunts us all."

"Does anyone else here need to talk about Seeger's
death?" Vick asked.

There was no immediate answer.

"Listen," I said, sensing an investigatory opportunity.
"If anyone needs to share about Seeger, or needs help with
their grief, my door is always open."

"Thank you, Cally," Vick offered. "That was very gen-
erous of you."

"And now . . ." Oralia began.

And before you could say "intimacy," we embarked on
our final exercise for the night, traversing a circle and
holding every participant's hands, bowing, and moving
on. It was very quiet. And very peaceful . . . before I got
to Roy.

Once Kapp had pried me off Roy, I went back to my
cozy room with relief. The rose tones and greenery and
bronze were still there. I put all thoughts of murder and
Roy out of my mind and checked out the quilt on my bed.
Each panel had a scene from nature: flowers, birds, trees,
night sky. It was beautiful. I wondered how much the
room was costing Trica. She had paid for both Kapp and
myself. Dee-Dee had insisted on paying her own way.

Suddenly, I needed to talk to one of my siblings. I
called Geneva first, but there was no answer. There was
no answer for York either, except an answering machine
for his martial arts studio. And Melinda's and Arnot's
respective spouses told me that each was on vacation. I

tried not to feel lonely as I undressed and slid under the cover of my lovely quilt. I pictured light enveloping me with love. I thought of my goats, and I was asleep.

The next morning, I had blueberry muffins and honey from the breakfast buffet at the inn after lifting weights in their tiny weight room. I had a couple of hard-boiled eggs, too, being assured by Rhoda that the eggs were from happy, free-range chickens. I was a fowletarian by diet. I ate fish and chicken occasionally, but couldn't bring myself to eat cows or sheep or pigs. It was probably the influence of my goats.

Aileen and Linda were at the buffet, too. Aileen had her arm around the frail woman's shoulders. It didn't seem to be the time to intrude. So I made small talk with Rhoda.

"Been here long?" I began.

"Only four generations," she answered.

"Did I just step into that one?" I asked, and she laughed, turning to pick up some plates.

And then Eddy came in.

I rose from my chair, hoping I didn't look like I was fleeing, and fled. I reminded myself that there was goodness in everyone, but I still didn't feel like listening to Eddy. My body was moving before my mind could even finish the argument.

When I got back to my room, the phone began ringing. It was Dee-Dee's sweetie, Ben, my favorite body repatterner. But he seemed to be trying to repattern my mind.

"I didn't want to worry Dee-Dee," he began.

"About what?" I asked carefully.

"Roy's there?" he answered my question with his own question.

"Yeah," I said tentatively.

"It's dark there," he muttered. "I can feel it."

Son of a lizard, were the dark forces catching? For Dee-Dee's sake, I hoped not.

"Where Roy is?" I tried.

"Yeah, keep your eye on Dee-Dee for me. She won't leave till she figures it out."

"Figures out who killed Seeger—?"

But Ben hung up before I could even finish my question.

I left my room, still thinking about our conversation, and walked slowly down the hall to the lobby. I tried to think positively for the time being. No spooks, no dark forces. No murders. No angry auras. Just good intent.

I walked out from the lobby into the sunlight and breathed in the smell of the sea. Salt and seaweed, flavored with floral overtones. And sunlight, yes! Harley sat across the patio. He smiled at me and raised a beckoning hand. I lifted my cane, waving it in his direction. I wasn't about to join him. Talk about searching for goodness. Searching in Harley was probably a job that could last a lifetime. Or two or three.

His smile widened, and he pointed up at a balcony. I looked up where he pointed and then back down, recognizing the all-too-real terra-cotta tile beneath my feet.

In an instant, I felt myself falling through the sunlight and thick sea air.

FOUR

The terra-cotta tile rushed toward me. I wanted to scream for help, but my mouth didn't work.

So I stuck out my cane—and realized that I was still upright. I hadn't fallen at all. That was the good news. I hadn't hurt myself. I wasn't splattered on the tile. But I had experienced the falling sensation again. That was the bad news. I didn't want to use the word hallucination, but still . . . I closed my eyes, listened to my all-too-rapid heartbeat, and meditated on the tale of the guy with the glass house who threw stones. Maybe Roy wasn't the only one who could conjure up "dark forces."

"Hey, Lazar!" a voice shouted, way too close to me. "What the devil's the matter with you?"

Kapp. I opened my eyes. Warren Kapp was staring at me, his bulldog face all scrunched up. It took a few more instants for me to identify the scrunching as a facial indicator of concern.

"Nothing," I answered finally, shaking my head to clear it. It didn't clear the trembling in my body though.

Kapp's face uncrumpled. And I saw something else in his eyes as he moved forward, something more familiar. I gripped my cane lightly in trembling hands and began to move.

By the time Kapp had raised his cane fully, I already had my own up, executing a horizontal circle to block his strike.

"Heh-heh," Kapp barked. "Just checking your reflexes."

"Yeah, right," I shot back.

"You're just fine," Kapp added.

I laughed. Because now, I was just fine. I wasn't shaking anymore. And I wasn't going to hide from the spooks and the dark forces anymore either. If I could take on Kapp while I was still in shock, I could take on anyone. I felt a sense of protection like a warm blanket settling around my shoulders. I was going to find out who—or what—killed Seeger Snell. It was time to visit the police chief of Fiebre.

Kapp offered to go with me, but I told him I was saving the big guns for later. It was just a leetle white lie. Actually, I was afraid Warren Kapp might intimidate Chief Dahl.

I got the directions to the police station from Rhoda Neruda. She gave me the directions, but not her customary smile. I had a feeling she knew why I was asking. And a lot more. I promised myself to grill her later. Or maybe beg her for some answers. Grilling probably wouldn't work on Rhoda, even if I knew how to do it. There were many reasons I was no longer an attorney. Being grill-challenged was just one of them.

Chief Dahl had an office in the old stone building Kapp and I had passed on the way into Fiebre. And that building was midgin old, let me tell you, built before the turn of the century. It still had its original jail (which was mercifully empty), although the computer on the desk in Chief Dahl's tiny office looked a little newer. Though not much newer.

"What?" the chief challenged me as her sergeant escorted me through the door. She didn't even turn around but sat with her back to me as she typed. She didn't sound very friendly. I looked at Sergeant Zoffany for reassurance, but his round, dark face had stopped smiling the first time Chief Dahl opened her mouth. He crossed his arms and glared down at me. Keerups!

"Chief Dahl," I began, keeping my voice low and firm. "I've come about Seeger Snell."

At least she turned to face me then. She was a small woman dressed in a navy blue suit with a white blouse. Her boiled blue eyes, long nose, and large teeth might have been bred for the British aristocracy.

"What about Snell?" she demanded. "What's your relationship to him?"

"Um, I'm the deceased's wife's energy worker, and—"

"What the hell's an energy worker?" Chief Dahl asked.

"Well, a medical intuitive, some people say—"

"You mean, like a psychic?"

"Well, not exactly—"

Chief Dahl tossed back her head and neighed with laughter. "And you thought you'd channel old Seeger up for us," she finally finished my sentence for me.

Actually, that was a little too close to the truth.

"No," I told her anyway, shrugging my shoulders uncomfortably. "But Trica feels that her husband might have been murdered—"

"Murdered?" Chief Dahl grasped the armrests of her chair melodramatically. "What have you been smokin', girl? Seeger Snell jumped. No one pushed him."

"But Trica said he had absolutely no reason to jump—"

"The boy was a user. Did your little friend, Trica, tell you that? He had needle marks as old as this office."

"Still, if he always did drugs, why jump this time?" I argued. It was the best I could do. I couldn't tell her the real reason I thought he'd been helped to his death.

"You talk more like a lawyer than a psychic," the chief accused, squinting her boiled eyes.

I flinched. Now, *that* was an ugly accusation.

"Look, Trica is understandably upset," I plowed on angrily. "Her husband died in front of her eyes, and no one really even investigated—"

"Hold your horses, there," Chief Dahl commanded, holding up her hand. "Are you accusing me of not doing my job right?"

I took in a breath, wondering how I'd already managed to get into an argument with this woman. It was true she'd made the lawyer crack, but still.

"Ma'am," I said, keeping my voice contrite. "I'm certainly not accusing you of anything. I came down here today so that we could work on this thing together. There were plenty of people in Seeger's group that didn't like him, and—"

"Tell me something I don't know," she interrupted and turned her back on me again.

I looked up at Sergeant Zoffany once more. His arms were still crossed, but there was amusement in his eyes now.

"Don't you care what happened to him?" I asked the chief's back.

"Girl, I know what happened. He got hopped up on drugs and jumped off his balcony. Case closed."

"But—"

"No buts," the chief said. "Tell Trica to send a lawyer next time."

"But—" I tried again.

"Time to go," Sergeant Zoffany suggested quietly. Quietly but firmly. "You've had your chance, now you'd best get out of here."

I got out of there.

I was fuming by the time my feet touched the sidewalk. And remembering why I'd quit the law business. I really believed that we all shared a warmth of heart. Really. But working with the law made that stance as unsteady as my weak leg. I wanted to go back to my cozy little house and pet my goats, maybe do a healing or two. I tried to remember how I'd gotten into this. And then I thought of Trica weeping. And of the voice that I'd heard. I straightened my shoulders.

Maybe I'd been thrown out of Chief Dahl's office, but no one had thrown me out of Fiebre . . . yet. I sniffed. There was definitely a tang of salt in the breeze. I stood for a moment, just breathing. Here was the warmth of heart. It radiated in the sunlight, scented the air, and grew in the weeds and flowers. Just as long as it didn't bite like Chief Dahl, I thought as I reached my car.

Driving back, I remembered worrying that Kapp might intimidate the chief and laughed. If Dahl wanted me to send a lawyer, maybe I would. It would be interesting to see the two of them in the same room. Interesting, like introducing a new dog into an old cat's territory. Dog barks, cat scratches, and then what?

Dee-Dee was waiting for me when I drove up the circular driveway of the inn and parked.

I jumped out of the car, ran, and hugged her, practically knocking her over. Sometimes I forget that there are people smaller than me.

"Whoa, Cally," she squeaked and hugged me back. She was warm and smelled of chocolate and concern. What a combo. The only thing that could have been better was Roy—

"The chief of police beat you up?" she asked, tilting her head as she moved back from our embrace.

And she was an intuitive as well as a hypnotherapist. I sighed and nodded my own head.

"Where do you want to go to work?" she asked.

"Work?" I repeated.

"Yeah, work." She grinned. "I've been asking people questions all morning. Now, we put together what we know, and . . ." She waved her arms and snapped her fingers like a magician's. ". . . voilà, the case is solved."

I smiled back at her. And people accuse *me* of being an optimist.

"Did you hypnotize them to get their answers?" I teased.

She shook her head seriously. "Man, it was tempting," she admitted. "But you know I never hypnotize anyone who doesn't agree to it."

"Still, I'll bet you can tell who's nervous or lying," I said hopefully.

"Everyone is," she answered me.

I let the hope drain away. Because I was sure she was right.

We walked out toward the ocean, past the carefully tended bougainvillea, and sat on the jagged rocks in the sand, surrounded by wild mustard, anise, and dry grass.

"So, give," I ordered once we were seated.

Dee-Dee's voice deepened into her hypnotherapist mode.

"Seeger came out on the balcony with no one in sight behind him," she began. I shivered and put my hands palms down on the rough rocks, absorbing their heat. "Trica and Aileen were sitting together down below. Seeger climbed onto the railing, waved, and jumped. Aileen remembered that Trica screamed, and then everyone seemed to come running at once."

"Who was there first?" I asked.

"No one can really remember," Dee-Dee answered, her voice still low. "It was a circus."

"So the only two it can't be are Trica and Aileen," I murmured.

"We still don't know what exactly was done to make Seeger fall," Dee-Dee reminded me. She was kind enough not to add, "if anything."

"But what could they have done from two stories below him?" I asked.

"Hypnotism," she answered. She ought to know. "Pulled a wire, I don't know."

"Still, I don't think either of them could have concentrated hard enough to pull it off while they were talking to each other."

"Not unless they conspired," Dee-Dee threw in.

I opened my mouth to argue. Why would Trica have hired me if she was a conspirator in this thing? Then a new thought hit me. "Did anyone actually see them there together?" I asked.

"Yeah, they were there when the others came, Trica screaming and Aileen trying to calm her down. Cally, are you sure he was murdered?"

I hesitated. Was I?

"I know you," Dee-Dee went on. "Ms. Goodness and Light. You probably can't imagine anyone killing anyone."

"Oh, no," I replied, shivering again. "I can imagine someone killing Seeger. I heard him."

And Dee-Dee didn't argue with me. I was glad she was here at the inn. I thought of telling her about Ben's phone call and then let it go. If Ben wanted to call Dee-Dee directly, he would. But I worried for a moment. Could a person who had killed once kill again? Was Ben worried about Dee-Dee for a good reason?

I put my hand on Dee-Dee's. "Be careful," I told her.

"Now you sound like Roy," she said and grinned.

"Dee-Dee," I began. "Maybe you shouldn't be here—"

"Forget it, Cally." She stood up from her rock. "We have people to see and arms to twist."

On the way back across the beach to go twist arms, Dee-Dee asked me how much Trica was paying me for this exercise.

"Um, she paid for my room . . . and Kapp's," I answered.

"That's all?"

"Criminy, she said she'd pay me for my time," I defended, realizing that *optimist* might just be another word for *sucker*. Trica had never actually mentioned how much she'd pay me. Then I remembered something else. "She offered to pay for your room, too, Dee-Dee, but you wouldn't take the money. Why not, huh?"

"Because if Trica murdered her husband, I don't want to be bound by confidentiality," she answered quietly.

I stopped walking, shocked to the tip of my cane.

"But—"

"Don't worry about it," Dee-Dee said lightly. "We have plenty of other suspects."

I was glad Dee-Dee's brains weren't as scrambled as mine by the time we reached the inn.

Rhoda was setting up the buffet for lunch when we got there. Good smells were drifting in from the kitchen as she stacked plates and arranged silverware.

"Ms. Neruda," Dee-Dee began.

"Please, call me Rhoda," the innkeeper said, turning with a welcoming smile lighting up her face. The woman was beautiful. There was no doubt about it. Her bronze skin and black, silken hair accentuated her delicate features and rosebud mouth. Today, her hair was pulled up into a knot on the top of her head.

But when she turned, the smile disappeared. And the light. I hoped it wasn't me. I looked over my shoulder. There wasn't anyone else behind me. It was me.

"You're here about Seeger Snell," she stated without further ado. Her face was grim now, though still tragically lovely.

I just nodded.

"I was afraid you were," she added softly. "Are you from his insurance company?"

I shook my head. I was frantically trying to think of a way to describe myself besides "Trica's energy worker." I didn't want another Chief Dahl reaction.

"It wasn't our fault," Rhoda told me, crossing her arms. Apparently, she hadn't seen me shake my head. "The balcony is structurally sound, and no one would expect a grown man to climb up like that. It's childproof."

"Just not adultproof," Dee-Dee put in.

"Why should it be?" Rhoda asked, her warm voice anxious now. "It would be as if someone threw themselves in front of your car. How can you anticipate a thing like that?"

"You can't," I said gently, trying to bring her back to earth. "Rhoda, I'm not an insurance investigator, I'm a friend of Trica's."

"Of Trica's?" she asked, obviously confused. Was she weighing the relative merits of an insurance investigator versus a friend of Trica's? A faint purple aura surrounded her. Victimization? Or . . . I tried to keep my mind on our conversation, not her aura.

"Trica is trying to figure out what happened that day," I explained. "She can't believe Seeger just jumped."

"Nor can I," Rhoda admitted. "I didn't see the incident, I just heard all the commotion. I was in the kitchen with Dulcie and Phyllys. But . . ." She shook her head.

"But what?" I pressed.

"But I knew the man." She sighed softly. "He's been to a lot of these workshops. Seeger could be a real, um . . ." She threw up her hands as if reaching for the right words.

"Jerk," Dee-Dee suggested.

"Son of a lizard," I tried.

She laughed, and her face glowed again. "Yes, a real

son of a lizard. But despite that, Seeger loved life. I can't imagine him killing himself. Look, when he showed up, he tripped over my son Wiz's scooter. So he took his SUV and ran over the scooter. Back and forth, back and forth. Holy Mother! All because he tripped. But that was Seeger. He took out his feelings on others, not himself."

I stood there wondering how her son felt about the man running over his scooter. How old was the kid? Ten or something?

"Then, what do you think caused him to topple off the balcony?" Dee-Dee asked.

Rhoda made fists of her hands. "You don't think I've tried to answer that question? I've thought of very little else since it happened. People say it looked like he jumped, but he was smiling. It makes no sense."

"Could he have just been drugged?"

"Pah!" she snapped, waving her hand. "Seeger was always on drugs. He knew how to handle himself. I wondered if . . ." She paused.

"If?" I urged.

"If someone who couldn't be seen pushed the bottoms of his feet or something. The railing is solid from the balcony floor up. If they crouched low enough . . ."

She looked down at her own feet, as if ashamed of her explanation, before going on. "But that still doesn't explain why he climbed on the balcony in the first place."

"As a joke?" I suggested.

"Maybe," she said, considering the idea. "Seeger was a joker, all right. In fact, if he hadn't actually died, I would have thought the whole thing was some kind of joke. That man was a pain in the you-know-what from the day he first came here—"

"Rhoda!"

The voice from behind us made us all turn.

We saw a woman with pink skin and short red blond

hair, whose lack of pigmentation in her brows and lashes made her look like a large rabbit. A large rabbit, baring its teeth.

"Who are these people?" the woman demanded.

"Phyllys!" Rhoda returned her reprimand. Then she answered. "These people are our guests, Cally Lazar and Dee-Dee Lee."

I wiggled my fingers at Phyllys. Dee-Dee just nodded. Rhoda drew her shoulders up and extended a hand.

"This is Phyllys Nesbitt, my partner," she introduced.

But Phyllys didn't take the bait.

"I thought we agreed not to talk to strangers about Seeger Snell," she reminded Rhoda instead. She didn't wiggle her fingers *or* nod at us.

"They aren't strangers," Rhoda argued. "They're friends of Trica's."

"From the insurance company?" Phyllys enquired.

"Now stop that, Phyllys!" Rhoda snapped. "These people are not from any insurance company. Say hello to our guests."

"Hello," Phyllys said in a monotone. Then her eyes went back to Rhoda. "Do you believe everything people tell you?" she asked. It was a good question.

"We're not here to make trouble," I told her. "We want to protect Trica, to make sure she's safe."

"Oh, sure," she said, widening her eyes under invisible eyebrows.

Rhoda reached out and took her hand, as if she could transfer her own goodwill to her partner.

"Look, I'm sorry if I've been rude," Phyllys finally offered. "But how do we know if you're not reporters or something?"

"Oh, keerups," I blurted out. "I'm Trica's energy worker."

"Really?" Rhoda and Phyllys both said at once. I waited for the laughter.

But Phyllys actually seemed to soften.

"We have a great energy worker here in town," she put in. "He works with alignment of the chakras through tone and tempo."

"Oh, that sounds cool," I told her sincerely. "I work with feelings and auras mostly. Tone sounds like a good modality though—"

I stopped. Someone was laughing. It was Dee-Dee.

"Why didn't you just tell them that you were an energy worker to begin with?" she asked.

"'Cause Chief Dahl laughed at me," I answered indignantly.

"Oh, Debby's like that," Rhoda put in. "She was probably just trying to tweak you."

"Debby?" I asked; then, "You know her?" Immediately, I felt stupid. In a town the size of Fiebre, the two women were pretty much destined to know each other. I tried to remember if I had disclosed Trica's whereabouts to the chief. No, I was fairly certain I had kept that secret.

"Known Ms. Debby Dahl since grammar school," Rhoda assured me, rolling her eyes.

"So what do you do?" Phyllys asked, turning Dee-Dee's way.

"I'm a hypnotherapist," Dee-Dee answered. There was a note of defensiveness in her tone.

"Yeah?" Phyllis challenged, her voice distrustful again. "You hypnotizing anyone out here?"

Before Dee-Dee got a chance to defend her ethics, a boy with the features of an angel, an angel that looked very much like Rhoda, came racing across the room.

"Wow, that's really cool," he whispered. "Hypnotism. Do you do magic, too?"

"Wiz Neruda, I presume," Dee-Dee said.

"See, see, Mom," the boy squealed. "She knew who I was before I even told her. I'll bet she hypnotized me. Do it again," he ordered Dee-Dee.

"I'll bet I can make your eyes blink," Dee-Dee complied.

Wiz blinked, then stared, slack-jawed, at Dee-Dee.

"I think he's in love," Rhoda whispered to Phyllys. They both laughed.

Now we had them. It was time for information on Seeger Snell. I took a big breath.

"So, about Seeger—" I began.

Rhoda looked at her watch.

"Holy Mother!" she cried out. "It's almost time for lunch."

Less than a heartbeat later, she and Phyllys burst into frenzied activity. Within ten minutes, platters of homemade breads, cheeses, dips, spreads, and cold cuts were on the table next to fruit and cookies and drinks. A blond young woman in a halter top and nose stud brought out miniquiches and salads, complaining all the way about the intimacy workshop "perverts" who'd made her extra work necessary.

"Aunt Debby says . . ." I heard on her trip back to the kitchen. Could "Aunt Debby" be the police chief?

Oralia and Vick came into the room before I could chase after her to ask. The two workshop leaders were standing close together, but their expressions were grim. I had a feeling they weren't sharing their heart chakras. I walked their way, hoping I could overhear something.

". . . not about him," Oralia whispered.

"Then what?" Vick demanded.

Oralia turned his way angrily, saw me, and ground her face into a smile.

"Nice spread," I mumbled, picking up a plate.

Linda was next in the door, pale, shaking her head, but

not speaking. Flashes of yellow, blue, and green emanated from her auric field.

Eddy wasn't far behind her.

"This kind of stuff always happens to me," he was whining. "Seeger was so insensitive, and look at all he had—"

"Oh, use it in your writing," Oralia snapped.

Eddy dutifully pulled out his notebook and jotted something down, ignoring the venom in her tone.

Aileen and Kapp came though the door next. So many suspects, and no one knew I had anything to do with Trica, except Rhoda and Phyllys. I sighed with satisfaction. Private eye, Cally Lazar, I thought happily.

And then the door swung open again, and Trica Snell walked in.

FIVE

"Oooh, Cally!" Trica greeted me, rushing up and enveloping me in a moist, peach-scented hug. "You're here!"

Dack. I grasped my cane as I pulled back from her, feeling a sudden cold run all the way up my spine to the hairs on my neck.

"Trica," I whispered frantically, looking at her air-blue eyes. "You're supposed to be in hiding."

"I just had to see you, Cally. I was all nervous and everything." Trica was dressed in a bright blue jumpsuit that shimmered as she wiggled in place.

"Trica, leave before anyone notices," I commanded, whipping my head around as I spoke.

It was, of course, too late for that. If my mind hadn't been in blender mode, I might have realized that all eyes in the room were on us. Especially on Trica. With the reaction she was getting from the intimacy workshop people, she might have been the ghost of her husband, Seeger. They were stepping away from the buffet and looking at the exits, just for starters. Some, like Linda, looked pale enough to pass out. Others, like Aileen and Oralia, looked angry. And a few just looked dazed.

Trica finally seemed to notice that we weren't alone and proceeded to remedy the situation by introducing me.

"Oh, hi, everyone. This is Cally," she trilled, pointing at me and then clasping my hands together ecstatically.

"She is so cool. She's a psychic, and she's gonna find out what happened to Seeger."

I concentrated on invisibility, holding my breath and closing my eyes. I must have been as pale as Linda; I was sure of that. Still, pale wasn't invisible. I opened my eyes again. Everyone was still looking at us.

I needed a new strategy. Lying? That was another skill that I'd never mastered as an attorney. But this was an emergency. I could try.

"Oh, I'm not really a psychic," I offered in what I hoped was a genial, natural voice. "Just a healer like I said, an energy worker looking for a little relaxation. And when Trica told me about your intimacy seminar, it sounded . . . fun."

"Hah!" someone snorted. I couldn't tell who. Oralia? Aileen?

Before I could try any more lies, the dining room door opened again, and Harley walked in.

"Hi, Harley," Trica greeted him cheerfully. "Have you met Cally?"

Harley grunted.

"She's psychic, you know," Trica added. Just in case the whole room hadn't gotten it by now.

"In point of fact," a new voice piped up. Kapp, of course. No one else could sound that pompous without extensive preparation. "Cally is not so much a psychic as a healer. And, just in case you might wonder, she is also a martial arts expert, her specialty being cane-fu. However, her intuition is deep, and with my expertise in legal investigation, we may in fact be able to learn—"

"Oh, man," Harley moaned. He seemed to be turning yellow, and it wasn't just his aura. He rushed out of the room far faster than he'd entered.

Kapp tried again. "As I was saying, we have a number of experts here who might be able to assist Ms. Snell in her mission to find the truth surrounding her husband's death. To that end, if we all work together, we may well be able to pool our intellectual resources—"

"Jesus!" Aileen yelped. And then she jumped ship. Only, her face was red as she headed for the doorway, opening it just in time to bump into Roy, who was coming in as she went out.

"Sorry, ma'am," he said to her backside. Roy was always polite. I stared at him, at the worry and confusion on his narrow, freckled face, and forgot all about Trica. At least for a second.

"Hey, where's everyone going?" Trica called out. "I wanted you to all meet Cally so that she could—you know—like, investigate or something."

Eddy giggled shrilly just as Roy strode up to my side.

"I gotta get you outta here, darlin'," Roy whispered.

The "darlin'" almost made up for the sentiment. Just that one word out of Roy's mouth brought up the compressed memory of seven years of happiness. But *I* didn't need protection. *Trica* needed protection.

"Roy, I can't leave—" I began.

"Cally needs to help me figure things out," Trica put in helpfully.

"Maybe I won't be able to, Roy, but I have to try," I told him.

"Don't be such a wuss, Roy," Kapp cut in. "Give Cally some credit for her intelligence here—"

"I have to try, too," Roy interrupted. He squeezed my hand, gave me a wan smile, and left the room.

"So, what's everyone doing?" Trica asked those still in the room. Her friendly smile looked as genuine as her naïveté.

"Let's all get some food and sit down and eat," Dee-Dee suggested blandly. The smile on *her* face looked wooden.

Oralia and Vick were the next to leave. At least they both nodded and said hello to Trica before their exit. I wondered who would be left to eat the buffet offerings.

Eddy filled a plate and took it outside. There must have been someone out there, because the sound of his voice complaining reached my ears before the door shut.

Then Linda looked at the food, put her head in her hands, and went racing out after him.

Rhoda and Phyllys just stared at me across the emptying room.

"I'm sorry," I said finally.

"Sorry doesn't cut it—" Phyllys began angrily.

"No," Rhoda cut her off. "Let her be. It's the uncertainty that's killing us, isn't it? Maybe Cally can help us at the same time she helps Trica."

Phyllys opened her mouth and then shut it again. She sighed in defeat. "Maybe," she muttered.

"She's really cool, Phyllys," Trica assured her.

"Would you like something to eat, Trica?" Rhoda asked gently.

"Well, I don't know—"

"A beautiful woman like you needs food," Kapp threw in and extended his arm to Trica.

Trica giggled and took his arm, her buxom body swaying as they walked to the buffet together. Warmth returned to my body, and I remembered why I was so fond of Kapp.

I walked up to Rhoda and put my hand on hers. "An energy worker doesn't let her client go into danger. I have to find out about Seeger."

Rhoda rewarded me with a smile. Phyllys even nodded her approval.

Then Dulcie came in with another tray of salads.

"Where'd everyone go?" she asked.

Dee-Dee started laughing first, and then Kapp and

Trica. When Rhoda, Phyllys, and I joined in, Dulcie turned on her heel and walked back to the kitchen, muttering.

The food was good. I loaded up on the spinach miniquiches, coleslaw with raisins, and homemade millet bread. And the company was better than expected. Kapp was at his charming best, and Rhoda made everyone, including Trica, feel welcome. Within minutes, we were all talking like old friends about Fiebre, gardening, goats, and inevitably, Kapp's legal coups.

By the time I'd finished my cookies and tea, I was smiling despite the disaster of Trica's presence. At least she hadn't told anyone where she was staying. I hoped.

Kapp led Trica from the hall, chatting her up.

Dee-Dee and I were next to rise from our chairs.

"Thank you," I said sincerely to Rhoda and Phyllys. I hoped that they understood that I was expressing my appreciation for more than just the meal.

And then Dee-Dee and I left the dining room for the afternoon sea breezes.

We walked to the ocean again, our words sometimes caught in the wind, and found a spot near a cypress tree to stand.

"We need to talk," she said.

My chest clenched. Her tone was deep with solemnity.

"About Trica?" I asked timidly.

"No, about Roy."

My chest clenched even tighter. A gull cried above us, and I forced myself to relax.

"Roy loves you," Dee-Dee announced and lowered herself onto the sand beneath the cypress tree.

"I know that," I told her and flopped down next to her, my cane resting by my side. "Roy's the one who left me, remember?"

"He left you because you were making yourself sick

trying to control his life," she argued. "You wanted to heal him of his darkness. Well, maybe you can't."

"Dee-Dee!" I objected. "Is it controlling someone's life to worry if they obsess about 'dark forces'? Is it controlling to want to see them happy? Isn't that what healing is about?"

"He's not happy without you, Cally."

"Criminy, *he* left *me!*" I erupted. My body was trembling with something made of anger, frustration, and unshed tears. "How come you can't remember that? And now, he's afraid to be near me because he thinks his darkness will bring terrible things into my life."

"But he's trying to protect you, Cally," Dee-Dee insisted. "Can't you just accept him unconditionally?"

"Dee-Dee, I do accept him. I want to live with him no matter what darkness he sees. We were going to be married, remember? But it's hard to sustain a relationship with someone who refuses to live with you for fear of harming you."

"Well," she replied softly. "There is that."

"Did Roy put you up to this?" I asked finally.

"No, but he poured his heart out to me all the way down in the car." She paused, then shook her head. "I suppose if I'd ridden down with you, I might be arguing that the situation's just impossible."

"So, why *did* you drag him down with you in the first place?" I demanded.

"Ben," she mumbled.

"Ben?"

"You know him and Roy."

I did know Ben and Roy. They were as tight as Trica's blue outfit. Friends, like Dee-Dee and me.

I leaned over and hugged Dee-Dee. "I'm not sure about what you said, but I'm glad that you care enough to try to hypnotize me."

Dee-Dee drew back from my grasp for a moment, her elfin face a mask of horror. "I didn't try to—"

Then it was my turn to laugh. And finally, Dee-Dee was laughing, too.

After a while, we just sat there on the sand together, staring at the ocean.

I knew there was darkness in the world. But could there be lightness in darkness, like the stars in the night sky? I wondered. I tried, but couldn't remember a time I'd ever been in complete darkness. Light always seeps in if your eyes adjust to it. It's merely a matter of time . . . and trust. So—

"Those new guys," I heard, and my theories shattered. "They aren't here for the workshop. They think Seeger was murdered."

I saw Oralia and Vick striding across the sand, almost to us.

Without a word, Dee-Dee and I both scooted behind the cypress tree, out of sight.

"We can't be sure of that," Vick put in gently. Then he said something I couldn't quite hear. Finally, I caught his voice again. "They're just trying to find out what actually happened to Seeger. I'd like to know myself, if the truth be told."

"Oh, grow up, Vick," Oralia growled. "They think it's murder. It's obvious."

"But how could it be—"

"I don't know!" Oralia screamed. "But if anyone was ever looking to get murdered, it was Seeger Snell. I always knew that jerk would get us into trouble somehow."

"Seeger was okay," Vick put in. He might as well have waved a red flag under Oralia's nose.

"Seeger was not okay! Jeez, Vick, we should have blackballed him the first time he ever groped someone.

Remember that woman, Esme, who never came back? And Susan? And Myra—"

"He always backed off as long as someone called him on his actions," Vick pointed out. "He was just like a kid, testing . . ." The rest of his words were caught in the ocean's roar.

"Can you really be so naive?" Oralia demanded. "He was a complete and totally insensitive gorilla. Hoo-hoo, bugga-bugga." She reached up and scratched under her arms in an imitation of an ape. "If I had a nickel for every woman he'd offended in his lifetime, I'd be rich now. Our workshops are about love, not sleazy little power plays. God, Vick, why do you always defend him?"

"I felt sorry for him." Vick stopped walking within yards of us.

"Sorry for him? Well, how about you feel sorry for us? His suicide, or murder, or whatever it was, may just have put us out of business."

"I don't think he meant to kill himself," Vick mumbled. "He was—"

"You're doing it again! You're defending him. Even when he's dead." Oralia grabbed Vick's arm and swung him around so she could look into his eyes. "Did Seeger have something on you, Vick? Is that why you stuck up for the creep?"

"What do you mean by something on me?" Now, his voice was clear, almost menacing.

"I mean that no one could have taken all of his crap without being blackmailed or something, for God's sake," Oralia bulldozed on.

"I resent that," Vick said, and I, for one, believed him. Suddenly, it was clear that he was taller than Oralia, a fact that I hadn't noticed before. Oralia had seemed bigger up till now.

Oralia let go of his arm. "I'm sorry, Vick," she sighed.

"I know you wouldn't let anyone blackmail you. I suppose I just don't understand male bonding, or whatever it was that made you side with Seeger Snell."

A moment went by, with only the sounds of the sea to fill it. Then Vick pulled back his shoulders as if making a decision.

"Did you ever sleep with Seeger?" Vick asked.

Oralia stomped away from him, away from us. "I wouldn't have slept with that sleazoid for all the money in the world. It makes me sick just to think of it," she shouted.

"That's not what I asked, Oralia," Vick pressed. "I asked . . ." And then his words were gone as he followed her.

We heard one last, "How dare you?" from Oralia, and then there was only the sea again.

"What—" I began, stretching out from my crouched position.

"Shhh," Dee-Dee warned. Vick and Oralia had turned and were headed back our way. I crouched back behind the cypress tree.

". . . what's really wrong with you," we heard Vick say. "There's been something wrong ever since we got here."

"What do you care?" Oralia yelled. I thought I could hear tears in her voice, but maybe it was the wind.

Then she began quickly walking down the beach with Vick in hot pursuit.

Dee-Dee and I came out from behind the cypress tree cautiously, like groundhogs checking for our shadows. Once we were sure it was safe, we walked back to the inn and snuck into my room to talk.

"Do you think they're a couple?" Dee-Dee murmured, sitting on the edge of my bed, fingering my quilt. I wondered if her bedspread was as nice as mine.

"They sure act like it," I muttered back and took a seat

in my wingback chair, letting the warmth of the room sink into my chilled bones.

"Actually," she said, her voice resuming normal volume. "I think he likes her, but I don't think she knows."

"Yeah," I agreed eagerly. "I saw the way Vick looked at her at the workshop, but Oralia didn't seem to notice—"

"That's the way Roy looks at you."

"Dee-Dee!" I objected.

"Well, he does, but never mind. Okay, now we have more information to play with. Vick let Seeger get away with stuff, and Oralia hated Seeger."

"How about the rest of them?" I asked.

"I don't think Eddy liked Seeger," Dee-Dee answered slowly.

"Eddy doesn't like anyone but himself," I pointed out.

"Right!" Dee-Dee barked military style and saluted me.

We sat quietly for a while, hoping for inspiration.

"Let's go talk to Rhoda and Phyllys again," Dee-Dee suggested finally.

I groaned as we walked out the door.

We found Rhoda behind the reception desk. But before we could even start in with our questions, she beckoned us with a wiggling finger, and we followed her to the small, neat office behind the reception area.

"Debby Dahl just called," she told us. Her beautiful brown eyes were troubled, verging on panicked. "She asked all these questions about Wiz."

I thought back. Wiz was the one whose scooter Seeger had run over. Did Chief Dahl think—

"Wiz is just a kid," Rhoda hissed. "Holy Mother, every kid has to have a hobby. Wiz just likes magic."

I nodded and saw green tendrils of affection swirling around her head. She smiled gently.

"If you find any severed fingers in your soup or anything, he's just playing," she went on.

"Severed fingers?" I put my hand on my heart.

"You know, rubber ones, or eyeballs," she tried to explain. "He's just a kid. He does practical jokes, nothing serious. It's better for him than computers—"

"Rhoda!" Phyllys called out. "Have we got any more eggs?"

Rhoda was gone before she could even finish her sentence.

Dee-Dee and I walked back to the reception area without talking, finally splitting up in the hall. I finished the walk to my own room slowly, hoping a ten-year-old kid hadn't taken a practical joke too far. Could he and Seeger have been staging a joke when Seeger went over? A high-wire stunt gone wrong? Would Seeger even deign to play with a kid?

I was lying down on my beautiful bedspread when I heard a gentle tap on my door.

I put on my glasses, grabbed my cane, and peeked out the door.

The eyes that met me were golden and crinkled at the sides. Roy. He took a couple of tentative steps into my room.

"Hi, Cally," he murmured uncomfortably. He dropped his gaze.

"Did Dee-Dee send you?" I asked.

Roy looked genuinely confused.

"No, I just wanted to talk to you a bit," he replied. His voice carried a world of desire in it. My desire. "I didn't want you to fret, but I can't let you face the dark without warning. I truly wish that you would leave this place now."

I took a breath and reminded myself to be more understanding as I closed the door behind him.

"Roy, have you ever thought that darkness might be the backdrop for light?" I asked, my words covering the ones

I really wanted to say. But I'd tried "I love you," before. Roy wanted to talk about darkness.

Roy smiled, and he was my Kentucky boy again, years erased from his face.

"Thank you for admitting the darkness, Cally," he said, and I wondered what he meant exactly. But it didn't matter. He was smiling.

I reached out and held his familiar hand, so much like mine, long bony fingers—

"Cally," he sighed. He closed his eyes.

I moved closer, and brought my lips to his. One touch and I was gone. I didn't care about darkness and light anymore. I didn't—

Someone knocked on my door.

Dack, I *had* made an offer to be here for the others at the workshop. Was someone taking me up on it *now*?

Roy jumped away from me.

"Don't answer—" I began, but Roy was already reaching for the doorknob, polite as ever.

Linda Frey stood at the threshold. "Oh, I'm sorry," she squeaked, her cartoon eyes widening even further. "I just thought I could talk to you, maybe. I don't know, maybe it's a bad idea, but I wondered maybe if—"

"It's all right, ma'am," Roy told her. "I was just leaving."

Criminy, easy for him to say. He looked over his shoulder at me longingly before exiting and softly closing the door behind him.

Linda was blasting a rainbow of color like a strobe light. She moved around the room so fast that she was making me dizzy.

"I . . . I . . ." she tried.

"Calm down," I told her, falling into energy-worker mode. The woman was so clearly wounded, it was hard not to. "It'll be fine."

I didn't know where the words were coming from, but they seemed to be the right ones.

She flung herself in the wingback chair and stared at the carpet.

"I heard that you figure out these things. . . . I just needed to talk to you. I'm confused." She brought her head up suddenly. "Was Seeger Snell ever a spotter?" she asked.

"A what?" I asked back.

"For bodybuilding, the guy that helps you with your routine, you know—oh, it doesn't matter."

"I could find out," I told her, thinking of Trica. "I never heard anything about him being into bodybuilding though."

It's not important," she told me, shaking her head. "No, maybe I'm just being stupid. I just—"

The knock on my door this time was hard and definitive.

I opened the door again. I felt like a turnstile. So much for my offer to help the workshop members.

Aileen stood in the doorway.

"Hi Cally," she greeted me, smiling. "And Linda," she added.

"I'll be going," Linda yelped and jumped out of the wingback chair.

"I, you—" I tried, but she was out the door, shoving past Aileen, before I could finish.

I focused on Aileen.

"I wanted to talk to you," she said unnecessarily. "You know things."

"I don't really—"

She pulled a handkerchief from her pants pocket and blotted her eyes. Was she really crying? "Seeger was my business partner, a buddy." She took a tentative step into my room. "Sometimes, I think I'm the only one who really cared for him."

"There was his wife, Trica," I reminded her.

"Trica's an airhead sometimes," she told me. Was her dismissal of Trica cruelty or brutal honesty? Was there a difference?

"But I have to know. Have you found anything? Did Linda tell you anything?"

"Linda?" I asked.

I wasn't sure if we were having a conversation or not.

I stared at Aileen, looking for her aura. It wasn't evident to me, or maybe I was just too tired to perceive it.

"Are you guys really detectives?" she asked next.

"No, I'm a healer," I told her. I wanted her out of my room. I was tired.

A million questions later, she was gone.

It was dinnertime by then, but I couldn't bear a dinner at Marge's diner with everyone's eyes on me. I was no longer incognito, that was for sure. So I snuck off to the minimart and got a tuna sandwich. Once I'd eaten at my bedside table, I lay down on the top of my bedspread again, carefully removing my shoes and my glasses, hoping for a nice postdinner nap. The day had taken my strength away. Slumber called.

The world dissolved into softer focus, and then I was asleep. I dreamed of talking goats, bleating questions.

I don't know how much time had passed when I woke to the presence of someone in my room.

SIX

I sat up, my world a blur without my glasses. Then I felt my cane at my side. Once the cane was in my hand, that blur became something I could fight, something I could stop. I rolled off the bed. From a crouch, I swept my cane in a horizontal arc. A small jolt fluttered my hand when the cane touched flesh, and then the blur backed away. I hadn't really hit it, just grazed it. I stepped forward, raising my cane lightly but firmly in both hands. I would go for the strike this time. But the blur moved faster than I did. It flashed in what had to be a turn and slammed the door on the way out.

I shoved on my glasses and ran for the door. No one was in the hallway. I tried to remember what I had actually seen. A blur of indeterminate size, in beige—or was it shadowed white? I couldn't even remember the color. I squeezed my hands into fists of frustration. It was useless. It wasn't just myopia; it was being wakened out of sleep in the semidarkness of my curtained room. Had the blur been there a minute? Seconds? All my impressions were dreamlike.

For a moment, I even wondered if I *had* been dreaming. But when I came back to my room, I looked around and saw the familiar rose and greenery and bronze. And there, where the figure had been, the wastebasket where I'd thrown my sandwich wrapper. It lay on its side now, knocked to the floor. The blur had been real. And I didn't need Roy to tell me that it had meant to harm me.

I thought of Trica's luncheon announcement. Could this intruding blur have possibly been unconnected? Not likely. Trica. Dack. I sat and breathed in forgiveness. Trica was Trica. And what had been said couldn't be taken back now.

After a long meditation, my heartbeat was back to normal, and I remembered that whatever happened externally, it wouldn't matter as much as how I reacted to it internally. The light was not just out there but inside. Right.

Then the phone rang. For all the calm my meditation had brought me, I still flinched at the shrill bleat.

Dee-Dee was on the phone.

"Ben said he'd called you," she told me. "I don't know why he called you instead of me. I just hope he didn't scare you. You know Ben."

I smiled. Ben. He was a big, tall man, over six feet, and more than three hundred pounds of sweetness, serenity, and acceptance. He and Dee-Dee had a sure and confident love. When they stood together, I always thought that their disparity in size was the perfect foil for the commonality of their personalities. Earnest, kind, and intense. Buttinskys, both of them. They belonged together. Maybe Dee-Dee wasn't such a bad choice for advice on relationships.

"Ben's okay," I stated warmly. "More than okay."

Then there was a short silence.

"Cally?" Dee-Dee murmured.

"What?"

"I'm sorry for being so pushy about Roy," she finally spilled out. "I was talking out of my hat. I don't know what I'd do in your shoes, not really. I can't believe I was spouting unconditional love when I can't forgive Ben for stacking newspapers on the kitchen table."

I smiled again. "It's okay," I assured her.

"No," she insisted, her voice excited now. "It isn't okay. Friendship shouldn't get confused with romantic advice. I know better than that. And I know that 'dark forces' are a helluva lot harder to deal with than stacks of newspapers."

"All right, then help me be objective," I tried. "I've been thinking. Maybe my problem with Roy is his characterization of the darkness. He connotes darkness with evil. I've always known that darkness existed. It was the 'dark forces' I objected to, the implication of evil. I see the darkness. I just don't see the evil." I paused and took a breath. "When you ride back in the car with him, maybe you can explain the concept. And maybe you can suggest that the two of us can live with it . . . together."

"Whoa! Maybe you'll be the one riding back in the car with him," Dee-Dee teased.

"Dee-Dee!"

"Sorry, sorry!" she yelped. "I don't believe I said that. I am truly evil—"

"I don't believe in evil."

"Bad?"

"Nope."

"Naughty?"

I thought for a moment. "I'll go for naughty," I announced solemnly.

"I love you, Cally," she giggled. Then she stopped laughing. "But I hope you recognize more than naughtiness when you meet the murderer."

"I'm sure I will," I responded just as seriously. "Desperation. Confusion. Lack of empathy, maybe. Who knows? But I still don't think the person who killed Seeger Snell is evil."

"Oh, Cally, I just hope you're right."

I considered telling Dee-Dee about the blur in the bedroom then. But the words wouldn't come out. Was I afraid I'd make it real by putting words to it? Or was I just afraid of more gratuitous advice? Advice like, "Leave here right now." I wasn't ready to leave.

"What?" Dee-Dee questioned. "What are you thinking about?"

"Nothing important," I lied. "Tell Ben I understand. And you are now forgiven for past, present, and future unsolicited advice, but watch it."

"Oh, thank you, kind madam," she said with an auditory curtsy and hung up.

Should I tell *someone* what had happened? The obvious person was Chief Dahl. I imagined the conversation for a minute. "So you saw a blur?" "Right." "A blur that you remember no details about?" "Right." "Well, ma'am, we'll just keep a lookout for a beigey blur, then." My imaginary conversation was enough. I wasn't going to Chief Dahl with my story. But still, I needed to tell someone.

I called my sister Geneva, but again, no one answered her phone. Where was she when I needed her? Then York's answering machine greeted me again. I didn't have the heart to call Arnot or Melinda. When my parents had been killed, I'd been fifteen years old; Geneva had been thirty. And she'd taken me in and given me all the love and caring that I could have asked for. She'd soothed away the monsters. I was too young then to wonder how much she'd suffered herself. All her efforts had been turned toward me, and I had accepted them without thought, though with gratitude. And Geneva trained me in feminism and the politics of the sixties in a way few people my age have been trained. Maybe that was the trade-off for her. But right now, all I could think of was how I needed her. Friends were one thing, but my big sister was another.

I put down the phone with a sigh. It rang in an instant.

"Geneva?" I answered eagerly.

"No, sorry," Ben replied. "I can try to be your sister, but I don't think I'd fit in her gowns." My sister designed clothing that could make anyone look beautiful, but I thought I'd leave that discussion for another time.

"I talked to Dee-Dee," I told him.

"I know." I could almost see his big shaggy head dropping in shame. "I wanted to add my apology to hers. I was the one that suggested Roy surprise you at the seminar."

"I know that, too." I deepened my voice. "I know all."

"Oh, good, then you know who the murderer is."

"Maybe my subconscious does," I tried.

"Cally, be careful," he warned seriously. "And keep an eye on Dee-Dee. Together, you ought to be safe. Maybe you ought to bunk together."

I thought of the blur. What if I'd been bunking with Dee-Dee? Would she have caught the intruder? Or would she have been hurt?

"Ben, I—"

Someone knocked.

I told Ben I had to go and hung up.

I opened the door carefully, my cane in position, held a few inches off the floor in readiness. And saw Vick's handsome face staring back at me. I lowered my cane slowly and, I hoped, unobtrusively.

"Your phone was busy, so I thought I'd come to your door," Vick explained, all the earlier anger gone from his musical voice. "We're having another workshop evening, and I didn't want you to be left out."

"Oh, right," I chirped, hoping my lack of enthusiasm didn't flavor my tone too obviously. Could I claim I was sick? I felt kinda sick.

Vick stared at me, his dark eyes seeming to see and

understand my hesitation. What if Vick was a murderer? I shivered. Suddenly, I did want to go to the group. How else would I figure out what had happened to Seeger Snell? If he had been killed, someone at this inn had killed him, either one of the innkeepers or one of the workshop people.

"I'll be out in a second," I told Vick.

He nodded and turned, stepping farther into the hallway. The man knew his boundaries, all right. I measured him in my mind's eye for a blur match. Nothing. I closed the door and took a deep breath. A bit of fear subsided. I took another breath. Nope, that was it, that was as far down as I could push it. Maybe a little fear was healthy for this task.

Vick was waiting a respectful step away when I opened the door again.

We walked down the hallway quietly, but as we came to the bend that would lead us to the ballroom, Vick stopped and turned to me.

"Um, Cally," he began.

"Yeah?" I prodded cautiously.

"Oralia seems all out of whack lately," he spat out quickly. "I thought you might understand what's wrong with her, being psychic and all."

"You love her, don't you?" I asked.

Dark as his skin was, it still showed a blush.

"I suppose." He shrugged. "I'm sorry if I'm out of line, asking you."

"No, no," I assured him. "I just wish I knew the answers for you. But I'd really have to deal with her directly—"

"Don't worry," he told me, turning back, ready to walk again. "I know I shouldn't be asking this way, secretly. It's not right."

"Vick." I put my hand on his arm, stopping him for a moment. "It'll be fine, I know it."

I just hoped I was right as we finished our march to the ballroom and entered. But then, "fine" covered a lot of ground.

The ballroom was as dark as it had been the night before, given sensory reality by its vaporific incense, flickering candles, and silken hangings. Still, now that I knew who I was looking for, maybe I could recognize the characters in the dark. I scanned the room for the blur I had seen earlier.

Oralia came into focus as Vick went to take his place beside her.

"Tonight, we will be exploring something slightly different," Oralia announced, her prison guard persona back in place beneath her flowing, silver-threaded robes.

"We will be searching for Seeger Snell's spirit," Vick took up the script.

"In order to help him leave this plane—"

"Happily and peacefully," Vick finished. I had a feeling he'd been the one to add that last line. But happiness and peace didn't fill the room.

Instead, a rebellious murmur spread through the space.

Like an orchestra tuning up, small cries, groans, gasps, and sighs swirled together. The overall message was clear though. There were people here who didn't want to play with Seeger Snell's spirit.

Now I was beginning to see the people who stood in the flickering light.

Harley looked heavenward but not for Seeger Snell, as far as I could tell. Aileen glared next to him. Roy and Dee-Dee exchanged worried glances. Kapp looked avidly curious. Eddy opened his mouth. But Linda was quicker than he was. She turned to Roy and wrapped her arms around him, crying out, as if in pain. Roy's upper eyelids raised in panic.

"Linda—" Oralia began, whether to plead or reprimand, I wasn't sure.

And then Linda dropped Roy and ran to Vick, embracing him in a death hold. Vick was lucky he wasn't swimming. He would have drowned.

"Wait a minute, people," Oralia ordered, with a not-so-friendly look in Linda and Vick's direction. "There's nothing to be afraid of. We'd just hoped that a seventh chakra exercise might release some of the tension that people are holding about Seeger's death."

"What the hell's the seventh chakra?" Harley asked.

Finally, an intelligent question. And from Harley.

"The seventh chakra is our bodily connection to the realm of spirit," Oralia announced, pursing her lips.

"Oh, great, a connection to spooks." Harley shook his head. "That oughta ease tensions down real good."

"Listen," Eddy put into the moment of silence that followed Harley's comment. "I don't want to connect to Seeger. It's upsetting enough to think how he died. My grandmother was killed in a car crash. It must be awful to be crushed. Just imagine—"

"Crushed," Aileen cut in. "Bad as a mammogram, like getting your boobs slammed in a refrigerator door."

Oralia's face reddened in the dim light. I waited for her eruption, but it didn't come. Linda spoke instead.

"My poor sister," she whimpered. "She was all I had left. My dad died of a stroke, and then Mom died of cancer . . . and then my sister—"

The waterworks were flowing again. And she still hadn't let go of Vick.

"We would never ask you to do something you didn't want to," Vick assured the group. His voice had a strangled quality, which I assumed was due to Linda's grip on him. "The seventh chakra can guide you to your higher self, to guides and goals and information. Don't limit your idea of the seventh chakra to . . . um—"

"The deceased," Kapp finished for him cheerfully.

"I guess the higher self part might be nice," Linda murmured, her voice still thick with tears.

"Lead me to the seventh," Kapp seconded.

"I suppose," Eddy sighed. He reached for his notebook and sat, cross-legged on the floor.

Aileen rubbed up against Harley's leg suggestively.

"Wanna mingle our seventh chakras, honey?" she asked.

"If everyone would sit in a circle, we could prepare," Oralia suggested.

A series of thumps followed as each of us lowered ourselves to the floor.

"And now, if you will close your eyes," Vick ordered hypnotically.

"And as you close your eyes, imagine a place above your head, but still connected to your body—"

"A place that may look like a cloud—"

"Or a starburst—"

"It might be violet—"

"Or white or silver—"

"But you can feel it—"

"What do you feel?"

I opened my eyes stealthily. I was feeling the power of the seventh chakra, the connection that I used for my own energy practice, but I wanted to see how others were reacting.

I spotted a perfect violet halo across the room. Who—of course, it was Dee-Dee. And next to her, Roy, with black and silver rays jaggedly sprouting from his head like a punk hairdo. Eddy's energy was collected in a tight indigo circle around his head. And Kapp's aura was a medley of colors way too big for his body.

"Now imagine Seeger—"

Linda Frey gasped. Too many colors to count swirled around her.

"And tell him good-bye."

I turned to Oralia and Vick, willing myself to keep from feeling Seeger's fall again. Oralia was nestled in a gentle aura of silver and white that matched Vick's almost perfectly. They were the real thing. Not that their being in touch with their higher selves at this moment meant that they couldn't kill, too.

I closed my eyes again. For all of my impressions of colors and shapes, I knew nothing that told me about murder. And there were too many people in the room for me to feel them individually.

So I told Seeger good-bye.

And I felt and heard nothing. I searched further, telling myself that it was my fear of the falling sensation that was stopping me from feeling his presence. I consciously relaxed. Still, nothing. Was it because Trica was missing—

"And now you can all open your eyes again," Oralia told us. Her voice held a serenity that I wouldn't have associated with her before.

"Who would like to share their feelings?" Vick asked.

Surprisingly, Oralia was the first to speak.

"It took Vick to remind me that Seeger was human," she whispered. "Thank you, Vick."

"Oh, I wouldn't be too sure he was human," Aileen put in. Then her face turned serious. "But I miss the guy. He could make me laugh. And we made a good thing happen at The Sensual Body. Massage oils to tantra toys, we've got it all. I'll bet he'd be glad the business is still going."

Linda was uncharacteristically quiet, but not Eddy.

"I saw something that might have been Seeger, a flash of orange," he informed us. "But, of course, I'm unusually sensitive—"

"Dee-Dee!" a high-pitched voice squealed before Eddy could finish. "Cally!"

And through the haze, I saw Wiz running toward our group.

"Wow, are you guys doing magic?" he demanded.

Dee-Dee laughed and waved. Wiz was by her side in an instant.

"Maybe we can share magic tricks?" he suggested. "See, I can do lots of cool things. I've got a new one. You take this pretend mouse, see, and tie it on a wire. Then you put it in the walkway and when someone comes up, you jerk the wire."

Dee-Dee put her hand over her heart and widened her eyes. "Oh, yikes!" she yelped.

"Yeah, yeah," he said, his words tumbling out faster than his mouth could hold them. "And, and I've got this really cool Houdini rope—"

"Any severed fingers coming up?" Dee-Dee asked.

"Only for special occasions," he stage-whispered. "That's what my mom says."

"Wiz!" a new voice reprimanded.

I turned to see Phyllys coming our way now.

"Uh-oh," Wiz murmured.

By the time Phyllys had dragged Wiz out of the room, everyone was looking a lot better in body and in spirit, so to speak.

I cleared my throat.

"Now that we've said good-bye to Seeger," I began, "how many of you here want to really know what happened to him?"

"We know what happened," Harley growled. "He got stoned and fell off his porch."

"Well, I, for one, think that's not very probable," Eddy threw in. "The man was not the suicidal type."

"And what do you know about suicidal types?" Aileen challenged.

"Plenty," Eddy snapped back. "I'm a writer, remember. A writer knows people—"

"As if we could forget," Aileen muttered.

"I think maybe we shouldn't think about it," Linda said softly. "Remember, he had a wife, and you wouldn't want her to suffer."

"Anyway, the man fell," Harley finished up. Or tried to.

"Not good enough," Kapp plowed into the conversation jovially. "Remember, Cally here is psychic."

There was a short silence.

"If she's so psychic, why hasn't she figured out what happened yet?" Aileen asked.

"Ah," said Kapp, waving his hand. "The spiritual realm is not as simple as ours. What might be a blink of an eye here might be an hour there. It's only a matter of time."

Had Kapp started his career as a con man? I wondered momentarily. Or was that just another word for lawyer?

Meanwhile, Roy stood and made his way to a spot between Kapp and myself.

He bent over and whispered in Kapp's ear. But I could hear him easily. I wondered who else could.

"You shouldn't be talking about it," Roy hissed. "You're putting Cally in danger."

Kapp whispered back, loud enough for people *outside* the room to hear, "Shouldn't you be on meds or something?"

I jumped up and grabbed Kapp's arm myself, dragging him onto his feet and into the most secluded corner of the room I could find.

"Don't make fun of Roy," I told Kapp.

"Oh, do you think I should listen to his darkness, allow him his experience?" he asked in a flutey falsetto.

"Have you been talking to Dee-Dee?" I accused.

"Dee-Dee's been talking to me," he snapped back.

I paused for a moment.

"So what do you think, Kapp?" I asked. I really wanted to know. Kapp was a good people person, and he didn't pull any punches.

"My advice?" he asked.

I nodded.

His bulldog face went grim. "Keep your distance from that guy. He's bad news. Cally, you deserve better."

I felt tears spring to my eyes. I'd asked his advice, and I'd gotten it.

"Look, Cally. If I was a year or so younger . . ." He leered unconvincingly.

"So, if you're psychic, what do you do?" a voice from behind me asked. Eddy.

"I'm an energy worker, a healer," I told him, turning away from Kapp dispiritedly. "I'm not what you'd call a psychic—"

"Do you help the cops find bodies and all that?" Eddy continued.

"I just told you," I tried again. "I'm not that kind of psychic. I'm a healer."

"Then what are you doing here?" he asked.

It was a good question. And I didn't have a good answer. Not one that didn't involve Trica. And I was hoping that people would forget about Trica. Okay, I *am* an optimist.

But Kapp had an answer. "Ms. Lazar is here to research the paranormal effects of Seeger Snell's death," he began. And then, his mouth was off and running with exquisite pomposity.

Once he'd finished his dissertation, Kapp grabbed my

elbow and escorted me out of the ballroom posthaste.

I looked back over my shoulder and saw confusion, curiosity, and hostility as we exited. The hair on my arms went up.

We were barely out of the ballroom when we passed Dulcie, the kitchen help, smoking something very pungent in a corner. Something her aunt would not approve.

"So, what do you think of this bunch?" Kapp asked Dulcie with a shrug to the ballroom. He bared his smile.

"A bunch of weirdos," she answered nonchalantly.

"Does that include Rhoda and Phyllys?" he pushed on.

"Nah," she said. "They're all right. But the workshop people. They're the same ones who were there when Seeger died. Except for you and your snoopy friends."

"And?"

"And why would they come back, man?" Dulcie retorted. "Oralia and Vick usually do afternoon and evening workshops, but no one really wants to do them, so they're letting the whole schedule go to hell. Bunch of weirdos. Maybe they all figured out a way to kill him together."

"Why weirdos?" I asked

She shrugged, then spoke again.

"You don't like the dope I'm smoking. You should see the stash Harley has in his room. He practically had a cow when Kapp here said he was in legal investigation."

"And . . ." Kapp led the witness.

"And Aileen, always moaning, but I'm not sure she has sex with anyone, even Harley. Keeps him on a leash or something. And Linda. Whoa, next stop, loony bin. Gives me the creeps. And Eddy with that notebook, what a phony. Jeez, if I was going to do an intimacy workshop, I'd wanna do it with cool people. Cute guys, maybe." Dulcie smiled dreamily and took another drag on her joint.

"Get me Luke Perry or Peter Facinelli, and I'll come," she finished up.

She snuffed out the tip of her joint with practiced fingertips and stuck it in her pocket, then wandered down the hall.

"I hope she'll be okay," I muttered, not even knowing what I meant exactly.

Kapp turned to me suddenly.

"You okay, Cally?" he asked. "Did something happen to you?"

Ah irony, I thought. The least intuitive person in the circle from an outside view, and he had noticed I was shook from my run-in with the intruder. No one else had.

I told him about the incident, keeping my voice light.

Kapp ignored the lightness and began to question me.

"Could the blur be a child?" he began.

"No." I was sure of that.

"How do you know?"

"The blur wasn't small enough," I answered, thinking.

"So, it wasn't a very short person?"

I shook my head. Why hadn't I thought of that?

"Was the person excessively large in height?"

"No . . ." I said uncertainly.

"Did you smell anything?"

"Potpourri," I answered eagerly, suddenly remembering.

"Tell me about it—"

"Oh, rats," I remembered. "It was in the room."

"Did you hear anything?"

"A gasp, maybe?"

"Male or female?"

"I don't know," I answered dismally.

"Was there anything about the person's movements?" Kapp kept on. "A familiar rhythm, jerkiness, slowness, quickness?"

"The blur was fast."

"Faster than average?"

I shook my head. "I just don't know."

"Cally, did you see an aura?" Kapp asked.

"A tinge of red!" I yelped. How could I have forgotten? Now I remembered, but who—

"Configuration of aura?" Kapp prodded.

"Just the slightest haloing on the edges of the blur."

"Would you recognize it if you saw it again?"

"Maybe," I said hopefully. Then I dropped my shoulders. "But maybe not. You know how people's auras change all the time."

Kapp's face looked old and worried.

"Perhaps I shouldn't be playing the psychic card," he muttered. "I wanted to flush someone out. What if I have? Want me to sleep in your room tonight?"

"No such luck," I told him. I softened for a second. "Thanks, Kapp."

His cane was up in a moment, but it still wasn't fast enough. I knocked his cane to the side and put the tip of my own cane to his throat.

He said with a big smile, "I guess you'll be okay."

Dack, he was good. Not with his cane, mind you. But with everything else.

Kapp escorted me to my room and left. I lay down and thought how lucky I was to have such weird friends. And then I started wondering how the blur had gotten into my room. How had it unlocked my door? A mental image of Rhoda's reception area filled my mind. Old-fashioned keys lined up by number. And she wasn't always there at the desk. So who was it? I was just too sleepy to think. I began to get ready for bed when I heard a knock on my door. I looked at my watch. It was late, past eleven.

I shouted through the door, cane in hand.

"Who is it?"

"Oralia and Vick!" came the return shout.

Should I open the door?

SEVEN

I grabbed my cane in my right hand, holding it securely aloft in preparation for mayhem. And with my left hand . . . I opened the door.

I just couldn't think of a plausible reason not to open up besides "I don't open my door late at night to people I think might be murderers, especially when they come in pairs." There was something in me that just couldn't spit out those words. Especially since I'd said my door was always open. I wondered if there were statistics on the number of people who had died for the sake of politeness.

But by then, my door was open, and I saw Vick and Oralia. They didn't look like murderers, they looked scared, both of them. Oralia's square face was tense and oddly vulnerable. Vick's perfect features were scrunched, and he avoided my eyes.

"What's happened?" I asked, suddenly alarmed. "Are you two okay?"

Vick nodded, but before I could question him further, Oralia spoke.

"You have to find out what happened to Seeger Snell," she pronounced. Her voice was firm and clear but lacking the serenity it had held earlier that evening.

I almost laughed. Right. Someone else who thought I held the answer to Seeger Snell's death.

"Oralia has me convinced that if we don't put Seeger's death to rest, no one will come to our future seminars,"

Vick murmured. He sounded ashamed, embarrassed. Was he ashamed to be at my door again, or ashamed of Seeger's death? Or was it something else? Psychic, dack. I couldn't even figure out what people felt when they were speaking to me aloud. "We need help, and you seem to be it," he finished up.

I looked at their faces for a few more heartbeats, breathed in the incense that scented each of them, and finally ushered them into my room with a sweep of my cane. They may not have been there for a healing, but these two truly needed my help. The question was whether I could provide it.

Vick and Oralia sat on the end of my bed, their shoulders touching. I sat in my wingback chair, still holding my cane. I should have been comfortable in that chair, but I wasn't.

Oralia bent forward, her eyes intense under heavy brows.

"First, let me explain," she started. "Vick and I have regular jobs. I'm a nutritional counselor, and he's a fundraiser for charity. But these seminars are our vocation. Maybe that's what your healing is like for you?"

I nodded cautiously.

"Then you know how hard it would be to lose what we've worked for. We've spent years building our clientele, making our workshops important emotionally and spiritually as well as fun and, most of all, safe."

She paused and looked down at the floor. Vick took over for her.

"And the thing is," he told me. "We can't guarantee the safety of the workshops anymore. What if Seeger committed suicide? Was it because of some emotional issue that was raised by our group?"

"And worse yet," Oralia took over again. "If Seeger Snell was killed, the killer is probably here."

I nodded again. "Except for me and my friends, everyone here was at your workshop the last time," I stated.

Oralia's head jerked back in surprise. I guess she thought I hadn't figured that part out yet. Now it was her turn to nod.

"And then you add in Trica and the people who run the inn," I went on.

Oralia was nodding again. But I didn't have any further to go.

"Cally, do you know what happened?" Vick asked, a plea in his voice.

"No," I answered honestly. I was batting zero for two with Vick tonight. "Though I do have reason to believe that Seeger didn't commit suicide." A little shiver ran up my left side as if to remind me what reason I had for my belief. I wiggled my shoulder to shrug it off, fully expecting Seeger Snell's ghost to appear at any moment. I just hoped he had some answers if he did.

"Then you know something." Now, Oralia sounded excited.

"Just that," I told her, shaking my head apologetically.

They stared at me, waiting for more, like my cat, Leona, when the cat food isn't up to her standards.

"But, together, maybe we can learn more," I suggested positively. I always caved in with Leona, too.

"How?" Oralia demanded.

I stared at her. On the right side of her torso, red and blue radiated angrily from her breast. Was this the sign of a murderer? Or maybe illness—

"What do you see?" she asked softly.

I brought my own hand up to the corresponding spot on my own body and touched it lightly in answer.

Oralia paled.

"Oralia?" Vick questioned, his eyes opening wide.

"Nothing," she snapped. "Nothing." She drew in a

sharp breath. "Okay, how can we help you find the murderer, if there is one?"

I wanted to ask her what the "nothing" was that was upsetting her. But that "nothing" was her private business. So I answered her question instead.

"You can tell me more about the group members to start," I offered.

"But what do you want to know?" Vick asked. "We can't tell if any of them is a murderer."

Nor can I, I thought, but I pressed on anyway. "How long have they been with you? What are their idiosyncrasies? What have you noticed? Do you suspect anyone?" I wished Kapp was there to help me with the questions.

"Well, Seeger and Trica have been coming, off and on, for ages," Oralia began slowly.

"And Aileen," Vick threw in.

"That's right," Oralia confirmed, her voice gaining speed. "Aileen has been coming ever since she went into partnership with Seeger. First with another guy—Dave, I think—then with Harley. If she hadn't been sitting with Trica, I might have suspected her in Seeger's death. Seeger treated her badly at times. Of course, he treated Trica badly, too: made fun of her weight constantly, sometimes slept with other women, that kinda stuff."

"Linda and Eddy were new the last time," Vick told me, rubbing his chin. "Eddy found out about the group from one of the flyers our friend Felicia posted. And Eddy's some sort of acquaintance of Linda's. But not close, I think."

"And of course, Felicia didn't come this time either," Oralia interjected bitterly. "None of our regulars came who weren't here last time. They're afraid, and I don't blame them."

"Why do you think the rest came back?" I asked. Dulcie's earlier question had been a good one, one that just wouldn't go away for me. "You'd think *they'd* be even more afraid."

"Hmmm," Vick buzzed, stroking his chin again.

"Eddy's easy enough to understand," Oralia offered. "He likes the drama. For him, it isn't real. Just fodder for his eternal writing."

"And Linda really seems to need emotional support," Vick added. "I think she'd brave a lot for that support."

"How about Harley and Aileen?" I prodded.

"Those two are pretty thick-skinned." Oralia tilted her head in thought. "Maybe they just don't care. Or worse, maybe they're just as glad he's dead."

Vick's eyes opened. I could tell he didn't want to think that badly of Harley or Aileen. I sighed. He was clearly a fellow optimist.

"What if Aileen and Harley really thought it was just an accident?" Vick tried. "They wouldn't have any reason to be afraid."

"It's possible," Oralia conceded brusquely. Her tone told me she didn't think it was probable though. I was trying to keep an open mind, myself.

"Okay," I said. "How about the innkeepers?"

"Rhoda and Phyllys are two good women, a truly devoted couple," Vick answered, smiling. "They both love Rhoda's kid. They're always cool, never blink at any of our goings-on. I don't think either of them particularly liked Seeger, but they never said anything offensive to him or about him, as far as I know."

"Harley's an odd one," Oralia put in absently. "You gotta watch out for him. He's an aggressive SOB sometimes. And he gropes. But I don't know if he actually makes love to women. He gives me the creeps." She shook her head. "And Linda is strange, in some sort of constant state of despair. Actually, she acted really strange when Seeger introduced himself last time, but then she's always acting out, so I don't know if it meant anything or not. And Eddy . . ." She turned to Vick. "What more can you say about Eddy?"

Vick laughed, and when Oralia joined in, they looked like a couple for a minute. Vick went on. "Eddy is a Writer, with a capital *W,* which makes me suspect he's unpublished. I sort of like him though—"

"You like everyone, Vick," Oralia objected.

I laughed now. "You say that like it's a bad thing," I put in.

"But—" she began. Then she smiled, a truly warm smile. "I guess I ought to appreciate Vick more, huh?" she finished instead.

Vick blushed painfully. At least it felt painful to watch.

I changed the subject. "Someone told us that you guys usually put more time into your workshops, but that your scheduling has deteriorated. Is that true?"

Now both Oralia and Vick looked embarrassed.

"I guess we were more interested in finding out about Seeger's death than putting on our usual workshop," Oralia admitted. "I mean, you might as well have asked why *we* had the nerve to show up. I thought that Seeger's death wasn't right when it happened. Everyone who knew him felt that way. And I needed to know what happened. So . . ."

"So here you are," I finished encouragingly. I was beginning to like this woman a lot. There was a warm and ethical person under that prison-guard persona.

We sat for a while until I came to the important question.

"What did you think of Seeger?" I asked.

"Um," Vick murmured. Was he afraid to admit that he liked Seeger, too?

"Well, I hated him!" Oralia snapped. "He was my first boyfriend in high school—"

"He was?" Vick demanded, almost standing. Oralia tugged on his arm and he plopped back onto the end of the bed.

"He was as mean then as he was before he died," Oralia went on, her words fast and angry bullets now. "The only reason he slept with me was so he could tell all the guys he had. And I was 'in love.' " She made fluttery little hand movements like a Southern belle. "It's a wonder I lead intimacy workshops. Seeger almost ruined my ability to be intimate for life."

"Is that what's been bothering you?" Vick asked softly, wrapping his arm around her.

But Oralia was definitely still wanting in the intimacy department. "No!" she snarled and squirmed out of his embrace like a slippery cat.

Vick sat, stunned, on the end of the bed, his eyes full of hurt and confusion.

"Oh, Vick," Oralia whispered in a voice that made me feel as if I should leave the room. But it was my room.

Oralia stood, reaching for her fellow workshop leader.

"Come on, Vick," she murmured. "It's late."

She hugged me quickly, and then they left.

I lay on my bed and thought about what they had told me. And what they hadn't told me. And after a few minutes, my mind had drifted to Roy. Intimacy, it was catching.

Dee-Dee wanted me to take Roy as he was. Kapp wanted me to stay away from him. Who was right? I had once promised Roy that I would never force him into psychiatric care or medication. His childhood had been scarred. His mother had been institutionalized and had died in that mental institution. His father was a drunk. And from all this came a man of caring. My friend Oscar had suggested quite seriously that the darkness that Roy carried might be his form of the cross. But I didn't really accept the concept of the cross as a symbol of suffering. I truly felt the divine, whatever form it might take, as love and goodness. Blame my upbringing. If only I could convey what I felt to Roy, however nebulous. I sighed and told mys elf not to cry. Then I put on my pajamas and got under the covers, smoothing the quilt with my fingertips and giving myself up to that feeling of love and goodness. I was asleep in less than a minute.

The next morning, I woke up warm and sweating to the sound of someone knocking on my door. And something that smelled like apples.

I put on my glasses and looked at my watch as I yelled, "Who is it?" Ten o'clock. Oops.

"Room service!" the voice yelled back.

Every movie I'd ever seen where room service turns out to be a masked murderer carrying a knife, gun, or bomb flashed through my mind.

"What kind of room service?" I demanded loudly.

"Rhoda's kind of room service," the voice came back. And it certainly sounded like Rhoda, the voice warm and melodic, even as she yelled through the door. Then I heard a burst of laughter. It was Rhoda, all right. Not that Rhoda couldn't be a murderer.

"Hold on," I ordered and grabbed my cane. I looked down at my pajamas. They would have to do, yellow zebras and all. I didn't have a robe.

And then I opened my door once more to someone who might have been a murderer. At least the possible murderer had a cheerful smile on her face and a steaming tray in her hands.

"You missed the breakfast buffet," she told me.

She set the tray down on the small glass-topped table by the wingback chair and pulled back its domed cover with all the hand waving of a professional waiter. I looked down and breathed in spiced apple cider, tea, a fruit smoothie, three kinds of muffins, and what looked like vegetable frittata.

"I thought you might be hungry," she said simply.

My salivary glands gave her an inaudible answer. I smiled.

"And you wanted to talk in private," I added for her.

Her face lost its smile for a moment, then she laughed.

"Mother of God!" she exclaimed, dramatically clasping her hands to her chest. "You *are* psychic!"

"Just busy," I told her, giggling with her. "You might want to designate my room the private conference room for the duration."

"That bad?" she asked, eyebrows raised.

"Uh-huh—" I said, biting into a muffin. I tasted cranberry and maybe orange. "But this makes up for it."

"Oh good," she purred and sat on the end of my bed.

I took a sip of the hot apple cider. Yum.

"So, have you and Dee-Dee figured anything out?" she asked after I munched for a while longer.

I shook my head.

"You forgot my friend, Kapp," I reprimanded her. "And Roy. You need a course in better spying."

"And you're the one to teach it?" she questioned, her eyes sparkling with mischief.

"Oh sure," I played along. "Just let me know how to deal with Trica, and we'll be even."

"Duct tape," she suggested.

"Duct tape?"

"For her mouth," she said solemnly.

We both laughed then. Neither of us would ever last in spy school. We'd be thrown out for giggling in class.

"So how'd you end up an innkeeper anyway?" I asked after a gulp of the fruit smoothie.

"Well, you know all of this area was farming country," she told me. "Grain, baled hay, potatoes. That's what my great-grandparents exported. Then they brought in cows for a dairy. By the time my parents died, we were selling milk, Brussels sprouts, squash, and flowers—"

"You mean, you inherited this land?"

"Yep," she confirmed proudly. "I'm a fourth-generation Fiebrean. Debby Dahl is a veritable newcomer."

"Wow," I said. She and Chief Dahl obviously had their own history.

"So when my parents died, I decided it was time for a change. I sold off some of the land and used the money to refurbish the family house as an inn. Actually, then I had grand plans for a women's retreat. But the women didn't have enough money. So I opened the place up for all kinds of retreats and workshops. We've had Breatharians." Her eyes glittered. "At least Breatharians are easy to cook for since they don't eat. And UFO societies, environmental poets, healing dancers, Vedic astrologers, yogis, shamanic feminists—"

"And intimacy workshops," I finished for her. My head was reeling with the possibilities.

Rhoda sighed. "And intimacy workshops."

"And you don't want to lose your good reputation for all these groups because of Seeger Snell," I guessed.

She scanned me carefully. "Maybe you really are psychic," she muttered.

"I'll do my best," I promised her.

She took that as her exit cue.

As she was going out the door, I called out, "Thanks for the bribe!"

She laughed and waved over her shoulder.

And I finished my breakfast. Well, half of it. Maybe if I figured out who killed Seeger Snell, I could come here to live. I wondered how Rhoda would feel about goats.

I did my morning meditation, though it was getting

closer to noon. And finally, I dressed and left my room to go lift some weights.

I was just stepping outside into the sun and wind, when I smelled a familiar aftershave behind me.

I circled and swung the tip of my cane so that it touched Kapp's wrist. I could have knocked his cane from his hand, but I didn't. It was enough that he knew I could.

"One of these days, Lazar," he snarled, lowering his cane. "One of these days."

"Good morning to you," I sang back.

"You gotta tell me how you always know I'm there," he ordered.

I just smiled. If he couldn't smell his own aftershave, it wasn't my problem.

But Kapp wasn't finished with me. He lifted his cane again. Kapp's real problem was that he hadn't spent his teen and adult years studying potential lethal cane use with my brother York, the martial arts master. Not that I was going to tell Kapp that either.

"Okay, Lazar," he hissed and thrust his cane in my direction. But I wasn't there when his thrust arrived. Only my cane was, blocking his thrust. I turned my hand just enough so that his cane was tugged from his grip. It clattered to the ground.

"Damn—"

I heard a neigh of laughter somewhere nearby. I turned and saw Chief Deborah Dahl.

"Whoa, a little swordplay going on, Ms. Robin Hood?" she asked jovially.

Kapp stood in front of me, suddenly my advocate instead of adversary.

"You will note that we are not playing with swords but with canes," he answered the chief. "I don't believe there is a law against the use of canes in your city."

Sergeant Zoffany crossed his arms and stood behind his chief menacingly.

"So, Ms. Lazar," Chief Dahl sneered. "I understand you're a psychic." She closed her eyes and attempted a look of deep concentration. "Maybe you can guess what I'm thinking now."

I glanced at my attorney and kept my mouth shut.

Chief Dahl opened her eyes and waved a finger in front of my face. "Not very good. You wanna try again, girl, or shall I just tell you? Keep your nose out of Seeger Snell's death. Or else. I'm the law here."

"Debby!" Rhoda's voice rang out.

She stomped up and shook her own finger in Chief Dahl's face.

"Are you threatening one of my guests?" Rhoda demanded.

"This isn't your playground," the chief replied. "You're in Fiebre, my jurisdiction."

"And you're at my inn, on my property," Rhoda shot back.

"Not to mention the fact that your threats to Ms. Lazar might be actionable," Kapp threw in.

Chief Dahl crossed her arms and looked at her sergeant.

"Who is this clown?" she asked him.

But Sergeant Zoffany just shrugged his shoulders.

"Madame," Kapp introduced himself. "I am Warren Kapp, attorney at law."

Something flickered in the chief's eyes. I had a feeling she read *Newsweek*. She knew who Kapp was. It was one thing to threaten me but another to threaten Warren Kapp.

"Fine," she muttered. "Just fine." Then she looked at our innkeeper. "Just keep your guests in line, Rhoda," she finished, turned on her heel, and left, Sergeant Zoffany an obedient bear in her wake.

"And let that be a lesson to you," a new voice whispered. I turned my head and saw Phyllys, a grin on her pink face.

She and Rhoda went back inside after that, chattering like squirrels about lunch. I turned to go back to my room. I still had half of my breakfast to eat, and I'd worked up an appetite. It wasn't the cane-fu. It was the engagement with Chief Dahl. What if Kapp hadn't been there?

"Thanks, Kapp," I said once more to his back and walked inside and down the hallway to my room.

I had just eaten my third muffin and slurped down the last of my smoothie when my phone rang.

Oscar Suiza, another one of my energy worker friends, answered when I picked up.

"Did you call me about the 'dark forces'?" I asked, joking.

There was a silence on the other end of the line. Criminy, he *had* called about the dark forces.

"Cally, I care about you," he declared earnestly. "Roy may have foreseen your mission in Fiebre—"

"Oh, come on—"

"Really, Cally," he cut back in. "Be careful. Watch your back."

"What do you see exactly?" I asked.

"Danger," he answered. My stomach shrank around my muffins. "That's all I can say. I feel danger."

I hung up the phone. So much for Kapp saying Roy should be on meds. Maybe Oscar should be, too. Or maybe Kapp and I were the ones that needed help. Everyone else saw the danger but us.

I walked to my window, opening the blinds and letting the sunlight stream in.

And saw a six-inch-wide spider looking back at me.

EIGHT

Criminy! I'd never seen a spider that big. I stepped back in spite of the fact that the spider was on the other side of the window, my heart thumping loud enough to accompany a reggae band. After a moment though, I was drawn back to the window. There was something weird about that spider. It wasn't moving, and in fact, it looked like rubber. I saw the thread holding it extending all the way to the end of a stick. The thread wasn't gossamer. It was man-made.

I moved away from the window casually, then sprinted to my door. I wanted to see who was holding the other end of the stick. I ran as fast as my weak leg could take me, down the hallway and outside, doubling back around the building to the other side of my window. Whoever was holding that stick might be the murderer. Had they killed Seeger by somehow scaring him off that balcony? My questions raced as fast as my feet. I made the last turn and saw the culprit. Ratsafratz. I had to lower my eyes, not to mention my expectations.

Because the person at the other end of the stick was, of course, Wiz Neruda. And he smiled as I came limping his way. Not the behavior of a guilty felon.

"Did I scare you, Cally?" he asked eagerly, his eyes glittering in a familiar expression of mischief. Rhoda's expression. "Did I, huh?"

"Wiz," I answered solemnly. "You did scare me, and that isn't a good thing."

"Cool!" he whooped, waving the spider on the end of his stick. "See, I just got the spider yesterday. I ordered it in the mail. It took my week's allowance, but it was worth it if it scared you. See, scaring people is fun—"

"As long as you don't overdo it," I finished for him.

"Wow, that's what my mom and Phyllys always say, too."

"And do you listen?"

He tilted his head, pondering the question.

"I didn't overdo it, did I, Cally?" he finally asked, subdued. He put his stick on the ground, the spider with it.

I looked at his small, worried face. And I fudged.

"No, you didn't overdo it," I told him. "But that's just 'cause you tried it on me. Don't use your spider on anyone else besides me or your mom or Phyllys, okay?"

"Okay," he agreed unhappily.

I thought of adding Kapp to the list of permissible spider victims but then shook my head. What was I thinking?

"Wiz, your mom and Phyllys are having a hard time with their guests right now, and you don't want to scare a guest and mess up their business for them."

"But it did scare *you*, didn't it?" he persisted.

"It sure did," I assured him. "I jumped so high, I hit my head on the ceiling."

"You did? You did?" Wiz was jumping pretty high himself now, and laughing.

"Wiz, did you play any games with that Seeger guy?" I asked.

"Nah, that guy never wanted to play. He's like my dad."

"Your dad?"

"Yeah, he wants me to live with him. Yuck. He wants

me to use his stupid last name, too. But I won't. I'm a
Neruda."

"Does your father live around here?" I asked, suddenly
curious.

"Nah, he lives in Wisconsin. Mom says he was born in
a cheese vat."

I hid my smile. Rhoda was going to get in trouble with
her mouth someday. She probably already had.

"My dad says it's my mom's fault that I don't have
more friends. But, see, I have all the friends I want. Emily
and Taz, and all the neat people who come here. And I
can do all these cool things, too. So who needs a bunch
of friends? And who needs him?"

"Right!" I agreed stoutly. And I really did agree. I felt
a distinct aversion to Wiz's father already, and I hadn't
even met him.

Wiz laughed again and picked up his stick, making the
spider dance.

"Whoa," I said. "Can you make him do acrobatic
tricks?"

The spider had just executed an impressive backflip
when Phyllys came walking up to us.

"Wiz," she said severely. "Where have you been? Your
mother and I have looked all over for you."

"I've been showing Cally my spider, Phyllys," he shot
back, ignoring the severity of her voice. "Watch this."

The spider danced along the ground, then did a grand
leap, turned in the air, and landed like an Olympic pro.

Phyllys smiled as Wiz went on playing with his spider.
"Wiz is really a good kid," she pronounced.

"He's got my vote," I told her.

"He didn't scare you with the spider, did he?" she asked
suddenly.

"Only a little," I fudged again. "And I told him to only
scare me or you or Rhoda from now on."

"Thanks, Cally," Phyllys whispered, breathing out tension as she spoke. She reached out a hand impulsively. "Not everyone understands Wiz. Not everyone understands *us*."

"You mean, you and Rhoda?"

She nodded emphatically. "This is a small town. So far, no one has objected to our relationship. Sure, they whisper, but basically, they can tolerate the presence of two lesbians in their community. Still, I'm afraid that Seeger Snell's death could make us a target of suspicion, or worse. Rhoda's been here forever, and even that isn't enough to make up for her lifestyle."

I felt something molten fill my backbone, the resolve to investigate Seeger Snell's death so that all the innocent parties could carry on their lives again. I wondered if that's what made others become detectives, not the urge to find the guilty, but the need to free the innocent from suspicion.

"When we were in the city, it was different. Nobody cared what we did, but here . . ." She sighed. "Rhoda loves it here, it's her home. And running the inn is great. We do a little of everything: cooking, cleaning, remodeling, bookkeeping, plumbing, you name it. And in between times, we have the ocean, and each other. And Wiz." She smiled affectionately.

"Is it lunchtime yet?" Wiz asked.

"Omigod!" Phyllys looked at her watch. "I have a buffet to put together! Wiz, come on, we've got work to do."

Phyllys grabbed Wiz's hand and she, Wiz, and the spider rushed back around the building to the main entrance.

I would have followed them to be first in line for the buffet, but I'd already had enough breakfast for lunch.

So I lifted weights and thought about suspects. I didn't want to suspect anyone I liked, but it seemed that everyone I liked had a motive. I raised my barbell to arm's

length above my chest in a bench press. Seeger Snell had
demolished Wiz's scooter. Even something that little
might have given Wiz, his mother, or Phyllys a motive,
if one of them was crazy. I slowly lowered the barbell
until it touched my chest. And Phyllys was an angry
woman. Not to mention Oralia. And of all the motives,
Oralia's looked the strongest. Seeger had abused their relationship in high school. That must have festered. And
what had he done to her recently? I raised the barbell
again. Then there was Vick. What if Vick actually *had*
known about Seeger and Oralia's former relationship?
Dack. And what had Oralia said about Linda reacting
strangely to Seeger when they'd met? And how Seeger
had abused Trica and Aileen, while he was at it. And
Eddy was sensitive. Seeger could have set him off any
number of ways. I lowered the barbell.

I was beginning to sweat. The bench presses weren't
that difficult, but finding a murderer among the suspects
was going to be a lot harder. So far, I had yet to eliminate
anyone totally, even Trica. I lifted the barbell again.

Chest, shoulders, legs, stomach, biceps, and triceps
later, I left the weight room soaked with perspiration. The
breeze chilled my wet skin, and random conclusions
chilled my mind. Anyone could have done it. Or maybe
Seeger hadn't been murdered at all. My body was strong,
but my will was weakening. It was fine to intend to dis-
cover Seeger's murderer and restore peace to Fiebre, but
how was I going to do it?

I looked out toward the ocean and saw a group of pelicans flying in formation. Seagulls screeched above the
sound of the ocean's roar as waves traveled endlessly in
and out from the shore. I shivered in the wind and tasted
its salty edge. Slowly, the sun warmed my skin, and my
spirits rose with each wave that crested. Persistence was
the answer. The ocean knew it, and now, so did I. If I

kept bugging people, sooner or later, something would give.

I stood there, enjoying the play of water, wind, and sun. And then something new entered my line of vision. Oralia. She was jogging down the beach, her hands in fists and her shoulders hunched in anger. What made her so angry? I had seen her other side. She could be friendly, kind, even serene. Had it been something recent that had sent her into this angry place? Had it been Seeger?

Fists and hunching aside, Oralia looked strong as she ran, very strong. Strong enough to somehow topple Seeger Snell off his balcony without being seen? I watched her as she circled a cypress tree and returned, her eyes forward, focused on nothing but her path.

And then I saw Eddy walking toward me.

"So, what does a psychic see when she looks at the ocean?" he asked when he reached my side.

I just wished that Eddy wore aftershave like Kapp did. Then I could tell he was coming and leave before he got there.

"Do you see the endless despair?" Eddy went on. "The emptiness of life. The meaninglessness—"

"Actually I see hope, joy, and peace, not to mention beauty."

Now Eddy noticed me.

"You do?" he asked incredulously.

"How can you miss it?" I shot back. We might as well have come from different planets. "The colors, the exuberance—"

His sigh cut me short.

"I guess I'm too sensitive," he murmured. "And my current novel . . ." He sighed again.

To ask or not to ask? I knew I might be sorry if I rose to the obvious bait, but on the other hand, who knew what a synopsis of his current novel might reveal about him? I cleared my throat.

"What are you writing about, Eddy?" I asked and snuck a quick glance at my watch. Anything over a half hour, and I was out of there.

"You really want to know?" he demanded.

I nodded, wondering if I was the first person who'd taken the bait.

He ran a hand through his unruly hair, thinking. Finally, he took a big breath and began.

"There's a young man, you know?"

"Uh-huh," I encouraged.

"He was adopted when he was a kid. His parents were brilliant, but they died in an auto crash. The people who adopted him ran a grocery store. They never noticed how smart he was. By the time he was ten, he was doing their books for them. He wanted to go to college, but they wanted him to help in the store. So he left, flooded with guilt and despair. He made his way out to California and enrolled in the university. But even there, people couldn't understand his intelligence."

I nodded, wondering how old Eddy was. Probably around forty. But his fantasies hadn't made it much past adolescence.

"Finally, one night, a beautiful woman comes to his room. She's from another planet, but he doesn't know that then. She makes love to him and asks if he'd be willing to help the Earth. The president is a real jerk and has a plan that she has foreseen will cause a total apocalypse. The president's always joking and has all these women, but he's really stupid. But the young man understands this woman. Even when he realizes that she's an alien, he knows that she'll be making better decisions for the Earth than the president of the United States—"

"The president sounds kind of like Seeger," I threw in.

"Very observant," Eddy complimented me, a smile crumpling his frown-lined face. "I'm basing his character on Seeger's. He gets it in the end, but that would be spoiling the plot for you. Anyway, the young man is one of the few people on his planet who actually understands what's really happening. The aliens have warned the others, but they won't listen."

"It's hard to be an outsider, isn't it?" I tried this time. Then I noticed a blur of movement from behind a nearby cypress tree. Was someone else *voluntarily* listening to this story?

"Oh, but he doesn't mind," Eddy answered, his eyes going out of focus. A greenish aura floated around him like an evaporating cloud. "Because the aliens give him the ultimate weapon and the power to use it. They've finally found someone they believe can make the right decision."

"Does he?" I prodded, staring at the cypress tree.

"Of course, but it takes a painful toll. He is left with a few like-minded citizens on an Earth that has returned to Eden." Eddy sighed and opened his palms to the sky. "Remembering what had been and mourning."

Eddy's voice went silent then. Had he finished his story?

"So, how does the president get it?"

Eddy's eyes focused then. He frowned deeply at me.

"Why do you want to know?" he snapped. Reddish brown hair appeared and disappeared again from behind the cypress tree. Was that Roy?

"Oh, I just wondered," I replied defensively. "You really know how to build suspense."

"Really?" His eyes widened. "Sometimes, I worry people will steal my ideas, you know."

"It must be hard for a well-known writer like you," I purred.

Eddy's skin pinkened.

"Well, I'm not all that well-known."

"What are some of your recent books? I'd love to read them."

"My work is being considered by several publishers, but I'll tell you about it another time," he replied and edged away from me. "Catch you later."

As Vick had predicted, there were no published books. And I wondered just how much Eddy had disliked Seeger.

Then I remembered the cypress tree. My heart warmed. Roy had been looking out for me. We needed to talk. I took a deep breath and walked toward the tree. But there was no one left behind it. Maybe there never had been anyone there. Dack!

I was walking back to my room when I heard footsteps pounding behind me. I turned and saw Vick.

"Cally, we're doing an afternoon workshop," he announced as he skidded to a stop, clearly out of breath from running. "I'm gathering all the group members I can find." He looked down at the ground for a moment. "We're going back on schedule. We haven't been honoring our workshop commitments. Will you come? We'll be meeting in about fifteen minutes."

I told him I'd come. Here was a chance for me to see all the workshop suspects up close. *Give intimacy a chance,* I concluded.

Fifteen minutes later, I was in the ballroom with the silk hangings, the candlelight, and the incense. But it wasn't as dark as it had been the night before. The afternoon sunlight was doing its best to circumvent the curtains and the hangings. I could actually see all the participants. Vick and Oralia were stationed at the main candle. Eddy, Linda, and Aileen stood nearby. But no Harley, I realized. I wondered where he was. Kapp and Dee-Dee were there. And Roy, golden eyes wide and pleading. My body began to move toward him without thought. Then Oralia interrupted.

"Thank you all for coming on such short notice," she began. I put my foot back on the floor and kept it there. "We realize we might have been a little too . . . um . . . spontaneous this time around."

Aileen and Dee-Dee chuckled, and I realized Oralia was making an attempt at humor. But it was too late for a token laugh.

"Today, we return to intimacy—" she said, her clear voice low.

"Today, we learn to see—" Vick chimed in.

"How many times have you looked at someone and seen nothing but your own reflection?"

"Wouldn't you like to see more than that?"

"To share true sight—"

"Insight—"

"With another human being?" Oralia paused and then went on. "Today, we will look into each other's eyes—"

"Really look—"

"Seeing not only the eyes—"

"But the spirit."

I shivered. What did these people's eyes hold? Secrets? Guilt? Ruthlessness? Criminy, Roy and Eddy must have been wearing off on me.

"So, pick a partner," Vick ordered.

I looked at Roy, but Eddy was standing in front of me before I moved. Eddy. Interesting. I thought of his book synopsis and suddenly remembered something else. Eddy had said on the first night that he was writing a book about Seeger's death. And now, that book was bad science fiction with a president who might bear a resemblance to Seeger. Was he already distancing himself from the incident?

"Now, look into your partner's eyes—" Oralia commanded.

"Really look—"

"What do you see?"

I looked into Eddy's eyes and saw an attractive shade of blue. It was true. I couldn't have even told you the color of Eddy's eyes before. And they were squinted under dark brows. *Had* I only seen a reflection of myself earlier?

"Now, look beyond the eyes themselves into the soul," Vick whispered.

I looked and saw a murky swirl of color behind his eyes . . . and a darkness not unlike Roy's.

I took a sharp breath in, startled by the sight. Was Eddy truly sensitive? Could he even belong to the same species as Roy?

"I'm sorry," Eddy muttered. "I always blow people away like that."

"You do?" I muttered back.

"There's something dark about me," he said. "Right?"

"Dark forces?" I asked, my voice hushed.

"What?" he yelped. He looked closer at me. "Are you making fun of me?"

"No, no," I assured him, or tried to. "It's just that I have a friend—"

"Now, find another partner," Oralia ordered.

"But—" I said to Eddy.

He just turned his back on me and walked over to Dee-Dee.

I put my head into my hands for a moment. And then, Roy was there. I didn't even have to open my eyes to see him.

But I looked into his golden eyes when Oralia told us to. I saw them as I always had, the beauty, the shape, the kindness and intensity. Then Vick told us to look beyond the eyes. And I did. What I saw bore no resemblance to what I had seen behind Eddy's eyes. All the colors of the rainbow were behind Roy's golden eyes. The darkness was not in his eyes. It merely surrounded his body. In fact, it didn't seem to be *of* him at all, only traveling with him.

"Roy," I blurted out. "The darkness isn't yours."

"You see that?" he whispered.

"Yes," I whispered back. "It's not you. It's just attached to you."

"But if—"

A wail broke into his words. I turned to see Linda sobbing on Vick's shoulder. Oralia marched forward, intimacy paramedic to the rescue.

"It's okay to cry," she told Linda, and Linda took her advice. Aileen joined them for a while, stroking Linda's back, her usually irreverent face showing concern now. But Linda only cried louder.

I turned back to face Roy, but he was gone. Gone from his place in front of me and gone from the room. Dack. I thought about his darkness. Why hadn't I seen that it wasn't really him before? Just like Seeger's orange blob on Trica. And what about Eddy's darkness? What was that? Despair, true despair? Or the darkness of a murderer? But the person that had come to my room had worn a red aura, not a black one. My mind spun.

I closed my eyes. When I opened them, I was looking into Aileen's face.

"You okay?" she asked, her rowdy voice subdued.

"Fine," I lied. "Fine."

"Anymore fine, and they'll have to take you away in the loony wagon," she commented.

I laughed. I couldn't help it.

And Aileen smiled with me. There was good nature in

her face. Something about her steel-rimmed glasses made her look trustworthy.

"Everyone seems to be melting down here," she went on. "And I'm not just talking the candles."

"Where's Harley?" I asked.

"Baying at the moon," she answered. "It's his time of the month."

Then I really cracked up. I was laughing hysterically as Linda cried all the harder. It made for a good balance.

Once I'd stopped, I remembered my self-promise of persistence.

"You must have known Seeger pretty well," I led in. "What'd you really think of him?"

"Ah, let me count the words," she began. She raised a finger. "Jerk." She raised another finger, and she was rolling. "Peckerwood, pipehole, moron. And those were the nice things about him."

"Really?" I pushed.

"Really." Then her face turned serious. "But he was funny, too. He could make me laugh. Seeger Snell was a wild man. Lots of people thought he was too wild, but that's just how he was. A guy, you know, couldn't see beyond a good boob implant. He was always chasing some woman . . . or some dream. That's why *I* ran the business. It won't be a lot different without him, still selling lotions and potions. Still, he had a sense of humor. I keep wondering if he was doing some kind of joke when he fell. I mean, right there in front of me and Trica. It was just too weird." She looked at me to see if I understood.

I nodded. And I smiled. I liked Aileen better when Harley wasn't around.

"I think we'll break now for the afternoon," Oralia announced. Linda sat on the floor like an empty water balloon.

As we trailed out into the sunlight, I tried to put all the things I'd learned into context. But I couldn't. Roy was too much to even think about. And as for the death I was investigating, I knew what was missing. It was Seeger Snell. I'd never met him. It was time to visit Trica at her hideaway hotel to meet him secondhand. Even in my long heart-to-heart with Trica, I'd never quite understood who Seeger was.

I got into my Honda and drove down the highway to the Cypress and Pelican Inn. I was told I couldn't miss it when Trica had first talked me into this trip. And I didn't. The six-foot sign with the pelican and cypress were a good clue. Once I'd parked, I made my way into the lobby. This inn was very different from Rhoda's, all in white and sand colors. I was about to storm the registration desk when a familiar voice greeted me.

"Cally!" Trica yelled. "Come and join us."

I turned and saw that Cally wasn't alone. There were four other people seated with her: Geneva, York, Arnot, and Melinda. Someone had called a family reunion.

NINE

"Geneva?" I whispered tentatively. I still wasn't sure I was seeing what I was seeing. It didn't make sense in a reasonable universe that my four siblings would be seated comfortably with Trica Snell, the dead man's widow, in a cozy circle of beige couches.

Then I remembered that mine had never been a reasonable universe, no matter how hard I had tried to make it one. My young hopes of conventionality had died about the same time my law career had.

"Cally?" four voices said as one. They made a nice symphony: Geneva's resonant cello, Arnot's exuberant flute, Melinda's nasal saxophone, and the single note of York's deep drum.

"How'd you find us?" Geneva asked, rising from a deep sofa with the grace of a dancer. She was dressed in one of her own creations, a fluid pajamaesque pantsuit of ruby silk with a mandarin collar.

"I didn't really—" I began.

"You're okay?" York asked brusquely before I could finish. When he rose, it was with the precision of a tight-rope walker. Of course, York was a martial artist. He could probably walk a tightrope if he wanted to.

"Well, I suppose so, but—"

"Of course, you're okay," Arnot exclaimed, waving his hands. "You are absolutely superb, as ever." He hopped off the sofa and blew me a kiss. I never knew if the gay

act had to do with Arnot's exclusive cabinetmaking business or if he just liked to play. York was the one who
really was gay.

"But what are you guys—" I tried again.

"We just decided it was time to act," Melinda told me
with a little giggle. "We said, 'Cally's in trouble. We'll
just take the willy-nilly space machine and get her.' "

I smiled. Melinda was a cartoonist, her creation one
"Acuto from Pluto," an alien sent here from his home
planet as a punishment for his goof-ups. Only Acuto continued to goof up here, much to the popularity of Melinda's daily strip. She had become lost in his personality
years ago, down to the nasal whine of his voice. And yet,
somewhere in her words there was a hint of the reason
that my family was all here, sitting in the lobby of the
Cypress and Pelican Inn with Trica Snell. They were here
to help me.

Geneva reached me first with a hug that could have
held me for a thousand years. Then York with a quick
squeeze, Arnot with an expansive embrace, and Melinda
with an awkward arm around my shoulders. Especially
awkward since she was even shorter than I was.

Then they just stood and stared at me. All the Lazars
shared the same sharp, gaunt features, but on Geneva they
looked elegant, on York, almost predatory. Arnot's face
was softened somewhat by his receding hairline and added
weight. And Melinda just managed to look goofy under
her cropped hair. Criminy, I loved them.

"Roy asked us to come," Geneva finally announced,
breaking the silence.

"Roy?"

"He was worried." Melinda explained. "Son of a lizard,
sometimes I think he worries more than Acuto. That's
some asteroid he comes from."

"Still, there's real danger here," York reminded us.

"But we are here to serve you, my lady," Arnot finished with a deep bow. "The Lazars shall prevail."

"And you all came," I said in amazement, afraid I might cry.

"Your relatives are really cool, Cally," Trica shouted from the couch, and I forgot about crying. There *was* danger in Fiebre. But I couldn't talk in front of Trica.

"Tell me, Trica," I blurted out. "Are you absolutely sure Aileen was with you the entire time when Seeger jumped from the balcony?"

I hadn't known I was going to ask her that. But it had been bothering me. Of all people, Aileen appeared to have the most motive. Except, of course, for Trica.

"Sure, she was there the whole time, Cally," Trica insisted, her eyes reflecting hurt. "Remember, I told you all that."

"Right," I agreed, and remembered that I didn't want to talk to Trica in front of my family.

"Trica, maybe you should rest now," I managed in my most reassuring voice.

"Rest?" she asked.

"Lie down," I suggested.

"Or take a walk," Geneva added dryly.

"Oh!" Trica's blue eyes widened. "You need to be with your family. I'll go for a walk. I promise, Cally."

She bounced out the door, and five sighs of relief joined the piped music in the lobby.

"Sit down," I ordered. One by one, we each took our seats on the beige couches. I breathed in familial support for a moment, and then I told them about everything, ending with the story of the intruder in my room.

I might as well have thrown a bomb on the teak coffee table.

"And you wondered why we showed up," York hissed.

"Do you think we wouldn't show up? We're the cavalry, and you need us nearby."

"This person actually entered your room!" Geneva protested belatedly, bending forward, hands outstretched as if to dismember the described intruder.

"This is midgin awful—"

"You keep your cane by your side, don't you—"

"They'll have us to answer to if they harm a hair on your splendid head," Arnot finished, standing and flinging out his arms.

"But I'm okay," I tried.

"Still, this is serious," Geneva pronounced. She leaned back for a moment, lost in thought. All eyes were on her when she followed up. "We need someone on the inside."

"Right," Melinda agreed. She attempted a salute and bopped herself on the side of her cropped head.

"But how?" York asked.

"We'll think of something," Geneva promised, and somehow, I believed her.

"Honey?" Arnot asked me. "What else do you need?"

I looked around the lobby. It was empty, except for Lazars.

"Keep Trica out of my hair," I whispered.

"Heh-heh," Melinda offered, pretending to shoot Acuto's ray gun.

Geneva just shook her head.

"Duct tape," York growled.

"Especially over her ever-so-lovely midgin mouth," Arnot added.

"You're not the first to suggest duct tape," I told them.

All four of my siblings grinned. And I grinned with them. Dack, we were scary.

I drove out of the Cypress and Pelican Inn a lot more confident than I had been when I'd driven in. In fact, I was so pleased with myself that it wasn't until I made it

back to The Inn at Fiebre that I realized I'd never interviewed Trica about Seeger. As much as I wanted her out
of my hair, I still needed to know about the man. Of
course, I assumed that Trica knew herself. *Did* she know,
without realizing, whatever it was about Seeger that had
triggered his death?

I parked and walked toward the inn with the ocean
wind at my back, pondering. Did *I* know the factor that
had triggered Seeger's death? I had talked to so many
people and heard so many things. Had I ignored something vital?

I was almost to the front door when I heard someone
sobbing. And I immediately forgot all the safety warnings
my family had just given me. A sob was someone in need.
And that someone was, unsurprisingly, Linda, standing a
few feet away, near another parked car, doubled over as
she wept, her arms crossed over her stomach.

"Linda," I whispered, approaching her. "What is it?"

"I . . . I—" she tried, and then broke into fresh sobs.

I put my arms around her and gently rocked her.
"There, there," I cooed. Not original, but usually it
worked.

Usually. This time, however, Linda broke away from
me, rolling her cartoon-wide eyes and pounding the inside
of her elbow as if she wanted to tell me something.

"It's okay," I told her. "Take your time."

Her aura gave me no more clues than her words, a
tangle of colors so complex that I couldn't read it at all.
Charades in full knotty spectrum. I knew Linda was in
despair, but beyond that, nothing.

"I . . ." she sobbed. Then thickly, "My sister . . ."

She wept again. And I remembered from somewhere,
something. Hadn't her sister been killed in a weight-lifting
accident? Linda pounded the inside of her elbow again.
Was she miming her sister's death?

"Your sister," I tried as calmly as possible.

She nodded her head violently.

"She . . . I . . ."

"Linda, does what you're trying to tell me have anything to do with Seeger Snell's death?" I asked softly.

Linda's eyes widened even more. Acuto from Pluto had nothing on her. But she still hadn't answered me. I opened my mouth to prod her further when I heard the sound of bagpipes in the air.

Bagpipes?

"It's Harley," Aileen's strong voice said from behind me. "Harley plays the bagpipes when he's feeling moody."

"Oh," I answered. Maybe Linda's ability to speak, or not speak, was rubbing off on me.

"Of course, Harley's always moody," Aileen went on. "But he doesn't always play his bagpipes."

"How moody?" I asked. Now I was up to two words.

"Not moody enough to murder, if that's what you're thinking," Aileen snapped.

"No, I . . ."

Then I turned back around. Now that I was talking like her, I was suddenly aware that Linda was gone. In the short time that I'd been listening to Aileen, Linda had disappeared. Dack! I couldn't see her behind any of the parked cars. Or hear her over the ocean's growl either. Maybe she'd gone to her room. Had one of the front doors been opened?

"What are you looking for?" Aileen asked.

"Linda," I answered. "She . . . she was upset."

"Girl's always upset," Aileen told me. Then she grinned. "Harley's moody, Linda's upset. Not many of us are sane around here anymore."

"Um . . ."

"Hear about the mad cow?" Aileen inquired.

"What?" I said, totally confused now.

"One cow says to the other cow, 'Aren't you afraid of getting mad cow disease?' Other cow says, 'Why should I be? I'm a camel.' " Then Aileen leaned her head back and laughed deeply.

It took me a while to get it. Then I laughed, too. Aileen was a funny woman. I wondered if she was an observant one.

"Aileen, you knew Seeger," I began. "Was there something about him, some factor I can't see, that could have caused him to kill himself—"

"Or someone to kill him?" Aileen finished for me. She frowned for a moment. "Aside from being an all-around jerk, I can't really think of anything. But you never know, someone that manic might have had a depressive side."

Criminy, she was right. All the descriptions I had heard of Seeger might have added up to manic. I just hadn't thought of it that way. What if Seeger *had* killed himself? But if he had, why the intruder in my room?

Aileen stared at me as I ruminated. I had a feeling she thought I was a cow thinking I was a camel.

"Gotta go," I told her finally.

"See you later," she rapped out with apparent good humor, slapped my shoulder, and strode toward the front doors.

My mind was on overload. I turned so I could see the ocean from the parking lot. I needed its calming perspective. But instead of the ocean, I immediately noticed Vick and Oralia, silhouetted in front of it.

I watched as Vick leaned over Oralia, caring evident in his protective posture. Oralia curled her hands into fists. Vick stepped back. Oralia lowered her head, then held out a hand. Vick reached—

And then I smelled aftershave. I turned and knocked Kapp's cane out of his hand.

"Holy Mary, Cally," he snarled, picking up his cane. "How the hell do you do that?"

I just smiled nonchalantly.

"I don't suppose you're interested in what my fact-finding network found out about the Fiebre Intimacy inmates?" he tried. Dack, he might be lousy with his cane, but he was good with words. Was I going to have to beg?

"Come to my room and tell me?" I offered.

"Show me how you always know I'm there?" he countered.

I shook my head. Some secrets have no price.

His bulldog face went pink. I almost laughed. I wouldn't have to beg. Kapp was dying to tell me what he'd found out. Grumbling, he followed me inside the front doors of the inn.

I folded back the quilt before sitting on the end of my bed when we got to my room. Kapp lowered himself into the wingback chair across from me. I bent forward and settled my chin on the end of my cane.

"Well?" I tempted him.

"Too bad you left your law practice," he told me with a glare. "Could always use a psychic negotiator on my team."

I leaned back and laughed.

The glare faded from his face. Kapp liked a laugh.

"Okay, have it your way," he conceded. "Got some more information on some of the wackos here. Might as well share it."

I nodded encouragingly.

"Harley Isaacs is a piece of work," he began. "The SOB's got a record for assault, to begin with."

"What'd he do?"

"Two incidents," he answered, spreading two fingers in the air. "One was a bar fight some eight years ago. He beat up on some gay guy more recently though, no reason given. The gay guy dropped charges. Harley had Marv Figone for an attorney. He got lucky."

Kapp sounded admiring. I knew the admiration was for Marv, not Harley though. Marv was a good defense attorney from what I'd heard.

"Marv said Harley's been surly ever since his wife died. More than ten years, but he never got over it."

"Marv told you this?" I asked incredulously.

"Sure, confidentiality and all that garbage."

I shook my head. I was glad I wasn't a lawyer all over again.

"Asked Marv what the wife died of," Kapp went on. "Thought there might be a connection to Snell. But she died of cancer. No connection that I can see. And get this." Kapp leaned forward in his chair, his face lit with the joy of gossip. "Aileen Meyer's nobody's sweetheart either." He paused for effect.

I could have tapped him with my cane, but I just waited instead. It worked.

"Aileen used to be an anesthetist," Kapp told me. "Worked for some jokers doing plastic surgery. Got kicked out of her job for stealing drugs."

"Her attorney tell you this, too?" I asked.

"Hey!" he objected for the record before going on. "I got it from the receptionist. One of my informants dug her up. Anyway, Aileen was never prosecuted. They just threatened her with prosecution if she ever worked as an anesthetist again."

"Why didn't they prosecute?"

"They would have looked bad. Some tony plastic surgeons. They don't want anyone knowing they had a drug thief working for them."

I nodded, trying to look wise. And I'd liked Aileen. I probably still did.

"So Harley and Aileen are a matched set of losers. If

you're looking for a murdering twosome, I'd say they'd fit the bill," Kapp concluded.

"It's a long way from assault and drugs to murder," I pointed out.

"You've been out of the legal arena too long," was Kapp's only comment. Then he went on. "And if you're looking for another twosome, just look at our innkeepers."

"What?" I objected.

"Here's the story. Rhoda Neruda's ex-husband has been trying to win back custody for years. He's a piece of work, too. A druggie for one thing. So he hasn't been successful. Still, the woman's a lesbian. One slipup and, poof!" Kapp snapped his fingers. "No more custody for Rhoda."

"But—"

"You think she wouldn't kill to protect the kid, cover up a murder?"

I shut my mouth. I wasn't sure.

"And get this. Phyllys has a report on her record for assault, too. Guess who she beat up?"

I opened my mouth, trying to think of an answer. But I wasn't fast enough.

"Rhoda's ex, that's who. The wimp slapped the kid, so she slapped him. Did more than slap him. Broke his jaw. But he didn't press charges. Didn't want to admit a woman beat him up." Kapp chortled.

"The ex is still trying for custody, but he isn't getting very far. Wiz's age, he pretty much gets to call the parent he'll be with, and he wants Rhoda."

"Kapp, do you think Rhoda could lose Wiz if there's too much scandal over Seeger's death?" I asked.

"Nah," he said. "Ex has gotta find out first. But if Seeger had anything really heavy on Rhoda or Phyllys . . ."

"But what could Seeger have had on either of them?"

I pressed. "They're both devoted to Wiz. He's a great kid—"

"Hey, I'm not opposing counsel here. I just said *if.*"

"How about Linda Frey?" I asked. "Criminy, that woman is upset about something."

"Got someone working on Frey, and our writer friend, and the rest of them. But these things take time. Gotta get the networks in place just right to get good answers."

"Like with Marv Figone?"

Kapp waved his hand.

"Part of doin' business," he assured me. "I've done Marv some favors, too."

"So," I said seriously. "Who do you think did it, Kapp?"

"Too early to tell," he responded after a beat. "Wait till all the evidence is in, then we can take a better look."

It sounded good, but still . . .

"Is it possible that Seeger Snell really did just kill himself?" I asked in a small voice.

"Cally, anything is possible. Reasonable doubt and all. But I don't think so. Trust your gut on this thing. You think he was murdered. I believe you."

"Thanks, Kapp," I said. Then I stood up and gave him a kiss on the top of his balding head.

"Whoa!" he cried, jumping out of his chair. "Sneaking up on an old man like that!" He swiped at me with his cane. I parried.

He was still blushing when he left my room.

I smiled, and the phone rang.

I answered with a bright "Hello," expecting one of my siblings.

But no one answered my greeting. There was nothing but breathing on the line. And then the click as the connection was broken.

Son of a lizard. Was the caller the previous intruder in my room? Was it the murderer?

I dialed Rhoda at the front desk, telling her I'd just received a call.

"And?" she asked.

"And the caller didn't say anything," I told her. "A breather."

"Oh," she said softly. "No one called the inn in the last fifteen minutes."

"But my phone rang—"

"So it must have been someone *at* the inn," she went on. "Room-to-room calls don't go through the switchboard."

It was my turn to say, "Oh."

I hung up the phone very carefully. I had to leave the room. When I opened the door, I stuck my cane out first.

And collided with a body.

I looked up, startled, and saw Harley Isaacs grinning back at me.

TEN

"Gonna beat me to death for walking down the hall?" Harley whispered.

I considered it. I still had my cane in my hand. And Harley looked weird smiling. His dark reddish hair and white beard just accentuated the lines of his face, lines that didn't go with a happy face. I looked at his position. Was he nearer to my door than he should have been? The halls weren't all that wide. He might have just been walking—

"Or would you rather tie me up and whip me?" he went on suggestively.

It could have been something to laugh at, but what might have been funny coming from someone else's mouth seemed frightening from Harley.

Then I took a closer look at him. His aura was blue with what looked like a ripped seam in the back.

I put down my cane.

"Harley, are you sad?" I asked.

The demonic smile disappeared from his face. And I saw that the lines there were lines of despair, old despair. And I remembered his dead wife.

"You're really a psychic?" he growled uncertainly.

"An energy worker," I said, shrugging my shoulders. It wasn't the time to argue semantics.

"Okay, energy worker," he hissed. "Tell me about despair. How long do you think it can last?"

"Forever?" I guessed.

He stepped back from me.

"Yeah, that's right," he finally agreed. "Forever."

"Harley, would you like to reach out from the despair?" I asked him. Because if he didn't want to, there was no way I could help him.

He stared for a moment, then sighed. "I'm not really sure," he answered quietly. "It's a way of keeping her with me."

"Your wife?"

"Yeah, my wife," he snapped. "What the hell do you know about it?"

"My parents died when I was a teenager," I answered softly.

He shook his head and looked human for a moment, though not quite solicitous.

"Life gives you love and then tears it away," he stated. "If I met God, I'd rip his throat out."

Dack. This guy was scary even when he was sad.

"I forget for a while," he bulldozed on. "Smoke a little dope. Drink a little wine. And then, I remember again, and it feels like I've been shot in the gut."

I nodded. I knew what he meant. Only I felt it in my leg. And in my heart.

"Who the hell made this world work this way, anyhow?" he asked rhetorically. At least, I hoped he was asking rhetorically. I certainly didn't have an answer. "Why all the pain? Where's the joy?"

"There is joy," I told him softly. "Honestly. You don't betray the dead by feeling joy. And you can remember them without—"

"What do you know?" he challenged, moving way too close to my body. My hand tightened on my cane. "Maybe there's joy for you, but there's none for me."

"I heard you playing the bagpipes earlier," I whispered.

"And?"

"And there was joy in the music," I answered. "Sadness, too, but joy and wonderment—"

"You can hear that?"

I nodded.

"Then your hearing is better than mine," he finished brusquely and turned to stride stiffly down the hall.

So much for cheering him up. Anyway, what was I doing trying to heal a suspect? Dack. Could Harley have made the anonymous call to me and then rushed from his room in time to stand in front of my doorway? I thought of asking him, but he was gone from my view when I looked down the hallway. The man walked fast, stiff as he was. And I still wasn't sure if I'd really just surprised him walking down the hallway or if he'd been at my door, regardless of the phone call. I sighed. Briefly, I considered giving up my investigation into Seeger Snell's death. Whose idea had it been anyway? Trica's. And Trica—

I heard a rustling behind me. And I didn't smell aftershave. Slowly, I turned, placing both of my hands on my cane.

"Who's there?" I demanded.

"Me," a voice squeaked from behind a potted plant.

I lowered my eyes and saw Wiz staring up at me as he peeked out from his hiding place, his oval face filled with concern.

"What are you doing here?" I squeaked back. Criminy, it was bad enough that Harley had startled me, but now my heart was pounding over a ten-year-old boy.

Wiz looked off to the side, his face flushed. "I was protecting you," he muttered and walked out from behind the plant.

"Protecting me?"

"Yeah, see, I can protect people with my magic. Honest. It's really cool. And I saw you and Harley—"

"Did you see Harley walk to my room?" I interrupted.

"Naah," he replied. "You were already talking when I came up." Wiz looked back at me, the flush gone. "Harley is really spooky, huh, Cally?" he said.

"Uh-huh!" I replied enthusiastically and immediately felt unfair. "But he has problems," I added gently.

"Is he sad?" guessed Wiz. Or maybe he'd heard our conversation.

"Yes, he is, but he scares me, too."

I didn't want Wiz tangling with Harley, no matter how sad he might be.

"Didya hear him playing the bagpipes?" Wiz asked.

I nodded.

"Wow, was that spooky or what!" Wiz went on. "Like from another planet. In fact, I got to thinking maybe Harley *is* from another planet. I mean, all those mooing sounds and stuff. And look at him. His hair and his beard don't even match. See, I read this really cool book about invaders from space, and Harley could be one of them. Wouldn't that be cool, Cally? Maybe we could, like, catch him in a net or something—"

"No nets," I interjected.

Wiz's impish features looked sullen for a second.

"Watch him from a distance," I suggested instead.

He brightened. "Yeah, like in the movies. Sir-whatchamacallit."

"Surveillance?" I tried.

"Yeah, that, too. See, we can keep an eye on him, and if he, like, changes shape or anything, then we'll know. . . ."

I kept my smile inward. Melinda and this kid would get along great. Maybe Wiz would end up doing an outer space refugee comic strip when he grew up, too.

". . . Could we put him in a net, then, Cally?" Wiz was asking.

Ratsafratz, I hadn't been listening. Still, I was pretty sure I knew the answer.

"If you ask your mom or me first. Otherwise, no nets."

"That's cool," he agreed.

I looked at him more closely.

"Wiz, did you think Seeger Snell was from outer space?" I asked carefully.

"Seeger?" He shook his head. "Uh-uh. Was he?"

"No, no," I put in quickly. I didn't want to put the idea into his head. That was a rumor I didn't need to start.

"He was just mean," Wiz added.

"So I hear. . . ." I ventured, hoping for follow-up.

"Wiz, I've been looking all over for you."

Rhoda came down the hallway, looking less gorgeous than usual with a scowl on her face.

"Marcie's mother called," she announced and crossed her arms.

Wiz seemed to shrink.

"Marcie told her mother that aliens had landed and killed one of our customers."

"Wow," Wiz said, his round eyes feigning innocence.

"Now where do you think Marcie got *that* idea?" Rhoda asked softly.

"Um," Wiz mumbled. He shrank a little bit more. "I guess I told Emily, and maybe she told Marcie."

"Oh Wiz," Rhoda sighed. "Don't you understand that telling people these stories can hurt our business?"

"But Mom!" Wiz answered. "What if I'm right? Harley is really weird. Cally told me I couldn't use a net on him unless I asked you or her first—"

"A net?" Rhoda shifted her eyes to my face.

"Yeah, in case I catch Harley calling his ship or something."

Rhoda turned her head away.

I thought I heard a muffled laugh. But Rhoda's face

was serious enough when she turned to look at me again.

"Cally, don't encourage him," she ordered. "I know he's fun, but I'm nervous now. If he tells these stories and they get out, someone might think he knows more about . . . you know."

About Seeger's heading off the balcony, I thought, nodding my head vigorously. I hoped my face wasn't flushing, because *I'd* already wondered if Wiz had played an accidental part in Seeger's demise.

"Rhoda," I began, trying to infuse calm into my voice. "Wiz may think Harley might be from outer space, but he doesn't think Seeger was."

Rhoda's eyes softened slowly.

"It's okay if he tells me this stuff," I added.

"You, maybe, but not Deborah Dahl, Chief of Police," Rhoda reminded me. "Think what she'd make of Wiz's stories."

I thought. It wasn't much of a step from luring one alien into a net to tricking another into jumping off a balcony. That's what Chief Dahl would think. Maybe. But everyone knew that ten-year-olds have imaginations. Not to mention limitations. I still didn't see how Wiz could have pulled it off even if he'd tried.

"Mom, I'm protecting us," Wiz put in.

Wrong approach. I changed the subject quickly.

"Did you ever figure out who the call to my room was from?" I asked.

"No." Rhoda frowned again. "But whoever called you had to have called from within the inn, and they had to know your room number."

I wiggled my shoulders uncomfortably. The person who had called my room had probably been the intruder. And the intruder had probably been the murderer.

"So either they were checking where I was or trying to scare me off," I concluded.

Rhoda raised her brows. "Well, I'm scared," she put in.

Wiz pulled his infamous spider out of his pants pocket. "They bother you again, Cally, I'll scare them to death!" he proclaimed.

What Wiz had in gallantry, he lacked in timing.

Rhoda bent over and grabbed Wiz's arm. "Wiz, never say anything like that again!" she hissed.

"But Mom—" Wiz began.

"Wiz, aren't you listening to anything I'm saying? You've got to stop that kind of talk."

"I was just protecting Cally," he objected.

Rhoda gripped his arm harder. "I know you'd like to protect Cally, but don't talk about scaring people to death! Mother of God, we're in enough trouble as it is. You've got to start—"

But Rhoda's shoulder was tapped from behind before Wiz or I ever heard what he had to start. Rhoda dropped Wiz's arm and spun around, stopping short when she saw that it was Phyllys who'd touched her.

"What are you doing?" Phyllys demanded angrily. "Are you hurting the boy?"

"Of course not," Rhoda snapped. "Do you think I'd hurt Wiz?"

Phyllys just stared, her pink features coolly appraising.

"It's okay, Phyllys," Wiz put in. "Mom just didn't like me saying—"

"Don't say it again—" Rhoda threw over her shoulder.

Phyllys crossed her arms. Suddenly, I was afraid of her, afraid of her anger when it came to protecting Wiz. Rhoda was Wiz's mother, for criminy's sake. And I would bet she wasn't an abusive one. I looked at Wiz. He was cringing. What if I was wrong?

"Mom?" Wiz whispered. "Phyllys?"

"It's okay," Rhoda told him, and it was. "Phyllys worries about you. So do I. You know we both love you."

Wiz nodded solemnly.

Phyllys uncrossed her arms, and all the anger seemed to leave her body.

"I'm sorry, Rhoda," she muttered. "I don't know what got into me.

"We've all been a little tense lately," Rhoda said. Kee-rups. No kidding.

"Not me," Wiz argued.

Rhoda laughed. "That's what I'm talking about, you little scamp." She reached down and hugged him.

I let myself breathe.

"Rhoda, your sister called," Phyllys announced. "She's on the phone."

Rhoda let out a small groan.

"All right," she gave in. "Let's all go talk to my sister."

I decided I was included in the invitation and followed Rhoda, Wiz, and Phyllys out to the lobby.

Rhoda picked up the phone behind the registration desk while I sat down on a velvet couch. Wiz sat down across from me. Phyllys was still on her feet though.

In the silence, we heard Rhoda.

"No, Mona," she growled.

A pause.

"Don't believe everything you hear," followed. Then, "I know I live an alternative lifestyle. Actually, I'm quite aware of it."

Another pause.

"Mona!"

Phyllys winced.

"Aunt Mona's really weird," Wiz whispered to me. "She drives Mom crazy."

"I'm hanging up now, Mona," Rhoda said. And she did. Then she came out from behind the registration desk, her hands in the air.

"Was it bad, honey?" Phyllys asked.

"It was my sister. How could it be good?" Rhoda answered.

"What'd she want, Mom?" Wiz tried.

"She wanted to tell me not to get 'involved' in murder." Rhoda threw her hands even higher. "Like I tried to get involved in the first place. Then she reminded me that she was my older sister and this was all for my own good. She heard all about Seeger Snell from the biggest blabbermouth in town."

"Debby Dahl?" I guessed.

Rhoda laughed. "No, Fred Ziegenhagen. He sells real estate. He's our portable Internet. He hears something, everyone hears it. Of course, Fred probably heard it from Marcie's mom, thanks to my Wiz kid."

Wiz grimaced.

"Welcome to small-town living," Phyllys threw in.

"Do you have an older sister?" Rhoda asked me suddenly.

"I have two, and two older brothers," I told her.

"And I thought I had problems," she hooted, laughing.

"So, are we having fun?" a new voice asked.

The four of us all looked toward the door. It was Oralia who'd spoken, and she was walking in with Vick at her side.

"I'm having fun," Wiz finally answered.

"Good," she answered, a smile lightening her tough face. "Maybe you can be our lead act at our next seminar."

"Cool!" he yipped, leaping up from his chair. "I can do magic and everything."

"Hon, I think she was joking," Phyllys told the boy.

"Aw, I knew that," he answered, deflating.

"Seriously, Wiz," Oralia offered, "maybe the next time we're here, you can be our opening act, do a few magic tricks and then disappear."

"Really?" he asked cautiously.

"Really," she repeated.

"Wow, cool," he said solemnly. His eyes went out of focus. I could tell he was already thinking up his act.

"Cally?" Oralia turned my way. "Can we talk?"

"Sure," I answered, keeping my seat.

"Um, maybe outside," Vick suggested. I'd been afraid of that.

The first thing I said when we left the lobby and stepped into the ocean air was, "I hope you're serious about Wiz because—"

"Of course, I am," Oralia cut in. "I'm not gonna break the kid's heart."

We walked out past the bougainvillea toward the ocean. It was cool now, the breeze even catching my heavy braid and whipping it around to flap in my face. Vick gestured toward a group of rocks in the sand, and the three of us sat down as formally as if we'd been called to a summit meeting. I could smell wild anise here, and seaweed, as well as the ubiquitous salt tang.

"We've dug up some information," Oralia declared. "Thought you should know."

"Anything about Harley?" I asked, suddenly curious about the man.

"Lots," Vick said quietly, his voice almost swallowed by the wind.

"You ever notice how stiff Harley is?" Oralia asked.

I thought about it and nodded.

"Old motorcycle accident," she told me. "But he still rides the motorcycle. It's almost like he enjoys being in pain. Not to mention all the anger he carries in his body."

"Harley's wife died some time ago," Vick added. "I think he *is* in pain—"

"But his wife died years ago," Oralia argued.

"Is there a statute of limitations on grieving?" Vick asked.

"Well, Harley's a jerk, almost as bad as Seeger was," Oralia insisted. "He gets stoned and then makes passes at the women. Then he gets morose again. I tell you, if we didn't need the members, I wouldn't put up with it."

"Now, Oralia—" Vick began.

"No," Oralia cut him off. "We shouldn't take the weird ones. Like that new guy, Roy. He gives me the creeps."

"Um," I muttered, leaning forward into the wind. "Roy is my boyfriend. Well, my ex-boyfriend."

Vick just groaned and closed his eyes.

"Damn, I'm sorry, Cally," Oralia offered. "It was just a first impression, and—"

"No problem," I interjected. I didn't want to get in a discussion about Roy. "So who else?"

"Well, there's Trica," Vick tried. "Poor woman."

"Trica comes to all the intimacy and tantra workshops she can," Oralia explained. "We worry about her. Even before Seeger died. She's just so . . . so—"

"Helpless?" Vick tried.

"Something like that. Low self-esteem, too." Oralia sighed. "And then there's Linda. Her sister was killed by her own weights in some sort of bizarre bodybuilding accident. She's only been to two workshops, but I still can't get through to her. She's in a permanent pitch of hysteria."

"I noticed," I offered. "But it's hard to tell exactly what she's upset about."

"I can't get her to really talk either," Vick said sadly. "She just cries."

"Well, at least Aileen has been a rock through all of this," Oralia went on. "She seems to be able to handle Linda. They hang out together sometimes. And Trica. Trica's lucky Seeger left her such a capable partner to manage their store. Aileen will keep it going, no problem."

Vick looked out to the ocean. A seagull cried. I tried to remember who we hadn't talked about.

"How about Eddy?" I asked finally.

Oralia and Vick smiled together.

"You just have to laugh with Eddy," Vick began.

"Because he's so self-absorbed, nothing really goes in his brain," Oralia finished.

And then they each put their hands over their ears and said in unison, "my novel." That was enough to set them both off laughing hysterically.

I was truly glad to see them having fun together. I got up and brushed the sand off my pants. They needed some intimacy time . . . alone.

"Wait up," Oralia ordered. "Have you figured out anything yet?"

I thought of all I'd learned and decided it was really confidential. Especially since Oralia and Vick weren't off my suspect list yet.

"Nothing important," I temporized.

They looked at me expectantly.

"I had wondered one thing—" I started.

"What?" demanded Oralia.

"Could Seeger have been manic-depressive?"

"Bipolar," Oralia corrected me automatically. She frowned in thought.

"Not really," she finally muttered, but she didn't sound sure.

"He wasn't really moody," Vick put in helpfully. "He was just impulsive."

"Not to mention insensitive," Oralia completed the thought for him.

Vick put his arm around Oralia.

It really was time to leave them alone. I wished I was

with Roy for a moment, then said good-bye and walked away.

I was almost back to the inn, when I saw Harley in the parking lot on his motorcycle.

"Hey, energy worker!" he called out. He was almost smiling again.

I approached him cautiously.

The smell of marijuana was strong when I reached him.

"What's up?" I asked, my tone even.

"So, is that little creep, Roy, your SO or something?"

"First," I answered. "Roy is not a little creep. And secondly, he is not currently my significant other, but he is a good friend."

Harley seemed to find my response amusing.

"Go, mama, go!" he cheered.

"Listen, Harley," I began, ready to lecture him. Then I decided to interrogate him instead. "What do you do for a living, anyway?"

"You really want to know," he asked, bending close to me.

"Yeah, I do," I answered, tightening my grip on my cane.

"I'm in charge of the celestial discharge log for Saint Zuleger's Hospital," he proclaimed.

"The what?"

"I'm a morgue attendant."

And then he really smiled.

ELEVEN

I stepped back without thinking. Dack! A morgue attendant? Well, someone had to do it, I decided, and tried to relax.

"Wanna know anything else, energy worker?" he asked, rolling his bike to the right until he'd made up the distance I'd put between us.

"How'd you feel about Seeger Snell?" I asked. For all of his efforts, Harley didn't really scare me. And I had my cane.

"I'd file him under *A* in my log," he growled. "Ya wanna know what part of the body *A* stands for?"

"No," I told him, shaking my head. I already had a guess, and it wasn't *aorta*.

"So, energy worker, wanna ride my machine?" He leered. I was surprised he didn't twirl his mustache. He really was reveling in his bad-boy role.

"I don't want to ride your machine or your motorcycle," I shot back. "Not now. Not ever."

But he just laughed, kick-started his bike, and roared away before I could ask him anything else. Actually, I was just as glad. Harley might not have exactly scared me, but he wasn't a relaxing conversationalist either. I liked his bagpiping better than his talking.

Phyllys, Rhoda, and Wiz were all still in the lobby when I went back inside the inn.

"Did you know that Harley was a morgue attendant?" I asked the group at large.

Rhoda shook her head. Phyllys looked pointedly at Wiz.

"What's that?" he was already asking. Ratsafratz. When would I learn to keep my mouth shut?

"He keeps a celestial discharge log," I told Wiz. "Kinda like an accountant."

The word accountant seemed to cool Wiz down.

"Aw," he muttered. "Aliens should have cooler jobs."

"Wiz, I want you staying away from Harley," Phyllys ordered.

"But Phyllys—" he began.

"You'd better listen to her," a new voice insisted. It was Dulcie, nose stud glistening in place. "Harley's a real loony tunes." She looked behind herself for a moment, then turned back to us. "I got some uncool news," she went on.

"What is it?" Phyllys asked patiently.

"Aunt Debby says I can't work here anymore, 'cause of all the weirdos and stuff. Says I gotta clear out. So, I'll be seeing you."

She spun around and walked toward the lobby doors.

"Hold it right there!" Rhoda shouted.

"Whaddaya want, lady?" Dulcie whined, spinning back around. "It isn't my fault. Aunt Debby's on my dad, and he says I gotta clear out, or he won't let me keep the car. Not to mention my room."

"But your aunt said it was an accident," I objected.

"Well, maybe she doesn't think so anymore. She practically had a cow when I argued with her." Dulcie shook her head. "She's so weird, man. Told me it might be dangerous here."

"Did she say why?" I asked.

"Aunt Debby doesn't explain, she just orders. Ya gotta

understand, she's on some, like, power trip or something. Even my dad doesn't mess with her."

"But you can't leave," Rhoda argued. "Phyllys and I can't handle the kitchen without you—"

"I told you!" Dulcie yelled. "It isn't my idea. I'd like to stay with you guys. But I can't mess with my Aunt Debby. I'm outta here." And with that, Dulcie turned on her heel and sidled out the front doors of The Inn at Fiebre.

"Maybe Chief Dahl knows more about the situation here than we do," I threw out into the ensuing silence.

Rhoda and Phyllys just looked at me, their relative skin tones drained to a uniform ash.

"What are we going to do?" they asked simultaneously.

"I could help," I offered.

And then I saw it. A look that said I couldn't be trusted in their kitchen. I wanted to remind them that Seeger was killed before I'd ever heard of their inn, but I didn't blame them. Here I was, snooping and prying.

"We'll do fine," Phyllys insisted, color revisiting her cheeks. "I'll do up an ad and post it downtown at the town hall."

"And one for the local paper," Rhoda added, clasping her hands together as she thought.

"Someone's always looking for an easy job," Phyllys soothed. "I'll bet we have someone by tomorrow."

"But I thought Dulcie liked us," Rhoda muttered angrily.

"Debby's just protecting her," Phyllys said mildly. "The girl's only nineteen."

"Right," Rhoda agreed. "You're right. I shouldn't be so selfish."

"I can help," Wiz offered.

Rhoda smiled. "Maybe you can, my little angel," she whispered.

"Well, back to work," Phyllys announced.

I took that as my cue to exit and turned to go down the hall to my room. I had a lot to think about, and I wanted to lie down to do it.

But as I took my first step, I heard the front doors open behind me. I couldn't resist a peek over my shoulder. Two people I hadn't seen yet in Fiebre were walking in. Somehow, I could tell they were a couple, both nearly but not quite elderly. A woman with gray curly hair and wild eyes, and a man with almost no hair at all. They each wore somber, dark suits, hers with a skirt and sandals.

"Trica Snell told us we might find a woman named Cally Lazar here?" The man's voice was loud and a little shaky.

"And your name?" Rhoda inquired smoothly, not even looking my way.

"Don Snell," the man said, sticking out a big hand to shake Rhoda's smaller one. He nodded toward the woman with him. "And my wife, Mary."

"You're related to Seeger?" Rhoda asked in surprise, not so smoothly this time.

"His parents," the man agreed, the tremor in his voice again.

"I'm Cally Lazar," I announced, though it felt more like a confession. "I'm sorry for your loss."

"Loss?" Mary Snell muttered. Her wild eyes were haunted. "Loss."

"Thank you," Don Snell put in. I looked at him closely. His aura was that of an arrogant man, one who usually got his way. But a mantle of grief seemed to be wrapped around his usual self.

"Trica told us that you were looking into the reason for Seeger's death—"

"Informally," I interjected truthfully. "I'm not a private investigator or anything."

"What are you, exactly?" Mr. Snell asked. I could see his arrogance swell larger and larger, in deep red.

"I'm an energy worker," I answered.

"Madame Blavatsky," Mary put in and laughed in a high-pitched giggle that didn't match her tortured eyes or her barely visible green aura.

Don Snell turned toward his wife angrily. "What are you talking about, Mary?" he demanded, his voice booming off the walls.

Mary cringed but didn't answer him. Criminy. I was beginning to have difficulty with Seeger's father, and I'd barely met him. I liked to find the kernel of goodness in everyone, and Don Snell's was buried deeper than a gold miner's dream.

"Madame Blavatsky was a mystic and a spiritualist," I answered Mr. Snell. I didn't add that many people thought that Madame Blavatsky was a fraud. My own opinion was that she was for real, psychically speaking, but that she liked to have a little too much fun with her clients. So she embellished. A lot. Table-tapping was just an appetizer for Madame Blavatsky.

"So what's the point?" Mr. Snell persisted loudly. "Are you a mystic and a spiritualist, too?"

I was going to say no, but something about the question irritated me, so I just nodded and tried to look otherworldly.

"Then, why on earth are you looking into my son's death?"

"Seeger's on the other side," Mary Snell popped up.

Actually, she'd hit it right on the nose, but could I explain this to Don Snell?

I looked at his reddening face and decided on a different approach.

"Why don't we all have a seat and talk about your son?" I suggested.

Pretty soon, I was sitting in a wingback chair closely resembling the one in my room, and the Snells were perched side by side on a red velvet couch across from me. Wiz and Phyllys had disappeared. And Rhoda worked discreetly behind the reception desk. Mr. Snell glared at me, and Mrs. Snell scanned the ceiling for something only she could see.

"Let me explain," I began, injecting reason into my voice. "Your daughter-in-law, Trica, came to see me a little while ago for some healing work—"

"Healing work?" Mr. Snell interrupted.

"Yes," I continued. "She was very upset about her husband's—your son's—death. And as we worked, we realized that knowing more about what happened to Seeger the day he died would help Trica with closure."

"Closure," Mr. Snell repeated.

I took a big breath, wondering what to say next. But Seeger's father surprised me by speaking again. And this time, he didn't raise his voice.

"It's hard to lose a son," he whispered.

"It must be terrible," I agreed, and I meant it. Maybe the only way this man knew how to manage his grief was by raising his voice.

"Seeger was a great kid," he told me. "Smart, good-looking—"

"I always worried, even then," Mary interrupted, her wild eyes still glued to the ceiling. "The way he treated the cat."

This time, Don ignored her.

"We had a great time," he reminisced. "I taught him to play ball. Taught him about business."

"Don was never there for Seeger," Mary mumbled under her breath. "Maybe that's why it all came out so bad." I wondered if she was in shock or if she always acted this way. Her husband didn't seem to hear her in any case.

"Kid was a born businessman. . . ."

I saw Aileen out of the corner of my eye as Don Snell went on. She walked up to our little corner of the lobby and stared for a moment.

"Seeger knew how to make money," Mr. Snell was saying. "Learned it from his old man."

"Learned how to cat around, too," Mary put in.

"I used to sell stereo systems. Got into waterbeds in the sixties, then hot tubs and computers.

"Don, Mary!" Aileen exclaimed. "Is that you?"

The Snells both jerked on the red velvet couch.

Then Don seemed to remember where he was.

He stood up and stuck out his hand. "Arlene, isn't it?" he asked, smiling. "You worked for Seeger?"

"Aileen," she answered, smiling back, but her smile had a strain to it. "Seeger and I were business *partners.*"

"Well, Seeger always had an eye for the best," Don tried gallantly.

"The best in implants," Mary murmured.

"Yesiree," Don went on. "I taught Seeger that from the start. Pick the people you work with as well as you pick your product, and you'll never fail."

"Well, I'll take that as a compliment from you, Don," Aileen offered shamelessly. "The Sensual Body is doing great."

"And how about that winery Seeger was gonna buy?"

"I don't know much about that," Aileen admitted. "But he was doing a great job."

They sat and smiled at each other a little longer. Then time seemed to expand.

"Well, let me offer you my condolences," Aileen said finally. "We'll certainly all miss Seeger."

It was right as Aileen was about to leave that Linda came by, her round eyes red and staring.

"Linda," I said, as cheerfully as possible. "Would you

like to meet Seeger Snell's parents, Don and Mary?"

Linda let out a howl, and I decided I needed some assistance with my hostessing skills.

As Linda ran away, Mary Snell shook her head. "Poor girl. Depressed," she diagnosed.

"Do you know Linda?" I asked eagerly, bending forward.

Both of the Snells shook their heads as one. For all of their differences, they were definitely a couple.

"So, how's your granddaughter?" Aileen asked. I could have kissed her.

"Christie's great," Don said. "Seeger's girl, you know," he added as an aside to me.

"I didn't know Seeger and Trica had a child," my mouth babbled.

"They don't," Don stated emphatically.

"Don and Mary are raising Seeger's little girl from a previous marriage," Aileen informed me.

"Her mother left Seeger and Christie both," Don explained further. "Tramp!"

"But you're doing a great job with Christie," Aileen put in.

"Yeah, Christie's a champ," Don declared. "Reminds me of Seeger at that age. Into everything. Happy kid—"

"I hope she'll turn out better than Seeger," Mary threw in.

"Mary!" Don bellowed.

Seeger's mother went back to studying the ceiling. At least her husband had noticed her.

"Christie will miss Seeger." Don sighed. His voice shook a little. "His own little girl."

"Seeger never visited," Mary mumbled in a voice so small that Don seemed to miss it.

When Vick and Oralia came through the front doors, I

was afraid to introduce them to the Snells. But Aileen had
no problem.

"Oh my," Oralia tried after the introduction. "So you're
Seeger's parents. This must be a very hard time for you."

Don cleared his throat and nodded.

Vick sat down on the seat next to Mary.

"But you will begin to feel better in time," he assured
the older woman.

"Grieving is a process," Oralia chimed in, her voice
soothing as honey. "It is painful, but there are things we
can learn—"

"Hey," Don interrupted. "Didn't you used to go out
with my boy?"

"A long time ago," Oralia snapped back, her voice no
longer soothing.

"I never forget a face," Don told her triumphantly.

"Or a body," Mary added, moving her eyes up and
down Oralia's tall, square form.

"In high school," Oralia said through gritted teeth.

Vick stood up. "Oralia, maybe we'd better go check
out the hall for tonight," he suggested.

"Oh, right," Oralia agreed, smiling at him.

"I'm sorry for your troubles," Vick offered, and then
they were gone.

"So, you have a grandchild named Christie," I pressed
on, trying to get the Snells back on track. If there was a
track. I wondered if Seeger's former wife had anything to
do with his death.

"Carol was her mother," Mary declared lucidly. "Carol
Morgan. Lucky she got away."

Snell Senior opened his mouth, but I beat him to the
words.

"Did you ever see Carol again?" I asked.

"Never," Don Snell answered, sitting back down on the
velvet couch next to his wife.

"She sent cards," Mary said wistfully. "But Don burned them."

"Tramp!" he repeated. I assumed he meant Carol and not his own wife. I also assumed it was time to change the subject.

"So, you've seen Trica?" I prompted.

"Poor girl," Mary sighed. "Seeger was difficult, but he was her husband. We named him for Pete Seeger, you know."

"Trica's a cute little thing, a little on the plump side though," her father-in-law informed me. I bridled but kept out of it.

"She was good for Seeger," Mary pronounced, a little fire in her eyes.

"Girl's a ditz," Don argued. "Not really the right material for Seeger, but who could be? Seeger was brilliant. Went to law school, you know. Could have done anything he wanted, but he went into business like his old man."

Mary just sighed and looked at the ceiling again. I wanted to reach out to her, physically as well as emotionally. But Don was the one sitting next to her.

"Did Seeger have friends?" I asked.

Mary shook her head.

"Hey, I've got to get going," Aileen broke in. I'd almost forgotten she was there. "But it was good seeing you folks again. And my condolences once more."

"Thanks," Don and Mary chirped together, a couple for that moment.

Don turned to me after Aileen left. "That woman may claim she was Seeger's partner, but she just did the grunt work. Seeger was the brains of the outfit."

"The money, actually," Mary corrected him, but he was back to ignoring her.

"So you wanna know about Seeger's friends? He had friends everywhere he went. He was just that kind of guy.

One guy in particular, Gus Delaney, they were Mutt and Jeff."

"Oh, I'd love to talk to Gus," I purred. "Do you have his phone number?"

Don looked at me suspiciously for a moment, then smiled. "Oh, I get it. You want his phone number. If I were younger, I'd give you mine."

Mary rolled her eyes. But Don jotted down the number for me on the back of a gold embossed business card.

I grabbed the card unceremoniously. I needed to talk to someone who could tell me more about Seeger, and I was tired of torturing his parents.

I got up from my seat and walked over to Mary and gave her a big hug. She smelled of neglect and deodorant. Then I shook Don Snell's hand politely, offered my final condolences, and started back down the hallway to my room.

"Psst!" I heard halfway there.

I turned.

Rhoda was behind me, concern on her face.

"Are the Snells going to sue?" she asked.

"What?" I said.

"Isn't that why they're here, to sue?"

I thought for a moment, then shook my head. "I think they're here because Trica told them I was some kind of investigator. I think they're trying to understand what happened."

"Did they ask you about dangerous conditions or anything?"

"Not a word," I assured her.

In fact, once Rhoda was gone, I wondered exactly why they had visited. But I knew that grief took many forms. Maybe they needed closure, too, I decided, as I finished my walk down the hallway.

By the time I got to my room, my mind was buzzing

with the questions I was going to ask Gus Delaney. I even wrote down a few before I dialed his number.

1. Did Seeger have any enemies?

2. Were any of them staying at the inn when Seeger dove off his balcony?

3. Was Seeger suicidal?

4. How far would Seeger go for a joke?

Then I took a deep breath, whipped my cane around a few times in blows that could kill, and punched out the numbers for Gus Delaney on the telephone.

But I found out soon enough that Gus Delaney couldn't be led in a straight line verbally.

"Hey, babe," he answered when I asked him if it would be all right to talk about Seeger Snell. "You've got the money, I got the time." No wonder he and Don Snell got along.

"So," I told him. "I'm looking into a few things for Trica—"

"Far out," he cut me off. "I can tell you this, Seeger was a babe magnet, no question. And he was going to open this winery. I was just drinking to his memory, man."

I'll bet you were, I thought, but I said, "So what can you tell me about Seeger?"

"Women, women, women," Gus slurred. "That was Seeger, man. They were all over him."

"Did he have any particular woman he was seeing besides Trica?" I demanded.

"No, man." He burped. "He loved them all. But Trica was his wife. She was always with Seeger, but that didn't stop him. He was a real lady's man, a real stud—"

"And Aileen?" I prompted.

"Nah, no nookie there. Jeez, what a nothing she is. But she's made him a lot of money in his biz, not that it'll matter when he starts his winery."

I didn't remind Gus that Seeger wasn't going to start a winery now.

"Man, wherever Seeger was, things were happening. Here's to Seeger, man. We had a lot of good times together. Good times . . . good, good times . . ."

I waited for more and realized that Gus Delaney was snoring.

"Gus!" I shouted into the receiver.

"Whaa?" he mumbled.

"Hang up, Gus," I told him, and he did.

I slammed down the receiver, and it promptly rang.

It was Oralia, ordering me back to the workshop room.

TWELVE

"It's an emergency, Cally," Oralia said. "We all need to meet and work together—"

"What kind of emergency?" I asked.

There was a pause, then she answered, "We need to help the Snells," and hung up.

I sat in my chair and wondered if the Snells had been attacked . . . or worse. I was feeling less like Madame Blavatsky now and more like Cassandra, the prophet of doom. Something seemed terribly wrong.

Someone had died! *But what if Seeger wasn't going to be the last to die?* I jumped to my feet. Where had that thought come from? I reviewed my day. Had there been anything to support such an idea, something my conscious mind wasn't processing? No one answered my question.

Well, I wasn't going to find the answer to my question by hiding out in my room, that was for sure. I gripped my cane and made my way out into the hallway, a hallway that was becoming way too familiar to me. With a physical pang, I thought of my little house and my goats and my cat. I wanted to go home.

I just walked faster. I was here to find out how Seeger Snell had died, and I would.

I passed through the lobby and into the ballroom. A cacophony of voices greeted me. There were no candles burning today, and someone had pulled down the Indian silk hangings that usually covered the windows. Stark light outlined the intimacy workshop players.

"Why?" someone demanded. I recognized the voice as Kapp's.

"Are you crazy?" another voice put in. I wasn't sure whose that was.

The ballroom door opened again, and Dee-Dee glided in, Roy in her wake. I stared for a moment, then turned my head back to watch the action.

Oralia and Vick were at the center of the voices. Oralia wore a flowing silk outfit that had the look of a sari. But her voice wasn't silky.

"Because of compassion," she argued. She lowered her voice. "What are we learning in this group?"

"Nothing?" Harley sallied.

Aileen laughed next to him.

"We are learning how to care for each other," Oralia went on, as if she hadn't heard the interruption. "We are learning true intimacy."

"And sensitivity to the feelings of others," Vick added from his place behind her. "We ought to be able to calm their pain, to offer them solace."

"With all of our energy, don't you think we could find a way to spend a session helping Don and Mary come to grips with their grief?" Oralia demanded.

"Don and Mary Snell?" I asked incredulously. Was Oralia really going to invite Seeger's parents to an intimacy workshop?

"Yes, the Snells," Oralia snapped impatiently. "They've checked into the inn."

"Do you really think they checked in so that they could share in this group?" Dee-Dee asked, her voice unnaturally slow and reasonable.

"They must have," Oralia insisted. She crossed her arms across her bosom emphatically and scanned the group.

"Oh, God!" Linda yelped and began sobbing.

"I'm with Linda," Harley threw in. I could smell his smoke-drenched sweat from where he stood. And the incense permeating the whole room. And each person's scent—

"Have you asked the parents of the deceased if they would actually agree to come to a session?" Kapp asked.

"Not yet," Oralia answered. "But I will."

"We wanted consensus first," Vick expanded. "We wouldn't want to force anything on this group—"

"Then why are you asking us?" Eddy whined. "It's awful enough that Seeger had to die, but do we have to talk to his parents? What good will it do?"

"It might do *them* good," Oralia stated. "That's the point."

"And think of the material, Eddy," Aileen added maliciously. "A whole scene for your novel. Weeping parents find solace from a group of do-gooders. Or maybe they lash out and accuse us of luring him to his death. Or maybe—"

Linda's sobbing intensified.

Eddy made a motion to find his notebook.

"I was just kidding," Aileen announced, her voice softer. "Listen, Oralia. I know you're trying to help, but I think we ought to leave the Snells alone—"

"They're shocked and confused already," Roy put in. "I believe it would just fret the Snells unnecessarily to bring them into a group of strangers. They're still in hell, you see."

There was a short silence after Roy spoke. It was the silence that follows uncomfortable truth.

"But—" Oralia began again.

"I think we have our answer, Oralia," Vick told her softly. "We have no consensus."

"Why don't you and the energy worker just go heal

them of their grief?" Harley suggested, and headed out of the room, laughing. "That oughta be simple," he threw over his shoulder before the door closed behind him.

Roy was next to leave. Then Dee-Dee and Eddy.

I caught the lemming train and left after them. Only I went outside instead of returning to my room.

The wind was fresh and scented by salt and seaweed outside. I breathed in and tried to clear my nostrils of the anger, pity, and fear I'd smelled in the ballroom. I walked toward the ocean. The sound of the waves' eternal pounding roared louder and louder the closer I got. I let myself be seduced by the sound as I reached the water's edge. *Infinity,* it seemed to say. *What is this death compared to the infinity I've seen?*

It could have been an hour or a minute later when I felt someone behind me. Lulled by the waves into the embrace of what felt like goodness to me, I didn't even jump when I felt a hand on my shoulder. Because by then, I knew whose hand it was.

I turned slowly and looked into Roy's golden eyes.

His eyes were smiling, and they warmed me like the sun. I took his hand impulsively and kissed the back of it. It was such a good hand, strong, with long, square fingers.

Then I sighed, remembering how much time had passed since we'd truly been together. I heard the waves behind me, chiding. *Infinity, infinity,* they roared. Dee-Dee was right; I loved this man.

I tilted my head up until our lips were touching. He didn't draw away. His mouth was warm and moist on mine. And then his arms reached around me, pulling me in closer. I reached up with my own hands to touch his familiar face, to remember its bones as we kissed. And then I buried my hands in his hair.

By the time we'd let go of each other, our lips were raw from kissing.

"Cally," Roy sighed and closed his eyes.

I took his hands and held them. I wouldn't let him get away this time.

"Roy," I answered. "Roy, how could I live without you?"

"The same way you always have," he answered. "With joy and hope and laughter."

"No, Roy—"

"Yes, Cally, 'cause that's how you live life, with or without me. Don't you see, darlin', I never want that to change that."

I could see a conversational train wreck coming up, so I changed tracks.

"I liked what you said back there at the workshop," I told him.

His golden eyes looked confused for a moment.

"About the Snells," I reminded him.

"Oh that," he muttered. "It needed saying. All those folks arguing and not really thinking about what Seeger's mama and papa were going through. It didn't seem right."

"But you saw it," I insisted. "You said what no one else did."

He smiled.

"I don't lie," he stated. "I may be crazy, but I don't tell untruths."

I didn't know how to answer that. *Was* he crazy?

"Roy, come to my room." I just wanted to be with him, to feel the warmth of his love once more.

"Cally—" he began, and stopped abruptly.

He was staring intently over my left shoulder.

"No, Roy," I told him, my insides clenching. "No."

"The darkness is here, Cally," he announced. "You're just too good to see it."

"No!" I shouted. Then I took a breath. "Roy," I said, filling my voice with calm. "We went through a lot of stuff together in seven years. I'm not just going to forget you and throw you away now."

"Oh, darlin'," he murmured and kissed me again. "Please come away from here. This place is evil. I can see it."

"There is no such thing as evil," I began.

He held my hand. "That's why I love you, I guess," he admitted. "You really believe there is no evil. But that's why you're in danger. And I'm probably making it worse for you."

"But—"

"Shhh, my darlin'," he whispered. Then he slowly let my hand go and walked away.

I didn't really cry until I reached my room.

I was lying on my bed, hot tears trickling from my eyes. The tears spread across my face, some of them even landing in my ears. But I didn't try to stop the tears. I didn't even want to. At least I was still feeling something.

And then someone knocked on my door. Criminy! Did people think my room was the lobby? I groaned, remembering my ill-advised workshop offer once again.

"Who is it?" I shouted.

"Linda," came the muffled reply.

Oh great, we could cry together. She was a lot louder than I was. Maybe I could take lessons.

Still, I yelled back, "Give me a second!" and washed my face in the bathroom before opening the door.

Linda practically fell into my arms. I caught her and concentrated on not falling over myself. I wondered if she'd been eating enough. She'd looked tall and sinewy at a distance, but she felt like a bird in my arms. A very big bird. She tilted her head down at me, her large eyes already filling with tears. I led/dragged her to the wing-back chair and set her down.

She began to cry. Her aura was a flickering mixture in a gardener's variety of colors.

"Linda," I interrupted. "When did you last have a meal?"

"I . . . I . . ." she tried.

"You need to eat," I told her. "Then maybe you'll be able to think more clearly.

"Cally," she forced out. "I need . . . need . . . a friend."

"You need a friend," I repeated back. It was the most coherent sentence I'd heard from her since she'd come in.

"Talk, I need to talk. . . ." Then she began to cry again.

"Is this about Seeger Snell?" I asked gently.

But she just kept crying. She slammed her own fist into the inside of her elbow. Then she raised it to hit herself again.

Not in my room, I decided, and grabbed her fist before it crashed down again.

"Bad things . . . my sister . . . I can't—"

"Your sister was killed in some kind of weight-training accident?"

"Yes, yes!" she cried out, as if I'd gotten the answer in charades.

"And so, you're upset," I tried, on a roll.

She nodded.

"And then Seeger died?" I couldn't seem to put the two events together, unless they both appeared to be accidents.

But Linda seemed to, upping the sobs. How did her eyes take it? I wondered if you could get an eye infection from crying.

"Were you close to Seeger?" I asked.

"No . . . yes . . . I can't . . ."

"Linda," I instructed, taking her hands in mine. "I want

you to concentrate on breathing now. Don't try to talk.
Just breathe in."

And miraculously, she did.

"And out."

We breathed in and out together for a while. Linda
actually seemed to calm down. In fact, her eyelids began
to droop, as if she were falling asleep.

"Linda, why do you need a friend?" I asked as quietly
as possible.

"Need to talk," she said, her voice slow and deep.

Dack, I must have picked up Dee-Dee's hypnosis skills.
This woman was under.

"To talk about what?" I prompted.

"Death, names . . ." Her voice trailed off, but at least
she wasn't crying any more.

"Seeger's death?"

"Seeger. How many could there be?" she answered.

How many deaths? Was that what she meant? I shivered. Maybe she was feeling like Cassandra, too. I wanted
to ask the big question. Had this woman killed Seeger
Snell? But I was pretty sure that would just start the waterworks again.

"How do you think Seeger died?" I asked instead.

"Off the balcony," she answered, spreading her arms
like she was flying.

"Did you push him?" I asked and held my breath.

"No."

Ratsafratz. I let my breath out. I'd almost been hoping
for a confession. Even though it didn't feel quite right to
me. Linda was a few sentences shy of a paragraph, but
she still didn't seem ruthless enough to kill.

"Linda do you cry all the time?" I asked.

"No."

"Are you crying about your sister?"

"Yes . . . no . . . both, I don't know."

"Linda can you tell me, calmly, one thing that's bothering you?" I asked.

"My sister died," she told me.

"Okay, can you tell me a second thing that's bothering you?"

"Nightmares."

"Nightmares about what?"

"They're chasing me through the woods in the nightmare—" Linda began.

Someone knocked on the door to my room before she could finish her sentence. Why not? My door was always open.

Linda's eyes popped all the way open. She wasn't under anymore.

"Who is it?" I shouted for the second time in an hour.

"It's Aileen," came the answer.

Linda's eyes opened even wider. She was beginning to look less like a cartoon character and more like a baby seal.

"Linda," Aileen cooed when she walked into my room. "How are you doing, baby?"

Not good was my guess. Linda was crying again.

Aileen knelt down and put her arms around the crying woman. Then she whispered something in her ear.

"Cally," Aileen said, turning her head away from Linda as she continued to embrace her. "I wanted to talk to you about Harley, but it looks like Linda needs some help."

I nodded. Now, there was an understatement.

"Do you think you could find some food for her?" I asked.

"Food," she repeated, and then, "You're absolutely right, Cally. I hadn't thought of food."

She turned back to her charge.

"Linda, do you think you could eat?" she asked.

"I . . . I . . ." Linda looked over Aileen's shoulder at me as if asking for my advice.

"You need to eat," I said authoritatively.

Within moments, the two women had left my room. Oralia was right. Aileen was a rock. Maybe she could calm Linda down better than I could. And then I began to feel guilty. I shouldn't be letting Aileen do all the work. I was supposed to be the healer around here.

I took a big breath in and reminded myself not to let my ego take over. If Aileen wanted to take care of Linda, that was her business. I stood for a moment and surrounded myself in a column of white light. It felt like a good shower. Only the slime I was washing away was energetic. I wasn't sure where I'd picked it up, but I wanted it off of me.

Once I was finished with my energy shower, I decided to get out of my room so I could have a little peace and quiet. The lobby had to be less crowded than my room.

But I was wrong. When I walked into the lobby, I saw Sergeant Zoffany at the desk, talking with Rhoda. The tension between them was high. I didn't need to see any auras, Rhoda's shoulders were raised like a cat's back who's about to hiss and claw.

"Zoffy!" she rapped out. "You know me. You know Phyllys. You know Wiz. I can't believe you're asking these questions!"

I sat quietly in a green velvet chair in the farthest recess of the lobby and proceeded to eavesdrop shamelessly.

But I couldn't hear anything but the low rumble of the sergeant's voice.

"Fine!" Rhoda snapped. "Go search the room. Check the balcony. You don't need a search warrant." She reached back over her shoulder and flung a key at him. I assumed it was the key to Seeger Snell's room. "Just tell Debby the truth. We don't know anything about this. The man jumped. There were witnesses. And we can't be blamed for not knowing why he jumped. We're not psychic, you know."

I flinched in my chair.

But Sergeant Zoffany was turning now. I tried to make myself invisible. It didn't work. The sergeant homed in on my position and grinned at me. I shivered. I hoped I'd never cross him.

Once he was gone, I approached the reception area warily.

"Damn that Debby," Rhoda said, but there wasn't any real venom underlying her words. What I felt from her was worry, not anger.

"What's up?" I asked tentatively.

"Now Debby wants to investigate," she told me. "I think the Snells must have talked to her."

"They're staying here, aren't they?"

"Yes." Her body seemed to deflate. "I can't blame them for wanting to know what happened to their son. Oh, Cally, do you think we'll ever know?"

"Of course," I began, but then I shrugged my shoulders. "I'll do my best to find out," I amended.

"That's all we can do," she muttered. "That's all anyone can do."

I left the building feeling less than upbeat. What had Roy said about how I lived my life? With joy and hope and laughter? I tried to breathe some in now. There *was* the ocean, I reminded myself. And standing in front of it, my friends Kapp and Dee-Dee. I trotted as fast as I could over the sand to be with them. There were times when I felt loneliness as well as the qualities Roy had imbued me with. And this was one of them.

Kapp saw me coming and raised his cane. I smiled. Friends were a good thing to have.

"So," Kapp demanded when I made it to them. "Have you figured it out yet?"

And there were times when friends just got your goat. But I had goats to spare.

"No," I snapped back. "Have you?"

"We've just been going over the suspects," Dee-Dee told me, her voice back to its normal high pitch and speed. "Seeger was completely self-absorbed, didn't know when he was giving offense. That can be dangerous."

"Not to mention his attitude toward women," Kapp put in. "I could bring a class action suit for all the sexual assaults he's perpetrated."

"Too bad he's dead," I put in.

"Oh, we could probably sue his estate," Kapp answered me seriously.

"I was kidding," I told him.

Kapp raised his cane again; I gave it a little tap with mine. He sighed.

"Have you met his parents?" I asked.

They both shook their heads.

"You might find it interesting," I hazarded. "I think Don Snell was the prototype for Seeger."

"Yuk," Dee-Dee replied.

"Or then again, you might not want to meet Don Snell," I assured her.

"So who?" I threw out into the ensuing silence.

And then I heard the sound of bagpipes.

"Him," Kapp answered, raising his cane and pointing a few sand dunes over where Harley stood, squeezing the bellows.

"Why?" I asked.

"I can't stand the SOB," Kapp shot back.

"Not enough evidence," I lectured him. But Harley was the most violent, the most volatile, the most—

"See you two later," I said, and started the trek across

the sand to where Harley stood. "I just love a man who plays bagpipes," I threw over my shoulder.

Dee-Dee giggled. Kapp didn't. But I knew they were both watching my back.

When I reached Harley, he threw his bagpipes to the ground.

"Hey, energy worker," he hissed. "It's way past time for you to give me that little ride you promised."

I didn't even have a chance to ask what he meant, on the off chance I didn't already know, when he reached out a hand and touched my breast.

My cane came up hard between his legs before I even knew I was lifting it.

THIRTEEN

Harley fell to the ground on top of his bagpipes. They moaned as he squirmed. And then he started yelling with them.

"What are you doing, woman?!" he bellowed. "D'ya want to ruin me for life?"

"No, just for a few minutes," I replied serenely.

"Ya coulda cut short my manhood with that thing," Harley pressed on.

"It's a thought," I said, softly hefting my cane.

"Hey, energy worker!" he shouted, sitting up now and inching backwards on his bottom. "Back off! I just thought you'd be interested in a little foolin' around, considering your boyfriend is a wacko—"

It was my turn to shout now.

"My boyfriend is not a wacko!"

Harley scrambled to his feet now.

"You are one dangerous lady!" he yelled, hefted his bagpipes, turned, and ran across the sand.

I stood for a moment, chuckling. Me, one dangerous lady! There in the salty breeze, I absorbed the description. And in that moment, I liked it. Then I heard the cheering behind me. Dee-Dee and Kapp were whistling and hollering and clapping. I could feel my cheeks glow with pride and embarrassment, but mostly with affection for the two disparate friends who'd watched my back and applauded my actions.

I bowed briefly, shook my cane, and made my way back to the inn.

My feeling of triumph was fading as quickly as my adreneline by the time I walked into the lobby. Was it an act of light and love to have hit Harley in his, well, his manhood? My own body cringed. Even lacking the equipment, I could imagine the pain. And what had I learned about Harley as a suspect in Seeger's death? Nothing. Only that Harley had poor impulse control, and somehow I believed that Seeger's death had been planned carefully, not impulsively. Harley was angry, aggressive, and unpleasant, but that wasn't enough to make him a murderer. Criminy, if anger, aggression, and unpleasantness were the only prerequisites to homicide, there would be a lot more dead bodies lying around. And with that thought, I shivered.

I wandered through the lobby, waving absently toward Rhoda at her station, and made my way to my room. I sat on the end of my bed. Was Harley a true suspect? Then I remembered. Hadn't Aileen tried to say something about Harley to me earlier before she'd gotten enmeshed in Linda's presence?

I stood up, adrenaline renewed. And then I sniffed. Whoa, that acrid smell was coming from me! My encounter with Harley had left me olfactorarily challenged. A quick sponge bath and some deodorant later, I was back down the hall to the lobby.

"Hey, Rhoda," I greeted the innkeeper when I got to the reception area. "Have you seen Aileen around?"

"No," she answered quickly. "Is there any more trouble?"

Abruptly, I knew I wasn't the only Cassandra at the inn. Rhoda was nervous, too. But then, Rhoda had real problems, running the inn understaffed, having Chief Dahl on her case. Then I saw Aileen coming through the front door.

"Looking for *moi*?" she inquired, her voice flippant. She must have overheard me asking for her.

"Yeah—yes," I answered.

"So, whaddaya want?" she asked reasonably.

"Um," I began, suddenly embarrassed. "I wanted to talk to you about Harley."

Her smiling face looked blank behind her glasses momentarily.

"Didn't you have something you wanted to tell me about him before?" I pressed.

Aileen looked over my shoulder pointedly. I turned and saw Rhoda behind her desk, eyes down but ears open. She might have been a Vulcan, the way her ears pointed toward us.

"Shall we sit down in the lobby?" I asked Aileen, hoping that would be enough privacy for her. There just weren't enough places to talk at The Inn at Fiebre: my room, the lobby, or outside. I vowed to find new ones soon. Though I wasn't ready for the redwood hot tubs yet.

"Sure," Aileen agreed, and together we walked toward the familiar chairs. An interrogator had to do what an interrogator had to do. Aileen took the love seat, and I took the wingback.

I let in a big breath. *How to ask a woman if she thought her boyfriend was a murderer? Hmmm . . .*

"So what's the deal?" Aileen prodded.

"You know Harley?" I began stupidly.

Aileen nodded impatiently.

"He assaulted me."

Aileen just stared.

"At least, I think he assaulted me first," I went on.

"First?" Aileen questioned, her eyes widening behind her steel-rimmed glasses.

This was shut up or put up time. I wondered just how close to Harley Aileen really was.

"I got him with my cane after he touched me," I told her.

Aileen grinned. Maybe she wasn't too loyal.

"I got him between the legs," I followed up in a burst of bravado.

Aileen leaned back and started laughing. The loyalty issue seemed to be moot.

"Poor baby," she said finally. "You didn't hurt him too bad?"

"I don't think so," I told her, I hoped honestly. Her grin was infectious. "I think his bagpipes suffered the most."

And pretty soon, we were both laughing hysterically. And then as I laughed, I wondered. How could Aileen care so little about Harley? Were they truly lovers? I certainly wouldn't be laughing if Aileen had hit Roy. But then Roy would never give a woman cause to hit him. Except maybe me. I shook off the thought.

"So what *is* your relationship to Harley?" I couldn't resist asking.

The grin left Aileen's face. She shrugged her shoulders.

"He isn't the love of my life," she answered. "We're friends. Once in a while, we end up in bed. But no one's going to take the place of his wife as far as he's concerned, so it goes no further. And he likes to spread it around, if you know what I mean. So, no monogamy forthcoming."

I hadn't been able to read Aileen before, but right now bitterness was evident in a wisp of her aura. As if I'd have to read her aura to guess that she was bitter.

"So what were you going to tell me about him before?" I ventured on.

For an instant, Aileen's eyes were shuttered. Then she spoke.

"Just that he was getting a thing for you. I know the signs. So, I was going to warn you." She leaned forward and stared into my eyes. "But I guess I didn't have to warn you, did I?"

I dredged up an answering smile. It was time to ask the hard questions now.

"Aileen?" I began softly. "Do you think Harley could kill a man?"

"Under the right circumstances, sure," she answered without great concern. Then she shrugged. "But I don't think he killed Seeger."

"Why?" I pressed.

"Why should he have?" she lobbed back. "He didn't have any beef with Seeger. Actually, I think Harley kind of admired Seeger. Two cock-of-the-walks having a great time with the ladies and the drugs. Male bonding at its finest!"

I nodded. Aileen made sense. Then I remembered Linda.

"Hey, did you ever get Linda to eat?" I asked. A better suspect than Harley was already forming in my mind.

"Yeah, Phyllys took pity on her and took her to the kitchen for leftovers. Linda scarfed up like she hadn't eaten for a week."

"Maybe she hadn't," I put in guiltily.

"Nah." Aileen shook her head. "I've watched her. She doesn't always eat at the right times, but she manages to eat."

"Well, that's a relief," I sighed, then turned my face full to Aileen's. "What do you think Linda's problem is, anyway?"

"Hard to tell. I don't think Linda's ever been wrapped very tight anyway, but her sister's death really unhinged her. She says all these crazy things. The only thing to do is keep her fed and let her cry it out."

"Do you think Linda could have killed Seeger?" I kept on.

"Oh, jeez, I hope not!" Aileen exclaimed, seemingly more upset by this idea than by the accusation of her part-time lover, Harley. "Cally, don't say anything to her, okay? Linda's so buggy right now, she'd admit to the JFK assasination." Aileen paused. "Poor kid."

I sighed internally but nodded. Linda certainly didn't look like a woman who needed any more grief. At least, not today.

"On the day that Seeger dived, you were sitting down below with Trica, right?" I asked. I knew she'd already told me, but I needed to ask again.

"Lucky for me and Trica," Aileen agreed, nodding. "Trica's cool. You don't suspect her, do you?" I shook my head, wondering if I did suspect Trica. "Good, 'cause she's totally copacetic about me continuing The Sensual Body shop without Seeger. And the business is going gangbusters. Trica acts a little goofy, but she's got a good heart."

Still, I didn't really want to talk about Trica.

"Who else did you see around when Seeger dived?" I asked instead.

"Jeez, Cally. Talk about a blur. I think I saw Wiz, and maybe Linda."

"And Harley?" I threw in quickly.

"Oh, I didn't see Harley," Aileen answered quickly enough. Then she grinned. "But I heard him, honey. He was playing his bagpipes right when Seeger went over the balcony."

Apparently, that was the end of the interview as far as Aileen was concerned. She rose from her love seat with a solid stance, said, "Catch you later," and strode out the front doors of the inn.

I sat for a little longer, alone. Rhoda wasn't behind the

reception desk anymore. She was most likely too frustrated by her inability to stretch her ears far enough to hear Aileen and me talking. I tried to put together all the information I had learned from Aileen. And I kept coming back to her words about Harley. Had she given him a bagpipe alibi honestly? Did she really love the guy? I would have thrown up my hands if I hadn't been in public.

Instead, I headed back down the hall to my room, bubbling with frustration. I counted off my fingers. As far as I could tell, Trica and Aileen were in the clear. And possibly Linda, Wiz, and Harley. But I wasn't completely comfortable about the last three.

When I closed the door to my room and sat down in my wingback chair, I decided I needed help. And not from any spirit guides. I needed logical, analytical help. I called my best friend, Joan Hussein, attorney at law and cynic at large.

Just hearing Joan's brusque voice with its underlying tone of harmony relaxed my shoulders. But her reaction when I started in with motive, opportunity, and character knotted them back up again.

"Leave it to the police, and get out of there," she commanded before I was even finished.

"But, I have to—" I sputtered

"No, you don't, Cally," she stated with no uncertainty. "You just think you do. You don't owe this client your life—"

"But—"

"No buts!" she snapped. "I know the world for you is made of light, but it isn't for everyone else."

"Still, I can—"

"Leave now," she repeated.

"I can't," I told her, firming my spine and chin even though she couldn't see me over the phone.

She let out a little operatic scream. "Cally!"

"No," I repeated.

"Then be on guard," she advised seriously. "I care about you."

And finally, she hung up.

Keerups! So much for an analytical discussion. Was Joan right? I stood up. I was the psychic around here, not her. Well, at least I was the closest thing to a psychic around here.

What I needed was a timetable of where everyone had been when Seeger took his dive, I decided. I'd already picked up a lot from Aileen. It was time to talk to Rhoda again.

When I got to reception, no one was there. I rang the bell. Both Rhoda and Phyllys came out from the back, looking flustered. I wondered what I'd interrupted.

"Can I ask you guys some questions?" I tried.

Phyllys groaned, but Rhoda said, "Of course."

I went with Rhoda's answer.

"When Seeger fell, where were you all?"

Even Rhoda didn't look very happy with that question. Her impish features drooped.

"Why do you wanna know?" Phyllys challenged, rolling her shoulders forward.

"I'm trying to set up a timetable, listing everyone's whereabouts," I explained, keeping my voice low and conciliatory. "I'm not sure what it'll tell me. But . . ." I paused. "Wouldn't it be neat if there was just one person missing from everyone's account?" Then I went for the kill. "What if *we* can tell Chief Dahl who it was?"

Rhoda and Phyllys looked at each other. Something passed between them that I couldn't see, and then Rhoda began to talk.

"I didn't see Seeger fall," she told me. "I was here in

reception when I heard the screams. And Phyllys was in the kitchen with Dulcie."

Phyllys's skin pinkened. "Actually, I'm not sure where Dulcie was," she said.

"What?" Rhoda demanded.

"You know Dulcie," Phyllys responded sullenly. "Dulcie was out doing whatever Dulcie does when she's slacking off work."

"How about Wiz?" I asked.

Two sets of heads jerked with that one question.

"Look, we don't keep our eye on Wiz all the time," Phyllys announced.

"It's okay," I told them. "Someone else thinks they saw him downstairs when Seeger went over."

The relief with which each body relaxed was identical. I only hoped I could trust Aileen's fleeting perception that she'd seen the boy.

"I think I saw Eddy going by right before the screaming, but I'm not sure," Rhoda offered.

"Listen, about Dulcie," Phyllys started up again. "Dulcie's a good kid. It's these crazy intimacy folks you oughta be checking out. That's who Seeger had links with. They're the crazy ones. You ought to leave us alone."

And with that, Phyllys turned and slammed into the back room.

Rhoda looked over her shoulder longingly and then back at me with a weak smile. But despite her friendly expression, it was now clear that separate camps had been set up. The innkeepers and the workshop people. *Us and them.* Which camp did I belong to? Or Roy, or Dee-Dee, or Kapp for that matter? But before I could ask, someone shoved by me and rang the reception bell.

A short, bowlegged man with pouty features stepped closer to the counter, pushing his luggage in front of him with one foot. I'd never seen him at the inn before, but still. Images of newsprint nagged at my unconscious. Dack, a reporter! I was sure of it. And I wasn't playing psychic. I'd seen that pouty face on a newspaper column somewhere.

I waited until Rhoda had checked him in, and he'd ascended the stairs, before I whispered my suspicions in her ear.

"Holy Mother!" she whispered urgently, and her skin went pale.

"It'll be okay," I tried.

Rhoda looked up at me and smiled a real smile, as if seeing me for the first time that day.

"Thanks, Cally," she said softly. I saw Eddy walking up, in my peripheral vision. "Please don't mind Phyllys. Love and loyalty are what keep her going. And she thinks of Dulcie as part of our family—"

"Hey, I just thought of something," Eddy interrupted.

That pensive whine couldn't belong to anyone but Eddy of the eternal notebook. And sure enough, he had it in hand. He started up again.

"See, I got to thinking about Wiz. Remember that six-year-old who shot that little girl—"

"That's enough!" Phyllys had returned from the back room. "If you're accusing Wiz of anything—"

"Say, back off!" Eddy squealed, stepping away from the desk. "I just thought maybe it might make an interesting character study—"

"Wiz as murderer," Phyllys hissed. "I don't think so. Wiz isn't even tall enough to push over a person, but you are."

"Me!" Eddy cried.

"Why not?" Phyllys pressed on, her arms swinging like a prizefighter's. "Then you could write it down in your little notebook, and stick it—"

"Listen, lady, I—"

This time we heard the interruption coming. Wiz came sighing heavily, dragging himself to the reception desk. He had something to say, and he said it.

"I didn't do it." He hung his ten-year-old head wearily. "I've been framed."

FOURTEEN

Rhoda looked down at her son. You could see her considering if he was really serious. No doubt she was weighing the consequences of asking him what he meant by being "framed" in front of Eddy.

Phyllys took care of the second point handily.

"You!" she bellowed, pointing at Eddy. "Go to your room!"

And miraculously, Eddy closed his mouth, tucked his notebook in his pocket, and left. The whole slope of his back told us that writers were misunderstood. Especially geniuses.

Then all our eyes were back on Wiz.

Rhoda squatted down till she was eye to eye with her son.

"What didn't you do, honey?" she asked gently.

"And who framed you for it?" Phyllys asked just as gently, putting her hand on the boy's shoulder.

"They said I killed Seeger Snell," he replied.

Both women's first chakras exploded with the yellow color of fear.

"Who said?" Phyllys demanded a little less gently.

"The other kids."

Now it was pulling-teeth time. Rhoda attempted an extraction.

"What other kids?"

"Tiffany Dahl started it." Wiz looked up, sure of his

audience now. "She said that if I knew all about spacemen and stuff, that I probably beamed them down to kill the Seeger guy."

"Is Tiffany related to Chief Dahl?" I asked.

"Niece, twice removed," Rhoda answered quickly. But she wasn't really interested in my question.

"That's all Tiffany said?" Phyllys pressed.

"Yeah, but Axel said all this stuff about me not being magic at all, and how I couldn't beam down a space guy anyway. And a bunch of other kids laughed."

"Oh, I'm sorry, sweetie," Rhoda told her son, giving him a big hug. I could see her yellow fear seeping away now. Though Phyllys's was still in place.

"Were these kids serious?" she asked Wiz.

"I dunno," he shrugged. "Marcie and Emily said the other kids were just pooper-scoopers. Emily and Marcie were really cool. Emily took my spider and waved it at the other kids. Axel almost fainted."

A little grin warmed Wiz's delicate features.

It was good to see. At least for me. And I think for Rhoda. She stood up, turning her sly smile away from Wiz. But Phyllys wasn't satisfied.

"See!" she cried, jerking her body up to standing position. "Fiebre's just starting! We're going to be the scapegoats for this. Just wait and see."

"But it was just a bunch of kids," Rhoda objected.

"And it was teenage girls that started the Salem witchcraft trials," Phyllys argued. "And look what a bunch of kids did during the Cultural Revolution in China. Trust is everything, and these folks don't trust us."

"Don't be scared, Phyllys," Wiz offered softly. "I'll protect you."

Two big tears ran down Phyllys's face.

"And I'll take care of you, Wiz," she snuffled and bent

down to embrace the boy who couldn't beam down spacemen.

I cleared my throat. This was clearly a photo op I wasn't meant to share.

"I guess it's time for dinner," I put in, and looked at my watch in surprise. It was time for dinner, getting a little past time, actually. My stomach growled in an affirmative.

"Thanks, Cally," Rhoda said absently.

It was definitely time for an exit, stage right. I went to my room and put on a light silk jacket, a present from Geneva that had swirling primary colors and frog toggles for buttons. I loved it almost as much as I loved Geneva. And for some reason, I wanted to make a good impression when I walked into Marge's. Because I was going to Marge's. No more dining in suite on convenience store food for me. I wanted to look at suspects this evening. For all her analytical abilities, my friend Joan couldn't have calculated the effect her warnings would have on me. If there was danger here, I wanted to know what it was. Confrontation was the path. Or, at least, observation.

It was only a block's walk down Highway 1 to the low-slung building that housed Marge's Restaurant. Marge's looked like it had been built in the fifties and never renovated since, but when I opened the door and walked in, the rush of good cooking smells convinced me that the kitchen was working just fine. And the hum of conversation told me it was a popular restaurant.

I closed my eyes for a minute and breathed in the smells of frying onions and fish and burnt grease.

And abruptly, the hum of conversation seemed to ebb a little.

My eyes popped open. Maybe I shouldn't have worn my nicest jacket. There were too many people looking at me.

Most of the tables were filled with diners I didn't recognize. But I couldn't miss Don and Mary Snell seated at a table with a red-checked tablecloth near the flapping doors of the kitchen. Vick and Oralia were at the same table, looking over their shoulders my way.

Don's voice came booming out, ending the ebb. "Named for Pete Seeger," he said. Something in me shrank, thinking of this odd twosome who had lost their only child. Vick and Oralia seemed to shrink, too, melding into their wooden chairs as they turned back to the Snells.

Aileen and Harley were nearby at a table for two, heads together, whispering. Harley shot me a look that could have fried his own motorcycle. Aileen just put her hand over her mouth. Was she still laughing at my assault on Harley? For her sake, I hoped not.

And then I saw Dee-Dee and Kapp at another red-checked table for four. A pulse of relief danced in my veins. I hotfooted it over to my friends as quickly as I could. So far, I hadn't seen a waitress, much less a host.

"Lady Lazar," Kapp greeted me, standing. Then he bowed and kissed my hand, his eyes flitting merrily over Harley's way. "Will you join us?"

Dee-Dee made a tiny sound like a quick shake of a breakfast bell that I knew was a suppressed giggle. Whether she was giggling at Harley or Kapp's grandstanding, I wasn't sure. But I relished the sound of lightness.

"I'd be honored," I answered and attempted a curtsy. Curtsies work better with dresses than with jeans, but still, I did have Geneva's jacket on to fancify the occasion.

Then I sat myself down on a rickety, old, wooden chair. There was no food on the table, but I was eyeing Kapp's and Dee-Dee's menus.

Dee-Dee handed me one. Actually, if there was a resident psychic here, it was probably Dee-Dee. I opened the menu up and saw that Marge's turned from a diner into a fish house in the evenings. The choices were endless, from fresh crab to squid and back upstream to salmon, and more. And fortunately for Dee-Dee, there were even a few vegan entrées.

Fresh grilled swordfish! Yum. The good thing about fish is that they have shifty eyes, unlike some of the higher forms on the food chain. They always remind me of Mafia dons when they swim by in the aquarium. So, tonight I'd splurge without guilt.

"Hey, you two decide or what?" a familiar voice called from my side. I looked up and saw Dulcie, former kitchen help at The Inn at Fiebre, diamond stud glinting from her nose.

"Dulcie, why—"

"Oh, man!" she cried. "Not you, too."

"What are you—"

"Listen, man," she told me earnestly. "Before you have a cow about me deserting the inn, let me remind you of something. My aunt is chief of police in this city. And worse yet, she's chief of my whole friggin' life right now. This is the only job she'll let me take. Okay with you, huh?"

"Well, sure—" I began.

But Don Snell's gong of a voice cut me off, even that far away.

"Kid could do anything, you gotta understand." He took a gulp of what looked like red wine. "Anything. Business, law, you name it."

Dulcie bent over me.

"Get the fish," she suggested. "Marge is great with fish."

"*I'll* have the fish, squid, and chips combination," Kapp

cut in. He looked thoughtful for a moment. "And a green salad, no dressing," he added virtuously.

Dee-Dee rolled her eyes and ordered a primavera pasta with seeds, nuts, and vegetables.

"Grilled swordfish, baked potato, and salad with blue cheese," I announced. I kept my eyes off of Dee-Dee.

"Hey, good choice," Dulcie complimented me. Maybe there was hope for her waitressing skills yet.

After the endless recitation of drinks, Dee-Dee and I got water, though Dulcie sold Kapp on a good Riesling. Well, actually, it wasn't a hard sell.

"Kid had the world by the tail," Don's voice dominated again. "What the hell happened?" He slammed his hand on the table. Mary mumbled something that seemed to calm him. "Right, right. He had a good life, the best life."

I wondered if the other diners who weren't from the inn could hear Don as well as we could. Was it knowing his son was dead that made his voice impossible to ignore?

Dulcie left our table quietly as Don Snell's voice continued to fill the room. "Did you see my son fall?" he finally demanded. I whipped my head around but still couldn't hear Vick or Oralia's answer. I thought I might have seen a negative head shake from Vick, but it was too hard to tell at this angle.

I looked back at my tablemates. Kapp's balding head was lowered. King of the sharks or not, Kapp was a man of compassion. Dee-Dee had pain in her eyes now. And I had a pain in my leg.

"We'll figure it out," I insisted in a low voice. "And when we do, maybe that will bring everyone some closure."

"How will we figure it out?" Dee-Dee asked simply.

"Keep asking questions," I tried.

Dee-Dee sighed.

"Look," I insisted softly. "I'm working on a timetable to track people's whereabouts when Seeger died."

Kapp's head came up. "Trica and Aileen were downstairs," he offered tentatively.

"And maybe Wiz and Linda, according to Aileen."

Even Dee-Dee seemed to brighten. "A timetable," she muttered.

"And," I followed up, "two people heard Harley playing his bagpipes at the time Seeger fell."

Kapp shook his head gleefully.

"Oh, they did, did they?" he questioned. "Maybe that horse's ass is smarter than he looks. He could have taped his own bagpiping, set it on Play, and killed Seeger while people thought they heard him."

"But—"

"Did anyone actually *see* him playing?"

"You win," I told him and turned to look at Harley. His eyes met mine in a way that was very unnerving, even across a crowded room.

"Motive's the key," Kapp began, on a roll now. "Alibis are too easy to fake." I saw Eddy moving toward us across the room.

"How about Aileen and Trica?" Dee-Dee asked.

"Trica and Aileen—" Kapp began.

But whatever wisdom Kapp was about to offer was cut off by Eddy's pleading, disconsolate tone. "Can I join you?" he asked.

Much to our credit, neither Kapp nor Dee-Dee nor I groaned. "Please, sit down," Dee-Dee offered, beating me and Kapp to instant graciousness.

So Eddy took the last wooden chair at the table. Then he sighed and ran his hand through his curly hair. I wouldn't have taken these signs as real distress, but for once, Eddy didn't have his notebook in hand. Something was really wrong.

"I didn't mean to accuse Wiz of anything," he told me. Was this what was bothering him really? "You know, I'm always interested in material for my writing. I just meant that I might base a little of my observation on Wiz, that's all." He paused. "Can you tell them Cally, please? Can you explain? I'm not insensitive, you know."

"What did you do?" Kapp asked. His voice was that of a prosecuting attorney.

"I don't exactly remember," Eddy admitted. "I just mentioned to Rhoda and Phyllys that Wiz might make an interesting character study like that kid who shot that little girl—"

Now Kapp did groan, cutting Eddy short.

"Eddy," Kapp started in. "Do you ever think before you—"

"Time to say good night," Don Snell's voice rang out. Even the other diners in Marge's stopped talking, his voice was so loud. He placed his hands on the table and pushed himself out of his chair with some difficulty. Mary scrambled up to take his arm. He lumbered away from his table in our direction, leaning on his smaller wife. I could see Vick and Oralia's muscles relaxing all the way from where I was. It couldn't have been a fun dinner for them.

And sure enough, Don and Mary came to our table.

"Cally, right?" Don boomed, towering over us. "Never forget a name. Thanks for whatever it is you're doing. Seeger was a great kid. He deserves some respect."

I just nodded solemnly. I didn't know what else to do in the sight of his and Mary's grief. Great grief can't be answered by a simple phrase or act. Or even a more complicated one.

"Warren Kapp," Kapp introduced himself, standing. "And this is Dee-Dee Lee."

"Either of you know my son?" Don asked.

They both shook their heads.

"Great kid," Don said one more time, and then he and Mary made their way out of the restaurant.

When the door closed behind the Snells, the very colors in Marge's seemed to lighten.

"So, will you talk to Rhoda and Phyllys, Cally?" Eddy asked again, drawing my attention back to our own table.

"Sure," I promised. I didn't add that I might not be the best emissary for the job.

"Thanks," he said. "Well, that was really something."

"What was something?" I asked. For a writer, Eddy was sure hard to follow.

"The Snells," he whispered confidentially. "Talk about irony—"

"Swordfish, heart attack special, and pasta primavera," Dulcie announced, interrupting him.

She looked way too small to be balancing the heavily loaded tray on one hand. It held our entrées, salads, and drinks, not to mention bread. She probably figured she saved time this way, but I was sure her muscles would be sore by the end of the night.

Dulcie slapped our dishes down on the table, looked at them critically, and finally rearranged it all, each entrée with a salad to the left of the dish and a glass to the right. Then she sighed with relief, massaging her carrying arm with her other hand. She turned to Eddy.

"So whaddaya want?" she demanded. Uh-oh, waitressing skills in decline.

"Could I see a menu?" Eddy requested diffidently.

Dulcie just put one hand on her hip and looked down her long, studded nose at him. In that moment, I began to feel sorry for Eddy. Did no one like him because he carried around a sigh and a notebook? Or did he carry around a sigh and a notebook because no one liked him?

"I'll have what he's having," Eddy capitulated, pointing at Kapp's plate.

"Good choice," Dulcie said for the second time that night. This had to be training from Marge. Maybe Dulcie might make good cult material. Then she glared at us all, challenging us visually to make her waitressing more difficult. Forget the cult idea. One order was probably about as much as she could follow.

"Thanks, Dulcie," Dee-Dee put in cheerfully.

And then Dulcie actually smiled, a smile that made her narrow features glow. Was Dee-Dee the first one to say something nice to Dulcie tonight?

"Thank you, man," Dulcie replied, and turned and walked away.

"Jeez," Eddy whined. "What's her problem?"

"Do you see another waitress here?" Dee-Dee answered.

I looked around. Dee-Dee was right. Dulcie seemed to be covering the whole dining room by herself. I wondered what she had done to get her aunt so mad at her. And I wondered if "Marge" existed.

I took a bite of salad. It was fresh, with real blue cheese, sunflower seeds, and sliced mushrooms. I savored the mixture of flavors. Who cared about the waitressing if the food at Marge's was all this good?

Kapp was ignoring his salad and stuffing fried fish into his mouth.

"So, you were talking about irony," Dee-Dee prompted Eddy before twirling some pasta around her fork.

"Oh yeah," Eddy said, eyeing our food. "It's just that Seeger Snell had it all, you know? Rich parents, only child. He could have done anything he wanted, and that father of his would have subsidized him. And did he do anything meaningful? No way." He paused for a moment. "Except for dying."

"How many brothers and sisters do you have?" Kapp asked through a mouthful of catsup-covered chips.

"None," Eddy admitted, reddening. "But that's not the point. My parents don't have the money to subsidize *my* work. And I'm a real artist."

"I thought you said you were a writer," Kapp objected just to be ornery.

"I *am* a writer!" Eddy bleated. "I meant that I have an artistic temperament. Listen," he whispered, bending over the table. "In my day job, I'm a waiter. Only I hope I do a more sensitive job than *our* waitress. Here I am, a writer, and I do a menial job 'cause I don't have money. Seeger could have done anything he wanted—"

"Maybe he was doing what he wanted," Kapp pointed out.

I refused to enter the fray. I took a bite of swordfish. It was rich and light at the same time, flavored with lemon and some herbs I couldn't identify. I was just lifting another mouthful to my face when Linda walked into Marge's.

Linda sidled up to the cash register, her face averted from the diners. A large, attractive woman with curly salt-and-pepper hair came out to the cash register from behind the flapping kitchen doors. Was this Marge?

I couldn't hear Linda, but I could hear the woman.

"Sure, honey. Takeout is just fine." She pulled out a pencil from her apron. "Seafood salad? That's all?"

And then the woman I took to be Marge disappeared behind the flapping kitchen doors again.

Linda kept her face turned away as she stood in front of the cash register. But her body was talking. She rolled her shoulders, clasped her hands, and jerked her head around as if she was on a leash.

I couldn't watch her anymore. It was too painful.

I looked over at Aileen. Her eyes were on Linda. Aileen

had been right about one thing. Linda did manage to eat. As I watched Aileen watch Linda, I realized that the Snells hadn't said good-bye to Aileen the same way that they had to me. Maybe Don Snell hadn't recognized Aileen paired up with Harley? That must have rubbed her the wrong way. For everything Aileen had said about See-ger, it was obvious that she was proud of her position as part owner of The Sensual Body.

I took another bite of my swordfish and tried to forget Seeger and Linda and Aileen for a while. And Eddy. I saw his mouth opening to speak again.

And then the kitchen doors flapped, and Dulcie came out with what had to be the fastest take-out order I'd seen in a decade. I had a feeling that Marge wanted Linda out of the restaurant as quickly as possible.

The minute the front door had closed behind Linda, I asked Eddy about her health.

"Who, Linda?" he asked, tilting his head as if confused by the question.

"Well, there's obviously something wrong with her," I tried again.

"I don't know about her health," he said, dismissing her. "Except that she's all upset over her sister's death. Now me, I have a really sensitive stomach—"

"Maybe you should eat a vegan diet," Dee-Dee sug-gested.

A look of horror crossed Eddy's morose face.

And then Dulcie snuck up behind him.

"Heart attack special number two," she announced.

Eddy reddened as Dulcie slammed down his squid, fish, and chips. Dulcie arranged his salad and water, winked, and left. So much for Eddy's sensitive stomach.

Eddy cut off a piece of fish and had it halfway to his mouth before Kapp started in on him again. Kapp had almost finished his own meal now and looked ready to interrogate.

"So, how well do you know Linda?" Kapp asked.

"Barely," Eddy answered and stuffed the piece of fish into his mouth.

"Where'd you meet her?" Kapp prodded before Eddy had time to swallow.

"At a support group," Eddy mumbled through his fish. He swallowed. "There was a flyer for the intimacy seminar at the support group, so we decided to drive down together and check it out." He shook his head, rolling his eyes. "Some companion she turned out to be."

"What kind of support group?" Kapp pressed.

Eddy took another bite and talked through it. "A grief support group. You know, Linda is really crazed about her sister dying in that weight-lifting accident. And boy, have I heard about it."

"Eddy, who did you lose?" Dee-Dee asked gently.

"Lose?" he repeated.

"You were in a grief group," Dee-Dee reminded him. "Did someone you care about die?"

"Oh no, no one died," Eddy assured us, spearing a chip. "I just thought the material would be good. And then this guy, Seeger, dives off his balcony." He took a bite. "Great stuff."

"So, you'd never been to the intimacy group before, either of you?" Kapp took over again.

"Well, I sure hadn't," Eddy said.

"How about Linda?" Kapp pressed on.

"I guess not," was his only answer.

But Kapp was still trying.

"Either of you ever meet Seeger Snell before the previous group?"

Eddy shrugged. "Not me. He wasn't a literary type, that was for sure. But the material! Man, Seeger's death is what good novels are made of." Eddy's eyes went out of focus. "Or even maybe docudramas. That's why I came back this weekend."

I was having a hard time liking Eddy right now, but my baked potato was good. There is always light somewhere.

"Why did Linda come back?" Kapp tried one more time.

"Don't know," Eddy mumbled, shoveling in food.

"But wouldn't she at least make a good character?" I asked in frustration.

"Nah," he groused. "All she does is cry. There's nothing there to write about."

"Where were you when Seeger fell?" I asked. I'm sure there was something to like about Eddy, but I didn't feel like searching for it now. I wanted a few facts.

"I was heading out to the beach for inspiration. I missed the whole thing. Heard that crazy guy bagpiping."

"Are you sure?" Kapp demanded.

"I think so," Eddy muttered, beginning his salad. "But I could be wrong. That guy is always bagpiping. It might have been another time." He ate a couple of bites and went on. "I did hear the screaming. I went running back to the inn. Whoa, Seeger was a mess. I wanted to write it all down, get the details, but it was . . . I don't know, too weird to really be there."

"Who was on the scene when you got there?" I tried.

"Trica, Aileen," he told me, wiping his mouth with his napkin. He'd managed to scarf down his entire meal while we questioned him. No wonder he had a bad stomach.

"Did you see Linda?"

He drew his brows together. "I don't think so. But I saw Wiz. He was running away."

"Did you—" Kapp began. But the interview was over.

"Thanks for sharing the table," Eddy interrupted and

stood. He walked over to the register, paid Dulcie for his meal, and practically ran out the door.

And he wasn't the only one. Vick and Oralia got up from their table and left.

It was then that I noticed a lone diner near the back of the room. It was the reporter with the pouty face. He sat still, just watching the rest of us. It was almost as if he were waiting for something to happen. But what? Suddenly, I remembered his name: Rick Ryan. I'd seen it on his column in an alternative San Francisco newspaper. His specialty was vilifying the New Age.

I turned back to Kapp and Dee-Dee to ask what they knew about Rick Ryan, but they were both getting up to leave, too. It was a rout.

I stayed a few minutes after Kapp and Dee-Dee left, then paid my own bill with a good-sized tip for the beleaguered Dulcie, waved good-bye to Aileen and Harley, and headed out into the hydrangea-blue twilight.

When I got back to the inn, I was surprised to find Phyllys and Rhoda waiting to talk to me in the lobby, sitting together on the love seat.

"We just wanted to thank you, Cally," Phyllys pronounced earnestly.

"Me?" I said. This wasn't Phyllys's usual script.

"We didn't even think to ask Wiz if he saw Seeger fall," Rhoda explained.

"Did he?" I ventured hesitantly.

"No," Rhoda said, relief in her voice. "He was out front, but his back was turned. When he heard the screams, he thought it was something he'd done—"

"It usually is," Phyllys explained with a smile.

"And he hightailed it out of there," Rhoda finished off.

"So thank you, Cally, for reminding us to ask," Phyllys said again.

I could feel myself blushing. And then I remembered my messenger job.

"Listen, guys," I told them. "Eddy wants to send his apologies through me for giving you the impression that he thought Wiz was a murderer. He was just blue-skying fictional ideas."

"Well, he can stop right now," Phyllys snapped.

"Don't worry," I assured her. "He got the point."

Phyllys grinned and pinkened. "I told him to go to his room, didn't I?" she remembered.

"You sure did," Rhoda said and laughed. "Cally, you can tell him his apology is accepted—"

"Till the next time, anyway," Phyllys added. But she was still smiling.

"Hey, Dulcie's working at Marge's now," I offered.

"Makes sense," Phyllys muttered.

And then a little voice spoke up behind us. Wiz, superspy, had snuck in without any of us hearing him.

"Dulcie got in, like, big trouble with her aunt," the boy informed me. "Dulcie got caught with drugs and, um, like guys, and stuff—"

"Wiz—" Phyllys tried. But it was too late.

"So her aunt didn't put her in jail, but Dulcie says she might as well be," Wiz finished.

"Drug bust," Phyllys amplified. "But Wiz has it right. Dulcie might as well have served time for what her aunt's doing to her. But don't spread it around. Okay, Cally? There still may be *some* people in Fiebre who don't know."

"I promise," I said, crossing my heart with my hand.

And then the front desk bell rang.

Rhoda hopped up from the love seat and walked over to the desk where two women stood. One was elegant with sharp features, the other smaller with dark, cropped hair.

"We've come about your position for kitchen help," the first woman declared. "We'd love a job for two, no worry about rates. We're just passing through. Do you suppose you could use us?"

Rhoda opened her mouth to answer, but mine just dropped open, unspeaking.

The Inn at Fiebre was going to have two new kitchen helpers. And I knew their names: Geneva and Melinda. Geneva and Melinda Lazar.

FIFTEEN

"Can we use you?" Rhoda repeated, throwing triumphant fists in the air. "You are a gift from God."

"But of course, we can't pay much," Phyllys added quickly. A gift from God might be mighty expensive for kitchen help.

"That will be perfectly fine," Geneva assured her. "My sister and I can come as a package. Two for one, so to speak." She laughed. It was a stage laugh. Geneva was enjoying this role. She sounded like a character from a Noel Coward play.

"We can't offer benefits or anything," Phyllys told them. She was looking the gift horse in the mouth, unlike Rhoda.

"Oh, perfectly fine," Geneva twittered. "Let's just do it under the table, so to speak. Cash, no bother."

Cash meant no names. I'd wondered how she was going to explain away the coincidence of having Lazar as a last name.

Phyllys looked at Rhoda.

"Yes," Rhoda whispered. "Please."

"We love to cook and clean," Geneva went on. I almost opened my mouth to ask how she could say such a thing, but it was still hanging open from the first shock of seeing them, so I closed it instead. "A frightful obsession, but true."

Melinda picked up a vase from the counter and mimed

polishing it. The vase dropped from her hands inevitably, but Geneva caught it before it hit the floor. Melinda's process of melding her personality into that of her cartoon character, Acuto from Pluto, had unfortunately imbued her with his clumsiness and goof-ups as well as his endearing personality.

"Well, I'd say you two are hired," Phyllys concluded. "How about eight dollars an hour for the two of you? I know that's only four dollars apiece for each of you. But if you're a package deal . . ." She let her sentence trail off enticingly.

"Oh, perfect," Geneva cooed.

Dack. I'd never heard Geneva coo before, and I hoped I never would again.

"Would you like to stay here?" Rhoda offered. "We're not paying you much."

"Oh, how kind," Geneva gushed. "But I'm afraid we've already arranged other lodgings. It's a shame. We just saw your advertisement on the bulletin board or we wouldn't have. I must say your inn is lovelier by far if this lobby is any indication."

A look of suspicion passed over Phyllys's face but then disappeared. Even Phyllys wasn't going to pass up much-needed kitchen help at these prices, despite the oddity of their lodging preferences.

"Well, let me just say thank you," Rhoda said, beaming.

"And I'll take you back to the kitchen and show you around," Phyllys added. "Though you won't want to stay too late tonight. You're going to have an early morning tomorrow."

Geneva's face quivered under her Noel Coward smile. Geneva was not an early riser by choice.

Phyllys led my sisters away to the kitchen, and Rhoda turned her beaming face on me.

"Maybe everything will be all right after all," she whispered. "This certainly is a good omen."

"I hope so," I told her sincerely, taking her whisper as my cue to leave. "Night-night."

Then I turned to make my way down the hall, wondering how much damage Melinda would inflict while she was working in the kitchen.

"Sweet dreams," Rhoda called out after me.

Sweet dreams, indeed, I thought as I walked to my room. Sweet dreams of competent kitchen help.

I smelled aftershave as I reached my doorway. Reflexively, I parried Kapp's cane thrust. He grunted.

"Where have you been?" he demanded. "I've been waiting for you. We have to talk motives. And I've got more information."

"I was watching my sisters get hired as kitchen help," I told him.

"Really?" he asked, raising his brows.

"Really." I explained what had just happened in the lobby as we entered my room.

Kapp flopped down onto the wingback chair while I took my usual position, sitting on the end of my bed.

"So what's all this about motives?" I prompted him.

Kapp tapped his cane on the ground. "Listen, Lazar, while *you've* been fussing around with bagpipers, *I've* been doing real research," he announced.

"Do tell," I murmured provocatively. Criminy, now I was doing Noel Coward.

Kapp flashed me a look, but he told.

"Betcha you thought Trica was a bimbo who married Seeger for his money, right?" he proposed, leaning forward with a smirk.

"Actually, I didn't think about it," I said. I considered Trica's childlike insecurity, her worries about her weight, her sweetness. She didn't seem like bimbo material to me.

Kapp just nodded as though I'd answered in the affirmative.

"Well," he began, leaning back in his chair. "Trica was the one with the big bucks. An heiress. Ever hear of Tinbergan Linoleum? Her father owned it. So she just bummed around, taking every self-help seminar she could find after Daddy Warbucks died. She even taught a few. Then she met her soul mate: Seeger Snell, the classic screwup. Went to law school but never practiced law." I flinched a little here, but Kapp didn't notice. "Started a bunch of businesses that never took off. His parents gave him just enough money for him to keep on screwing up. Or at least, his father did. And then he married Trica. He didn't have to scrounge off his parents after that. And he got lucky enough to find a competent business partner to help him spend Trica's money. Aileen's the one that makes The Sensual Body profitable. But Trica's the one with the money."

"But Trica's not a suspect," I pointed out.

"Still, it's interesting."

"How's it interesting?" I asked. I didn't get the point.

"I don't know exactly," Kapp admitted. "But it's part of the evidence. That's for sure."

"Okay." I gave in. "What else?"

"Trica was arrested a few years ago," Kapp obliged. "She was in some kind of naked protest about sexual liberation rights."

"Trica?!"

"Yeah." Kapp smiled libidinously, probably imagining Trica's short, size-eighteen, goddess body. He wasn't one of those men who admired culturally acceptable body types only. "Wish I could have been there. I would have done her case for free, not that she needs freebies—"

A knock on the door ended that fantasy.

Kapp whipped his head around. "You got a date with someone I don't know about?" he hissed.

"No, I just have an open-door policy," I answered.

Kapp chortled. "Bet you're sorry you ever said—"

"Psst, it's us," came a hushed but urgent voice through the door. "Let us in, quick!"

I opened my door to my two sisters with a sigh. Not that I didn't love them.

Geneva slunk in elegantly. Melinda tripped over the doorjamb while peeking over her shoulder.

"How'd you get past Rhoda and Phyllys?" I asked as I hugged Geneva.

"Out their dreadful little kitchen back door," Geneva answered me. "*They* are going to bed." She shuddered. "So *we* can start early tomorrow. Do you want to know how early?"

I shook my head and laughed.

"You're a good sister," I said instead. "You, too, Melinda."

"You need protection," Geneva stated, pinkening a little. Praise was always hard for her.

"And we're going to investigate," Melinda added, her voice excited.

"Well, join the team," I offered, pointing at Kapp. "Mr. Kapp here is just going over the suspects. But so far, he's just talked about Trica."

"Who isn't a suspect?" Geneva questioned, one eyebrow raised.

"Never take anything for granted," Kapp muttered.

"Yeah!" Melinda agreed enthusiastically. "It's always the one you don't suspect."

I sat down heavily on the end of my bed. Geneva lowered herself gracefully to sit on one side of me, and Melinda smacked down on the other side. Then we waited like three children for our bedtime story.

Kapp was only too happy to give us one.

"So I was telling Lazar . . . Cally . . . about Trica's nude protest," he began.

"Whoa!" Melinda burst out, her eyes widening.

"And she's an heiress," I put in. I didn't want to go over the same material again. Anyway, Kapp was far too excited over the thought of Trica in the nude to be sitting with me and my sisters in a hotel room. Me, fine. Kapp and I knew our limits. But I felt protective of my sisters, especially Melinda. "So what about the real suspects?" I prodded.

"Boy, you sure know how to take the fun out of life, don't you?" he snapped. But then he rallied. "With all due respect, your honorable energy worker, I will regale you with the naughty deeds of the 'suspects.' "

"Yay!" Melinda cried, clapping her hands. Geneva just curled her lip in something between a sneer and a smile.

Kapp bowed, then sat down in the wingback chair again.

"I didn't get a whole lot on Oralia from my sources," he began, all business now. "She's some sort of nutritional counselor for an HMO. Her only police record is for non-payment of parking tickets. Unlike Seeger Snell, who racked up a bunch of DUIs—"

"DUIs?" asked Melinda.

"Driving under the influence," Kapp explained. "He should have lost his license, but someone fixed it with the judge."

"Wow," Melinda whispered. "I didn't know people could really do that."

"Still," Geneva put in impatiently. "Seeger Snell isn't a suspect."

"Sure he is, Geneva," Melinda insisted. "He's a suspect if he might have killed himself."

"Thank you to the lady with the logical mind," Kapp said to Melinda.

I kept my grin internal. Melinda did often amaze with her convoluted logic.

"But, back to Oralia," Kapp went on. "Oralia went to high school with Seeger Snell." He paused dramatically.

"I knew that," I told him. "But how did you find out?"

"My computer hacker's doing personal histories on everyone and found the connection, that's how. How the hell did you find out?"

"Oralia told me herself," I said. "She and Seeger even dated for a while." Kapp rolled his eyes. I should have kept my mouth shut. I didn't mean to steal his thunder.

"Vick," he went on quickly. "Vick works for a non-profit called Help the Children, America as a fund-raiser. Ix doubt that they'd like hearing about him moonlighting in intimacy seminars."

"Why not?" Melinda asked.

"Oh, come on," Kapp chided. "All their touchy-feely is pretty sexual if you ask me."

"And some people can be very circumspect if they think sex and children are involved," Geneva threw in, nodding.

Kapp cleared his throat before going on.

"And then there's Harley," he growled. "Harley Isaacs, master of assault, bar fights, and excessive drug use. He'd be my pick for a murderer, even if it wasn't for his damn bagpipes."

"But why?" I asked. I'd driven myself crazy trying to think of a motive for Harley and hadn't succeeded yet.

Kapp shrugged massively. "How the hell do I know? But the guy's violent. You've seen it yourself. And he has an criminal record for assault."

"When was he arrested?" Geneva asked.

"Eight years ago, the first time. He was convicted. He

wasn't brought to trial on the more recent one," Kapp admitted. "But that's not the point. The man's probably a born criminal. For all we know, he's some kind of serial killer."

"One conviction for assault does not a serial killer make," Geneva put in.

Kapp glared at her. I didn't think my sister and my friend would ever be a love match. Their personalities were too much alike.

"So, who would you bet on?" he challenged.

"That weird woman who cries all the time," Melinda offered. "Something's really wrong with her."

"Well," Geneva said, standing suddenly. "I'd go for our innkeepers, just so I wouldn't have to get up tomorrow morning. Do you know they had us sign some silly piece of paper saying we'd stay a month or until they got other kitchen help?"

"They can't make us stay, can they?" Melinda asked.

Kapp smiled cruelly. "You," he announced, "have signed a contract. Probably a binding contract."

Melinda's eyes rounded. "But we didn't even use our own names," she objected.

"Oh, even better," Kapp added. "Fraud."

"Kapp!" I warned. "Stop it. You're scaring her. They can't hold my sisters to anything if they're paying them under the table."

"Legal is legal," he insisted.

"Don't worry," I assured Melinda. "I'm sure they won't hunt you down if you leave. They just want you to stay."

"They won't hunt you down, but would it be ethical to leave after you've given your written promise?" Kapp asked.

Geneva frowned. He'd pushed her button.

"Listen, Dulcie will be back working for them as soon as—" I began.

A rap on the door shut my mouth. Who was it now?

I opened the door carefully and not fully, shielding any view of the room.

Rick Ryan, the reporter, was standing on his short, bowed legs there in the hallway. Dack.

"May I come in?" he asked.

"No," I answered succinctly.

I stepped out of my room into the hallway and pulled the door nearly closed behind me. "What do you want?"

"You know who I am," he said. It was a statement, not a question. He paused, staring at me. I guessed he was trying to intimidate me. When it became clear he wasn't getting the response he wanted, he went on. "I hear you're a medical intuitive." Now he sneered. "So have you intuited a murder?"

"No," I said again. I decided to stick with that answer. I couldn't bring myself to like this man. In fact, he made the hair go up on the back of my neck. His aura was a thick murk of anger.

"I heard rumors that Seeger Snell's death was a murder," he went on. "Are you working with the dead man's wife?"

I opened my mouth to say "no," then shut it again. It would have been a lie. So much for the "just say no" strategy.

"Go away," I tried instead. "I'm not talking to you."

"So, are you certified in medical intuition?" he bulldozed on as if he hadn't heard me. Then he gave me that pouty sneer again. "Whaddaya take, an aura test?"

"No," I said. "But you just failed yours."

I lifted my cane ever so slightly.

"Give me a break," he objected. "There isn't any such thing as an aura test, or an aura for that matter. It's just a bunch of New Age bull—"

"Leave," I ordered and touched his knee with my cane.

He looked down at the stick touching his knee. Then he looked at my face. I don't know what he saw there, but he left without another word, slithering down the hallway toward the lobby.

"Whoa, who was that guy?" Melinda asked once I was back in the room.

"Rick Ryan," Geneva answered unexpectedly. "A blight on the earth. He'll try to blame Seeger's death on New Age abuses in his column. Just watch."

"Look, everyone knows that guy is a jerk," Kapp put in. "Nobody will believe him."

"Oh, but Acuto's a jerk," Melinda argued. "And people listen to him."

"But he's not a malicious jerk," I objected.

"And not even real," Geneva said, shaking her head, a glimpse of a smile on her face. Then she held out her hand and helped Melinda up from her perch on the bed.

"Well, we must fly," Geneva announced. "Pots and pans to clean. Places to go."

I went out and scoped the hallway. Rick Ryan was nowhere to be seen. Geneva and Melinda skulked away after a pair of sisterly hugs.

And then Kapp got up to leave.

"Your sister Geneva is worse than you, Lazar," he commented. And before I could argue, he added, "I like her. And your screwy sister Melinda. She's a hoot."

And then he was gone, too.

I put on my pajamas, thought of Roy, and finally, I was asleep under my beautiful quilt.

Sunday morning, I lifted weights and then had breakfast at an almost empty buffet in the dining room. I kept my eyes averted, not wanting to see the results of the bumps and crashes from behind me where Melinda was cleaning up . . . or trying to clean up.

Vick came walking up to my table. "May I join you?" he asked. "I wanted to talk, and you . . . well . . ."

"Of course," I said. I looked into Vick's dark eyes as he lowered his tall body into a chair. He was clearly troubled.

"I wanted to talk about Oralia," Vick dove in, ignoring the sound of a glass breaking behind us. "Cally, I love her. Maybe I always have. But there's something wrong—"

Vick stopped suddenly. I turned to see what Melinda had done, but it wasn't Melinda at all. It was Oralia, bearing down on us.

"Vick," she murmured, sadness in her voice. I looked at her, even felt her energy for a moment. A wave of grief and self-pity washed out from her, dousing me in the process. There *was* something wrong, but what? I just hoped it wasn't guilt over murder. Especially if Vick was in love with her.

Vick pushed his chair back and stood, his face even more troubled now. Had he felt the same wave I had? He nodded apologetically at me. I nodded back my understanding. Clearly, he needed to be with Oralia, and so they left the dining room together.

I heard Melinda's voice. "Dack," she muttered. "Stupid midgin asteroid."

I resisted the urge to give her a hug or even a look, and left the dining room myself. I took a deep breath. I was going to sit on the beach today. I thought about sitting out by the hot tubs, but I still couldn't bring myself to sit where Trica had seen her husband die.

So I asked Rhoda for one of her folding lawn chairs and dragged it out to the sand, near one of the cypress trees. Then I closed my eyes. Ah, bliss. I felt the sun and wind, heard the roar of the ocean and the screeching of the gulls, and smelled it all. But I wasn't alone for long.

Eddy came walking up. "Did you talk to Rhoda and Phyllys?" his voice interrupted my oceanic commune.

"I did," I told him. "It'll be all right. Just don't talk to them about Wiz, okay?"

"Okay." He sighed and switched gears. "Cally, they're saying the police are going to keep us here till they're sure how Seeger died—"

"Who is they?" I demanded.

"Oh, you know, people in town. But the thing is, I'm not rich like these other guys. I gotta get back to my job, or I'll lose it. I only put in for the time to do the seminar. It's not fair—"

"Hey, energy worker," Harley intruded. With his arm around Aileen, the two walked up to us. He looked almost sober. "My lady here says I should apologize to you for my behavior."

"So . . ." Aileen prompted, elbowing him none too lightly in the side.

"Fer God's sake, woman, don't I have enough injuries?" he asked her.

"No," she answered.

"All right, all right," he growled. "I'm a pretentious git. I was out of line. I'm sorry."

I turned my head for a second to hide my grin. Then I turned back. "Sorry about your . . . um . . . manhood," I said with a straight face.

"No problem," he replied curtly.

"Easy for him to say," Aileen put in with a wink.

Just what was their relationship about, anyway? But before I could answer my own question, I felt someone behind me: Roy. I closed my eyes again, wishing everyone but Roy away. He put his hand on my shoulder, and I felt our energies meet and flow together. And his energy felt light, not dark. I settled into the feeling, savoring it, his scent blending with the ocean's—

"Cally," a new voice greeted me, and I opened my eyes to see Vick and Oralia standing with everyone else. Criminy, what was this, a receiving line?

"We just heard that the police are actively investigating Seeger Snell's death," Oralia announced. She paled a little. "They're investigating the 'Love Workshop.' "

"Can they really do that?" Eddy questioned. "I mean, it's not our fault—"

"The cops can do anything they bloody well feel like, grasshopper," Harley said. "Especially in a small town."

"But they can't keep us," Eddy argued. "We have our rights."

"Ha!" Aileen snorted.

"Maybe we could do a group to process our feelings about this," Vick suggested.

We all just looked at him. Even Oralia. He'd probably do a group to process his feelings if he were in prison. That was an awful thought. What if it was Vick—

Abruptly, I noticed someone standing, watching us from across the beach. At first, I thought it must be a police official, and my pulse sped up. Then I looked harder. It was Rick Ryan. I could feel Roy see him at the same time.

"Oh, foot," he muttered, as close to swearing as he usually came. "That's Rick Ryan. I thought I saw the last of him in Kentucky."

I turned to look at Roy. Did he know Ryan?

But Eddy began to whine again before I could ask.

"The police can't hold us here." His voice grew higher in pitch. "What if I lose my job over this? It isn't fair—"

Oralia whirled around and turned on Eddy, thrusting her face into his.

"Of course it isn't fair!" she shouted. I saw tears in her eyes, and blinked my own eyes. What was going on?

"Life isn't fair. Don't you understand? Nothing is fair. Nothing! Okay?"

Then Oralia turned on her heel and went running down the beach, her flowing gown ballooning out behind her like a ship's sail.

SIXTEEN

Vick's head reared back when Oralia took off, almost as if he'd been slapped.

"Oralia!" he shouted finally, and then he was running down the beach after her.

The rest of us just watched, stunned.

"So what's her problem?" Eddy demanded. "Is everyone going crazy around here? I don't—"

"Of course, we're all crazy," Harley interrupted him. "Didya think otherwise, my man?" He laughed deeply but not happily. "We'd be crazy not to be crazy."

"Oh, I just love it when you're profound," Aileen chirped in an unnatural falsetto. She batted her eyelashes under steel-rimmed glasses.

Harley took her arm. "Let's go somewhere else and be bloody profound," he suggested.

Aileen gave a little wave, and the two of them walked away down the beach. I saw Harley drop Aileen's arm, put his hand around her waist, and slide it upward. Aileen gave Harley a shove. I didn't want to see any more. I turned back to Eddy, wondering how to gently encourage him to leave. Roy's hands were still warming my shoulders deliciously. We might actually have some time alone if I could get Eddy to walk away.

"Well, maybe Harley can afford to be crazy, but I can't," Eddy groused. "He's just like Seeger, doesn't take anything seriously. No sensitivity at all to what's meaningful in life—"

"Seeger or Harley?" Roy asked softly. I was surprised to hear his voice.

"Seeger was even worse," Eddy answered. "Seeger's parents had money; no wonder he could afford to be such a jerk."

"And how do you think his parents feel now?" Roy put in.

"Huh?" Eddy said, scrunching up his face as if to get a better look at Roy behind me.

"I just can't help but be curious," Roy went on, his voice still soft. "How can you ignore everyone's feelings, the real stuff going on around you, and be a writer?"

"What do you mean?" Eddy asked, his voice soft now, too. He sounded like he really wanted to know what Roy meant. And he wasn't whining.

"Seeger's mama and papa are hurting terribly," Roy explained slowly. "Each in their own way. They're grieving. That's what novels are made of: grief and joy, love and despair. But you haven't noticed their despair. Or this Seeger. I never met him, but there had to be something to his life, something that caused his death. Something you didn't notice."

Eddy got out his notebook and jotted down some notes as Roy went on.

"You gotta notice, if you're going to write. You have to really see people."

"Yeah?" Eddy prodded eagerly.

But Roy was finished with the main lecture.

"I just thought it needed saying, is all," he muttered.

"Thanks, man," Eddy said, closed his notebook, and walked away.

He turned after a few steps. "You know, Roy, you'd make a great character," he offered. "I'll start noticing."

Then he turned back and began walking again.

"Oh, Roy," I whispered and stood up from my beach chair. Roy came around to stand in front of me. He held out a hand. I clasped it and remembered its familiar feel once more.

"Oh, Cally, darlin'," he murmured. "You know you're still the only one in my heart. I wish I understood this darkness thing. I want to—"

And then I smelled aftershave behind me. I whirled around and lifted my cane, blocking Kapp's strike.

"Damn," Kapp muttered.

"What?" I demanded brusquely.

Because I could already feel Roy's energy drifting away. The moment was gone.

"Hell's bells, Lazar, I just wanted to talk to you." Kapp looked pointedly at Roy behind me.

I felt rather than heard Roy sigh.

"I . . . I guess I'll talk to you later, Cally," he murmured. "See you, Mr. Kapp."

And then, before I could object, he was walking away across the beach like all the rest had before.

I turned back to Kapp.

"You did that on purpose," I accused.

"Me?" he protested, putting his hand over his heart. But he didn't even ask what he was accused of. He *had* driven Roy away on purpose. And now I'd never know what it was that Roy had tried to tell me he wanted. Me? To get rid of the darkness? To never see my face again?

"I know you don't like Roy," I told Kapp, anger floating up in me. "But I have unfinished business with him."

"He's a crackpot, Lazar," Kapp pronounced. "And he sucks you dry. Find a man who appreciates you—"

"Roy does appreciate me," I objected.

"Okay, fine," Kapp gave in, his hand upraised. "I'll keep out of it."

I glared at Kapp. I didn't believe him for a second. Kapp didn't keep out of anything. And he really believed what he was saying about Roy. I willed myself to relax, to let the anger go. Kapp was trying to be a friend.

"So what's up?" I asked him. "Did you get some new information or something?"

"Just that your sister Melinda is going to find it easier to leave than she thought," he answered with a sly smile.

"Criminy, what did she do?" I demanded.

"Oh just minor infractions: spilling trays, breaking dishware, bumping into people—but Geneva's cleaning up after her."

That didn't sound too bad.

"Lady Lazar, would you be my guest for lunch?" he proposed with a bow.

Of course, lunch was paid for already. But Kapp was trying to make amends.

"Meet you in the lobby at noon?" he pressed.

I agreed, and Kapp left.

I sat back down in my beach chair, alone on the sand, and let my thoughts roam where they wanted on the question of who might have had motive to kill Seeger Snell. My logical mind wasn't working. Maybe a more intuitive one would.

So, why would someone want to kill Seeger Snell? His death left Trica a widow, a rich widow, even richer than before. Was someone in love with her? Did someone want to marry her for her money? Seeger was an irritant. But had he done something more, killed someone while driving drunk? Stolen someone's sweetheart? Made a pass at the wrong person? Threatened someone with damaging knowledge? This was more like it! My intuitive brain was engaged. I thought of Seeger Snell and dreamily imagined him approaching Harley, "You were the one who knifed that guy in a bar six months ago. Did you get way with it?" Or Eddy, "I heard you were caught plagiarizing in college. . . ." And then I really was dreaming, dead asleep in the sun and the wind.

I woke up a little before noon. So much for the intuitive approach. Maybe I was channeling Geneva's sleep deprivation. She was the one who'd gotten up early to work in the kitchen.

I folded up my beach chair and carried it back to the lobby. I could hear Rhoda's and Phyllys's voices as I neared the registration desk.

"We can't fire them," Rhoda objected. "Mother of God, we just hired them!"

"Then let's just fire the clumsy one and keep the other sister," Phyllys tried. "She seems efficient enough."

"And how do you think the one you fired will feel then?" Rhoda shot back. "Phyllys, how can you even think such a cruel thought?"

"It's easy. Every time I hear something else break—"

I couldn't stand it. I walked up to the desk and rang the bell.

Rhoda came out to answer, her bronze skin flushed.

"Oh, Cally," she said, her ready smile strained. "Thanks for bringing the chair back."

I wanted to tell her my sisters were spies, but I didn't. I couldn't. Geneva would never forgive me. And an unforgiving Geneva was even harder to bear than broken crockery. Anyway, at the wages they were paying my sisters, they could probably afford new dishes, or glasses, or whatever else Melinda had dropped. At least I hoped so.

So I strained, too, and smiled back at Rhoda. "Thanks for letting me borrow the chair," I muttered.

And then I smelled Kapp behind me. This time when I turned, he didn't even have his cane up. Was he feeling guilty about Roy? Or was he just tired of losing?

The dining room was filled when Kapp and I entered; filled with people and filled with chaos. Melinda was the chaos element.

Vick and Oralia were at one table, speaking in hushed whispers. Dee-Dee sat with Eddy at another table. She waved our way. I could just hear the tail end of Eddy's sentence: ". . . a writer notices," and then something splattered on the floor. I looked up. Melinda was carrying a tray, not nearly as well as Dulcie had the night before, and something that looked like guacamole was glopped upside down on the floor. She bent over to pick up the guacamole, and the rest of the contents of the tray began to slide. And then Geneva was there, grabbing the tray and carrying it to the safety of the buffet.

Harley and Aileen guffawed.

"Dack, I'm such a space cadet!" Melinda hissed to herself.

I closed my eyes for a moment, wishing Melinda just a little of Geneva's natural grace.

Kapp nudged me. My eyes popped open.

"Just pretend they're strangers," he whispered in my ear.

Geneva glanced at me as we approached the buffet. There were circles under her eyes.

I opened my mouth to say something and shut it again. *Strangers, these women are strangers.* Geneva winked a tired eye and turned away.

The food looked good for all that its preparation must have cost in breakage, temper, and time. Great bowls of salads from Chinese chicken to tabouli to Caesar, two soups, breads, cheeses, desserts. I wondered who had cooked what. Maybe Geneva had stayed up all night reading cookbooks. Somehow, I couldn't imagine anyone trusting Melinda with the actual cooking.

I filled my plate with tabouli, Caesar, and chunks of

cheddar and Swiss cheese, then topped off with a hunk of warm corn bread and a thick slice of whole wheat. Kapp heaped up his plate into a small mountain of everything all mashed together.

"You can come back, you know," I teased him.

He opened his mouth to retort.

And then someone screamed, and Melinda came running out from the kitchen and tripped, falling into a mercifully empty table. "What happened?" she gasped, rubbing her ribs.

"My soup!" Aileen cried out. "There's a severed finger in my soup!"

Harley reached over and pulled something flesh-colored and dripping from her bowl. "It's rubber," he growled. "It's a bloody gag." He glared across the room.

"I didn't do it," Melinda protested, her voice barely audible.

By this time, Phyllys was in the dining room, too. She looked at the rubber finger that Harley was holding and paled.

"Wiz," Aileen concluded. "Is this Wiz's idea of a joke?"

Phyllys practically ran from the room. When she came back, she was holding onto Wiz's arm.

"Tell her," she commanded Wiz.

"Someone broke into my magic bag!" he told Aileen. "They took out all kinds of stuff—"

"Like this?" demanded Harley, holding the rubber finger higher.

"Wow," Wiz breathed. "You found it. Did you find the rest of the stuff, too? The spider and the rope and—"

"You want us to believe that *you* didn't put this in the soup?" Aileen asked incredulously.

"Why would I put it in the soup?" Wiz replied.

"Why don't you tell me why," Aileen shot back.

"But I didn't," Wiz argued, his voice rising. He sounded close to tears.

"Somebody stole my stuff. I told you. And it was really cool stuff—"

"Oh, sure," Aileen snorted.

"If Wiz says someone took his things, he's telling the truth," Phyllys pronounced in a dangerously low voice. "Wiz doesn't lie."

"Who else but a kid—" Aileen started.

And then Kapp weighed in. "You have no proof that the boy put this in your soup," he reminded her. "He's admitted it was his. He's even given you a reasonable explanation of how it came to be out of his control. In this country, even children are innocent until proven guilty. Moreover—"

"Moreover, my rear end," Aileen snarled, rising. "I get the shock of my life and you're defending the kid—"

"I'm sure Wiz didn't do it," Eddy piped up unexpectedly. "I notice people, and Wiz isn't stupid. He'd know he'd be blamed. Someone is trying to get him in trouble."

"That's certainly possible," Vick chimed in. "We shouldn't jump to conclusions here."

There was a silence in the room for a moment. The dining room jury was considering the evidence.

I looked around the room and suddenly saw Rick Ryan in the back, just watching, no expression on his face. When had he come in? Did he put the finger in the soup? I shook my head. What was I thinking? I only wanted it to be him because I didn't like him. But I agreed with Eddy. Wiz wouldn't have done the finger trick, not after his mother had warned him that tricks were off limits. But who? And why? My leg twinged. I didn't like the feel of this.

"Fine," Aileen huffed. "Just fine. I'll forget I ever found a severed finger in my soup."

Phyllys turned to Wiz.

"Honey," she probed gently. "When did you find the things from your magic bag missing?"

"A couple of hours ago," he answered. "I left the bag out in the lobby yesterday. And when I opened it up to-day, all this cool stuff was missing. I was looking all over for it. That's why I was in the kitchen—"

"He was in the kitchen," Aileen interrupted. "You want evidence. He probably put it in the soup in the kitchen."

"Anyone could have put it in the soup right here in the dining room," Kapp shot back.

"That's true," Phyllys said slowly. She surveyed the room, telescoping her eyes on each person there, ending with a long stare at Melinda. Poor Melinda, the new klutz on the block. She had to be suspect number two by now.

"Criminy, don't look at me," my sister protested. "I may be from outer space, but I don't try to get kids in trouble."

She certainly convinced me, but then she was my sister. Still, Phyllys seemed to soften her stare.

"I have a suggestion," Vick offered. "Why don't we just take some time to access the wisdom of our sixth chakras right now? Maybe between all of us, we can fig-ure out what's going on here."

"We could do that," Oralia agreed.

"Sixth chakra!" Aileen exploded. "I say up *your* sixth chakra!" She stood, slamming her chair back, and stomped out the door.

"I don't think her sixth chakra's very open right now, my man," Harley put in, a glint of laughter in his eyes.

Now I wondered if Harley had put the finger in Aileen's soup. At least he had a personal relationship with her. Maybe he wanted to scare her for some reason. But I wasn't about to verbalize my suspicion. There had been enough accusations flying in the room.

"Why don't we just take a moment and close our eyes," Vick began.

"And imagine your third eye in the center of your forehead, seeing what your everyday eyes can't," Oralia went on, her voice hypnotic.

We were in session, and I hadn't even had a bite to eat. But I closed my eyes dutifully. That's how I missed Harley's exit. I heard it though, door slamming and all. When I opened my eyes, I saw that Vick and Oralia were the only others in the room with their eyes still closed.

"I move that we finish our meals in peace," Kapp proposed.

"I'll second that motion," Dee-Dee put in.

Vick and Oralia opened their eyes, annoyance in hers and a smidgen of hurt in his. They looked at each other for a second, then both nodded simultaneously. Had they realized that you can lead a horse to the sixth chakra, but you can't make him see through it?

Kapp and I took our plates to our table in silence. And around us, whispered conversations began.

"Phyllys, you believe me, don't you?" Wiz asked in a small voice.

"Of course I do, honey," she murmured, turning to go back to the kitchen. Abruptly, she swiveled her head around to look at those of us still in the room.

"Thank you Eddy, Kapp, Vick," she said. "And all of you who didn't judge."

I tried to think of something to say, but she and Wiz disappeared into the kitchen before I could.

"You were great, Kapp," I told him.

"Kid didn't do it," he mumbled nonchalantly through a mouthful of food. "I can always tell."

"But who?"

"I'm thinking about it," he promised.

I wondered if Eddy and Dee-Dee were asking each

other the same kind of questions. And Vick and Oralia.

And then I dug into my tabouli salad. By the time Kapp and I had finished lunch, everyone had left the dining room but Melinda, who was struggling with the leftovers. And I mean struggling. The leftovers seemed to be winning. I'd seen everyone leave but Rick Ryan. I wasn't sure when he'd slithered away.

Kapp and I split up once we left the dining room.

I walked outside, passing the hot tubs on the terra-cotta tile. I stopped for a moment, considering sitting in the chair that Trica had occupied when Seeger had fallen from the balcony. Would sitting there add anything to my understanding of what had happened? I shivered and turned my gaze to the hot tubs. Could I do it? Should I do it?

Then I looked more closely at the first hot tub. It was covered, but something was sticking out from beneath the cover. It was a hand. I thought of the severed finger. This had to be something else from Wiz's magic bag, right?

I crept forward and touched the hand. It felt real. Then I lifted the cover to the hot tub. I should have never done that. Because the hand wasn't a joke. Nor was the body it was connected to.

SEVENTEEN

A wave of dizziness rocked my whole body, leaving a resonance of wavering, overbright images. I wondered if I would pass out. Then my leg buckled underneath me. I cleared my head in time to catch myself with my cane and remain upright.

But even if I was upright, the body was still there floating in the hot tub. Linda Frey's body. Wet and bloated as it was, her face was still recognizable. And floating next to her was Wiz's giant spider from his magic bag.

I don't know when I started screaming. I just know that I did. And then other people came. Dee-Dee was first to arrive. There is good in the universe.

She looked at me questioningly, and then her gaze followed mine to the hot tub. She blinked and began to sway. I caught her, and we both held each other up for what might have been a minute or an hour.

"What happened?" she whispered when we finally let each other go.

"I saw her hand, and I lifted the cover, and—"

A look of renewed shock pulled her face taut.

"What?" I asked.

"The cover was pulled over her?" she asked back.

And then I understood. Linda Frey had been murdered. She couldn't have killed herself and pulled the cover back over her own dead body. Could she? Unless someone else had seen her and pulled—

"Oh, God," I heard before I could finish the thought. Eddy had arrived. "Linda!"

I turned to say something, but nothing came out of my mouth.

Eddy clutched his stomach and moaned. "Linda!" he cried again. "Oh, I'm so sorry. I never noticed you. I never—"

"Can I help?" Vick's musical voice asked from behind us. And then Eddy stepped aside, and Vick saw Linda's body in the tub.

"Vick, what—" Oralia began, standing beside him. Luckily, she was looking at Vick, not the hot tub.

Vick's glowing brown skin turned ashen. He turned and ran. Oralia sprinted after him and caught up.

"Vick?" she asked again, and I heard the sound of retching.

"Help, he wants to help?" Eddy babbled. He began to pace back and forth like a guard dog in front of the tub. "Linda's dead. I rode in the car with her, and I don't even know who she was. I just thought she was some kind of a nutcase. I never asked her what was wrong. I—"

"Linda's dead?" Oralia demanded, turning away from Vick.

"Don't look," Vick ordered.

"But—"

"Oralia, you don't want to see," he told her.

He spat and wiped his mouth with a handkerchief, his skin still ashen. Then he grabbed Oralia's arms. They stood frozen in time, staring at each other. Were they trying to comprehend what had happened?

Meanwhile, Aileen had appeared. Or maybe she'd been there all the time. She looked into the hot tub, unheeding of Vick's advice to Oralia. She was made of sterner stuff than Vick or myself. She just closed her eyes and took a deep breath after she saw what floated there.

"Poor Linda," she murmured. "Damn. She must have killed herself. I tried to keep an eye out for her but she—"

"She couldn't have killed herself," I heard myself say.

Aileen turned to me. I saw Harley behind her. "Why do you say that?" she challenged.

The cover, I thought.

But Dee-Dee shushed me before I could even say it. She yanked my hand. "If Linda was murdered, the murderer might be here. Keep quiet, honey," she whispered in my ear.

I didn't argue. Dee-Dee was right. Instead, I looked at the people from the intimacy group who had assembled. Was one of them a murderer? My skin felt clammy, cold.

And then Phyllys, Rhoda, and Wiz came running up, adding new suspects to my mental inventory. Phyllys got there first, saw Linda's body, and did an about-face.

"Wiz," she warned. "Don't—"

But she was too late. He had already seen. His face drained of color.

"Holy Mother of God," Rhoda whispered. She turned to Phyllys. "Get him out of here," she ordered.

Phyllys nodded and grabbed Wiz's hand. He let himself be dragged off like a zombie.

"That was my spider," his small voice trailed back as they went toward the doors of the inn. And then his voice was even smaller. "Was that person really dead?" he asked.

I couldn't hear Phyllys's reply, just the resonance of her hushed voice as she answered him.

Rhoda looked back at us and then at the hot tub. I could almost see her internal struggle. To be a responsible innkeeper or a mother: Which was primary now?

Finally, she seemed to decide and turned on her heel, heading back to the inn behind Phyllys and Wiz.

"Wait!" Kapp had arrived. I was glad to hear him. "Has anyone called the police yet?"

"I will," Rhoda tossed over her shoulder, and speeded up to a run through the doors of her inn.

"What a bloody shame," Harley murmured, his usually rough voice smoothed with what seemed to be genuine sorrow.

"This is awful," Eddy started in again, still pacing. "Poor Linda, I never really knew her, and now she's dead. Jeez, we came here together. I should have tried harder."

Suddenly, I felt Roy's presence. He stood a few yards away from the hot tub, yet he seemed to know what was in it. I looked into his intense golden eyes and saw a warning. He was distancing himself from me. But why? What was he afraid of?

Then I saw a figure standing next to him. The reporter, Rick Ryan, stood watching the scene with a ghost of a smile on his pouty face. Now I was really cold. I rubbed my arms, trying to warm up.

I tried to catch Roy's gaze again, but he turned his head away.

"I thought she'd be all right," Aileen said, shaking her head. "She was eating. I just thought she was upset about her sister. I didn't expect her to do anything like this."

"It's not your fault," Harley absolved her. Still, his tone was grim.

But it was someone's fault. Someone who was here at the inn. I looked around, my hands shaking now. My whole body was shaking. Investigating Seeger's death had been an exercise in intuition. This was more. I had known Linda. She had come to me for something, something I hadn't delivered. And now she was dead. Before I could blame myself any more, I heard a car start up in the parking lot.

I turned and saw Geneva's Volvo creeping out onto the

main road. Melinda gave a little wave from the passenger's seat. I inhaled deeply with relief. At least they wouldn't be part of what was to come at the inn. For a moment, I wondered why they were leaving, and then I remembered their phony names and phony stories. No wonder they were sneaking off. I was just glad Rhoda and Phyllys weren't around to notice their defection. Or maybe Rhoda and Phyllys might have instigated their departure themselves. They *had* hired my sisters under the table, not the best situation if police were going to be investigating.

Geneva and Melinda left just in time. As the Volvo sailed down the highway, we heard the faint whine of a police siren. The Volvo was out of sight by the time the police car screamed into the parking lot. Luckily, nobody ever notices the help. At least I hoped so.

Sergeant Zoffany and an officer I hadn't met before leaped from the car. The new officer was a pleasant, motherly-looking woman with salt-and-pepper hair who was dressed in full uniform, including a gun.

"We got a call," Sergeant Zoffany announced brusquely. "Where's the body?"

We all stood back from the tub, bumping into each other as we did.

"Oh, man," murmured Zoffany. When he saw the body for the first time, he looked almost as bad as Vick, but at least he didn't throw up.

"Walras, stay here," he ordered the female officer. She didn't look too healthy herself, her face paling under her salt-and-pepper hair.

"I'm Officer Walras," the woman confirmed as Zoffany stomped off. "Every one of you stay exactly where you are." Her words were as soft as their content was hard. "No one move." I wondered if she was conscious of the way her hand was resting on the butt of her gun.

"This is really upsetting—" Eddy began.

"No one talk until you're asked," she interrupted him, her voice louder and rougher now. She snapped open the strap that secured her gun.

I, for one, wasn't going to do any moving or talking.

Sergeant Zoffany came striding back.

"Okay, folks," he pronounced. "You listen to Officer Walras. Don't move. Don't talk. The chief will be here—"

And then another screaming car skidded into the parking lot. This one was unmarked except for the red flashing light placed haphazardly on the roof. Chief Dahl climbed out of the car with two male officers, one dark haired with a long white face, the other with Asian features. She didn't introduce either of them.

She swept through on high heels, already speaking; a well-dressed tornado in motion. She took one look at the hot tub and looked back at us, unflinching.

"Okay, who saw anything?" she demanded.

Silence greeted her. We were all still looking at Officer Walras's gun.

"Who found the body?" she asked next.

"Um . . . I did," I admitted, ready to dodge if Officer Walras pulled her gun.

"You?!" Dahl pointed at me, her boiled blue eyes widening in recognition. At least she didn't have a gun in her hand. "You're the psychic, right? Did the body call you on your little psychic cell phone or what?"

"I—" Then I actually wondered. Had the body called me in some way? Or the murderer's guilt?

"Well?" the chief prodded.

"I saw her hand, and . . ." I faltered. How much should I say in front of the crowd?

Maybe Chief Dahl wondered the same thing. She turned away from me and surveyed the group.

"Okay, who else has information for me?" she pressed.

But no one was talking, not even Eddy.

"Okay." Her voice hardened. "We'll do this the hard way. She turned to Sergeant Zoffany. "Any guess as to the time of death?" she asked.

He shrugged before speaking. "Gotta get the doc in. It looks like she's been in a while, but the heat of the hot tub water can change everything."

"You call the doctor yet?" she asked.

He shook his head.

"You, Yukawa," she said to the second officer to have climbed out of the car with her. "Call Dr. Strauss. Get him out here, pronto."

Officer Yukawa headed back to the police car.

Chief Dahl surveyed us again. She spotted Rick Ryan and frowned.

"You're not one of this group," she accused. "Who are you?"

"Reporter," he answered.

Chief Dahl's cheeks reddened as I wondered how she knew the faces of those who *were* members of the group. Had she been keeping a better eye on us than I'd thought?

"Okay, reporter," she hissed. "Nothing, I mean nothing, goes out to your paper about this until I say so. Got that?"

"I heard there was freedom of the press in this country," he replied, smirking.

"Listen, what's your name?" she demanded.

"Rick Ryan," he replied, pulling out ID. The other officer with the long face took the ID, examined it, and handed it back.

"Okay, Rick." She smiled. Her teeth looked like a wolf's in her British Isles face. "You're in my town now. You wanna be in my jail, keep it up."

Rick stopped smirking and went back to pouting. But he didn't raise an objection.

The inn doors opened as Chief Dahl was taking another look at us. Rhoda stepped out and walked up to the chief. Phyllys followed out the doors, holding Wiz's hand, but didn't move toward our group.

"You've seen . . ." Rhoda faltered, pointing toward the hot tub.

The chief nodded curtly. "Is that Wiz's spider?" she asked.

That was the wrong question.

"Are you accusing my son?!" Rhoda hissed. She took a few more steps until she was nose to aristocratic nose with Chief Dahl.

"I'm not accusing—" the chief began.

"Someone is trying to frame Wiz!" Rhoda went on. "And it better not be you. Someone stole his things from his magic bag and put a severed finger in the soup and his spider in the hot tub. Do you really believe he'd be stupid enough to put the spider there himself, Debby? Do you really think—"

"No, I don't Rhoda," Chief Dahl interrupted. "But I'd sure like to know who did."

Rhoda stopped, midscreed, and stared. Then she started up again.

"The kids in town taunted Wiz, said you suspected him—"

"Hold on," Chief Dahl objected. "What kids? Because I never said any such thing. I don't spread rumors, and you know it, Rhoda Neruda."

"Really?" Rhoda asked, her voice low now.

"Of course, really. Damn it, how long have you known me, Rhoda? Do you really think I'd accuse Wiz of anything?"

"I . . . I—" Rhoda tried.

"Okay, people, show's over," Dahl announced. "Now we're going to get down to work. First off, your friend's death may quite possibly be a suicide, but we have to make sure, so I'll be talking to each of you separately. If everyone cooperates, things will go much faster."

I wondered if the chief really thought Linda's death was a suicide. Would she twist the facts to accommodate that theory? It would be the easy way out for her. But it wouldn't explain the hot tub cover. Of course, she didn't know I'd pulled back the cover yet. How *had* Linda died exactly? Drowned, or dead when she was carried into the hot tub? Or— Dizziness assailed me again. My mind didn't want to go there. I straightened my body and took deep breaths.

I looked at Dahl. *Would* she try to cover up, or was she just mentioning suicide to lull people into cooperation? To lull the murderer into a false sense of safety? If she was, she was smarter than me about making murder announcements.

"This is my group," Oralia began. "I should—"

"You'll be interviewed in turn," Chief Dahl assured her.

"Everyone keep quiet until you're interviewed," Zoffany added.

"But Linda was—" Eddy began, his voice high with angst.

"Did you hear what I said?" Zoffany demanded.

Eddy looked at Officer Walras, her hand still on her gun, and shut his mouth. He reached into his pocket for his notebook.

"Zoffany," Chief Dahl ordered, pointing, and Zoffany yanked the notebook from Eddy's hand.

"Hey!" Eddy objected.

"Are you some kind of reporter, too?" Dahl accused Eddy.

"Me?" he asked, genuinely confused.

"Yes, you," Chief Dahl confirmed.

"No, no," he said, shaking his head. "I'm a novelist. I write about important issues. Despair, abandonment, you know? I'm writing about a boy who was adopted right now, but his adoptive parents didn't understand—"

"Fine," Dahl cut him off. "Zoffany, give him back the notebook."

Would it help a novelist's career to be involved in a real-life murder? Could Eddy have orchestrated one? *No,* I told myself. Eddy wasn't capable of that kind of action—at least I didn't think so.

"Eddy," Aileen piped up. "Just what was your relationship with Linda?"

"Whoa!" Chief Dahl put her hand up. "I'm the police around here, not you, lady."

"Don't you people ever listen?" Sergeant Zoffany added. "Stand still and keep quiet."

Kapp raised his hand. "Permission to speak?" he requested.

"Granted, but keep it short," the chief agreed. Maybe she remembered he was a lawyer.

"Perhaps we could all go back to the lobby to be interviewed?" Kapp suggested politely. "It might help move things along."

"All right, Counselor," the chief said.

And then we all marched into the lobby with our baby-sitters.

"Rhoda, we'll use your office as the interview room," Chief Dahl announced once we were all seated. "You first, and then I'll want to see Wiz and Phyllys."

"Wiz?" Rhoda flared.

"He might have seen something," Dahl explained impatiently.

Then the two women disappeared behind the reception desk into Rhoda's office.

The rest of us sat with four police officers watching us. If anyone wanted to talk or move, they weren't going to get very far.

Roy sat across from me, still avoiding my eyes but watching me all the same. When I looked his way, I saw an aura of fear surrounding his body. I tried not to over-analyze. Fear seemed right for the occasion.

"Um, officer?" Oralia asked, holding up her hand.

"What?" Sergeant Zoffany barked.

"May I go to the bathroom?" Oralia asked. And suddenly, my own bladder felt full.

"Officer Walras can take you," Zoffany pronounced.

Now, hands went up all over the room. I shot up mine belatedly.

"One at a time," Zoffany ordered, writing down a list in his notebook, a list which I was afraid might be comprised of our names in order of hand-raising.

And so we all sat, on variously filled bladders. I don't know what the others were thinking of, but I was thinking of Linda Frey. Dack. What had happened to her? My mind filled with questions. Too many questions. I looked at Roy again. This time I caught his eye, but only for a moment. He was afraid for me. I was sure of it. But why for *me*? Out of habit, or did he have a good reason? I felt cold again.

I tried to empty my mind with no more success than getting a chance to empty my bladder. My hand hadn't been as fast as the others. Ages later, after a few more suspects got to go to the bathroom, the officer with the long face called my name. I jumped up, hoping it was finally my turn for urinary relief, but instead, he led me into Rhoda's private office. There was no toilet there, only the Chief of the Fiebre Police Department.

Rhoda's office was a pleasantly arranged, small room with a desk, two chairs, file cabinets, plants, and photos of Wiz and Phyllys. I sat in the chair in front of the neat desk and faced the chief.

"Officer Xavier, you may go," she told the long-faced man.

Once the door closed behind him, she turned to me.

"First question," Chief Dahl began without further ado. "Did you pull back the cover on the hot tub?"

I looked at her. How had she known?

"Well?" she prodded.

"Yes, I did," I babbled. "I saw a hand and I thought it was one of Wiz's jokes, so I pulled back the cover, and then . . . I saw her."

My mind filled with images that I tried to banish.

"So, it couldn't have been a suicide," I added.

"Leave the conclusions to us," Dahl ordered. "So tell me again, from the beginning."

"I saw the hand—"

"No, from the beginning," she corrected me. "What were you doing by the hot tubs? What time was it? Was there anyone with you?"

And that was just the start. Chief Dahl led me through the scene so many times, I knew details I hadn't even known I'd known.

Then she leaned forward.

"Okay, psychic lady," she challenged. "Say it was murder. Why? Who?"

"I don't know," I told her honestly. "But don't you think she must have known who killed Seeger Snell?"

"Assuming Seeger Snell was killed," she put in.

"But Linda tried to tell me something," I said.

Dahl's boiled eyes widened.

"What did she try to tell you?"

"I don't know that either," I answered, trying to keep the wail out of my voice. "Whenever she tried to talk to me, she started crying."

I closed my eyes, remembering the day in the parking

lot and the time she came to my room. What had she been trying to say?

"What did she actually say?" the chief kept prodding. I opened my eyes.

"That she needed a friend," I remembered out loud.

"What else?"

And then I remembered that Linda hadn't just talked. She'd made that weird motion.

"She kept pounding her fist into the inside of her elbow," I offered with new excitement. "Like this." I mimed the motion.

Dahl frowned. "What do you think she meant?"

My excitement drained. "I don't know," I said for the thirtieth time.

"What else?" Dahl kept on. "Did she say anything else?" There was almost a pleading note in the chief's voice now. And I remembered something more.

"She asked if Seeger had ever been a spotter," I whispered, amazed at my own remembering.

"A spotter?"

"For bodybuilding, I think."

"Wasn't Linda's sister killed while weight lifting?" the chief asked, looking through her notes.

"Yeah," I murmured. I hadn't put that together before. But Linda couldn't have been Seeger Snell's murderer. She was a victim.

"What else?" Dahl pushed me.

I concentrated, but all I could remember was Linda's constant crying.

"I wish I knew," I told her. "Criminy, I wish I knew."

"This Eddy guy was her friend, right?"

"Not really, according to him," I answered. "They just rode in together. He met her in a grief group or something."

"Okay, what else can you help me with?" Chief Dahl asked.

I just shook my head. I was out of ideas.

"Hear you assaulted Harley Isaacs," she said.

"Me?" I squeaked. "Oh, you mean with my cane . . . well, he assaulted me first—"

"All the felons say that," the chief put in.

It took me a second of forever to realize that Chief Dahl was joking. Then finally, I realized that she was smiling for the first time in the interview.

"Thank you, Ms. Lazar," she said formally. "You are free to go. But don't leave Fiebre."

As I got up from my chair, she added in a softer voice, "Don't worry, Cally. I'm taking this very seriously. No one gets way with murder in my town."

"Thank you," I said and held her eyes for a moment. "Thank you."

Officer Xavier escorted me out. And then Sergeant Walras took me to the bathroom. Ah, sweet relief.

Then I was back, waiting with the others. It seemed an infinity of time. I tried to meditate as people went into the office and came out again, but instead of communing with any divine presence, my head was filled with the image of Linda's body. I began to cry. Poor Linda. She had tried to tell me something. In the parking lot, and then later in my bedroom. *Had* she been trying to tell me the identity of the murderer? Had she seen the killer and been killed herself for it? Had she been trying to identify the murderer with that motion, fist to elbow? Criminy, what had she meant? I had never taken her seriously, dismissing her as deranged. Had she been a witness—

"Okay, people," a voice interrupted my thoughts.

Finally, the chief had come out of Rhoda's office.

"Everyone stays here until this is cleared up, under- stand?" she commanded. And suddenly, I saw the power in this small woman with the face of the British aristocracy. Now I was sure she wouldn't cover up a murder. "No one, I mean, no one, leaves town. You will all stay here at the inn—"

"No!" someone yelled. It took me a second to locate the source of the voice And I cringed when I did. It was Roy's voice.

EIGHTEEN

"Oh, Roy, no!" My words came tearing out before I could stop them. "Everything will be all right. Just keep quiet."

Chief Dahl raised her brows, motioning Zoffany to silence as Roy replied to my warning.

"No, it won't be all right, Cally," he murmured, his head tilted my way, eyes downcast. "You're in danger here. The darkness is all around you. You can't stay."

"The darkness?" the chief asked, her voice soft and manipulative. Dack, now Roy looked like a suspect.

Roy turned back to Dahl, his golden eyes wide and even more intense than usual.

"Cally is in danger," he told her. "Don't you see it, the darkness around her?"

"No, I don't," the chief answered casually. "Is the darkness associated with the death of Linda Frey?"

"I don't know!" Roy cried. "I don't know how to protect her. What if someone here is the murderer? What if they go after Cally next?"

"Hey, you know, he's right," Eddy put in. For once, I was happy to hear Eddy's voice. It took attention away from Roy. "We're all in danger here. We can't stay."

"Hold it right there," Chief Dahl ordered. "We will do everything we can to protect you. I'm leaving two officers on patrol here at the inn." She shifted her attention to her staff. "Walras, Yukawa, you'll set up shifts."

The two officers nodded. Walras tapped her gun.

"But can they really protect us?" Eddy objected. "What if there really is a murderer loose?"

"Yeah," Aileen put in. "Your officers can't be everywhere, every minute. How can they—"

"One officer will be in the lobby at all times," Chief Dahl told her. "The other will patrol."

"And when do they sleep?" Harley Isaacs asked. It was a good question.

"Listen, people," the chief sighed. "Let us figure out the logistics. The best thing you can do to protect yourselves is to be careful. Don't let anyone in your room alone. Check in with an officer if anything suspicious happens. Be sensible." Her voice held impatience now but also a hint of anxiety. It wouldn't look good on her résumé if someone was murdered under her officers' noses.

"It's not enough," Roy announced in the voice of doom.

"It'll have to be enough," Chief Dahl declared and turned to go.

"Wait!" Roy cried. "You can't leave Cally here. She's in danger."

"The subject is closed," the chief said over her shoulder and made her way out the double doors of the inn. Zoffany and Officer Xavier followed her out. Walras and Yukawa exchanged a look. I didn't see a lot of confidence in their exchange.

Nor did Roy. He started toward the doors after the chief.

I grabbed his arm. "Roy, come stay in my room if you want to protect me. If you're always with me, then—"

"No, Cally, can't you see? *I'm* dangerous. I attracted this to you somehow. I have to get the chief to change her mind." And then he tugged out of my grip and went running out the doors.

Walras glanced at Yukawa, all the while handling her

gun and tentatively walking toward the doors. Did she think she ought to shoot a possible fleeing felon?

"He'll be with the chief," Yukawa reminded her. Walras paused and finally nodded. I let out the breath I was holding.

I smelled aftershave nearby.

"Kapp," I begged. "Go with Roy."

"Why should I?" he asked, shrugging.

"For me," I argued. "Make sure he doesn't end up in jail or—"

"Or the loony bin?" Kapp finished for me.

I sighed and nodded in agreement. "Or the loony bin," I conceded. "He's not crazy, Kapp. He just sees things we don't. He's trying to protect me."

"Well, he's not doing a very good job—"

"Please, Kapp," I tried again.

"Lord, the things I do for young love." He groaned melodramatically. "Okay, Lazar. But you owe me."

He turned to the officers on guard. "Permission to follow the young man outside?" he asked.

Yukawa nodded.

Kapp turned to me and whispered. "Give me your car keys."

I fished the keys out of my pocket and made the transfer. Kapp went limping out through the inn doors. I followed him to the doorway and looked outside. Roy and the chief were arguing. Finally, the chief gestured impatiently to the backseat of her car. Roy climbed in back with the long-faced officer. Zoffany took the driver's seat, and the chief slid in the front passenger's side.

Kapp seemed to take forever, but he was in my Honda Accord in back of them by the time they finally exited the driveway.

"Listen up," Walras announced as I watched the parade disappear. "You may stay here in the lobby or go back to your rooms. You heard what the chief said. Be careful. And talk to us first if you want to leave the inn."

No one seemed to have the heart or the energy to challenge her now that Chief Dahl was gone.

I started down the hall to my own room as suspects began to scatter, some muttering but most quiet. I held my cane carefully. Roy may have looked crazy. Still, I couldn't help but wonder if he saw a real danger for me. I could hear Walras and Yukawa whispering behind me. Maybe they were trying to figure out how they were going to set up their shifts so they could be in two places at once and sleep as well.

When I got back to my room, I put my wingback chair against the door and my head into my hands. Then I sat on the end of my bed. It was fine if Roy talked about the darkness he saw while he was with my healer friends, but what would Chief Dahl make of it? Would she equate his beliefs with the delusions of a murderer? He hadn't even been present when Seeger Snell had died. But then, I still wasn't sure if the chief was convinced that Seeger had been murdered. What if she thought that Linda's was the only murder and Roy was the killer? My thoughts circled and dived like the seagulls outside and then circled some more.

Finally, I lifted my head out of my hands and told myself to think. If I could figure out who the murderer was, I could clear Roy, assuming the chief actually suspected him in the first place. But how? I found a piece of stationery and wrote out names: "Rhoda, Phyllys, Wiz, (Dulcie?), Oralia, Vick, Eddy, Aileen, Harley." I thought for a moment and added "Trica." Trica was fearful and seemingly naive. But what if the fear I perceived in her was the fear of discovery of her part in her husband's murder? What if she was in league with someone else? Sitting with Aileen had provided the perfect alibi.

I almost put my head in my hands again. And Dulcie? Could I eliminate Dulcie? She knew her way around The Inn at Fiebre. She could have returned to kill Linda. But why would Dulcie have killed either Seeger or Linda?

Motive was the real issue here. Everyone had opportunity as far as I could tell. Except for Aileen and Trica. But even those two could have conspired with each other or someone else.

Motive and temperament, I reminded myself. The amount of motive that would cause someone to resort to murder had to vary with temperament. How many of us could kill at all? I squirmed on the end of my bed, alone in my own room. I couldn't place myself in the murderer's shoes. I didn't want to. I didn't want to imagine what kind of mind, what kind of spirit, could commit murder. Keerups. The deaths were bad enough, but a person who could kill . . . I didn't believe in evil, but I was beginning to believe in something close to it, something born of desperation and leavened with callousness. For an instant, I could feel it, a coldness of the soul that I didn't have. I sent my psyche out, searching for the source.

The phone rang, shattering the connection, if there ever had been a connection beyond my imagination.

"Hello," I said cautiously into the receiver, as if the phone cord would jump up and wrap itself around my neck if I wasn't careful.

"Oscar here," a quiet voice reassured me. Just the sound of Oscar's voice, the voice of someone who wasn't here at the inn, was soothing. "Dee-Dee called. I had a dream."

"And?" I prodded. We had murders, and Oscar was having dreams.

"It was an important dream," he told me. "It had to do with your murders."

"Yeah?" I tried again, getting interested now.

"There was a kitchen blender in the dream. And inside

the blender there was a human being. The blender whirled and the body was destroyed. But I hadn't pushed the button on the blender. How could I? I was the blender."

"Yeah?" I said again.

"Who pushed the button, Cally?" he asked.

"Who pushed *what* button?" I squeaked. I was beginning to feel like a victim of a Zen Buddhist inquisition. Trial by koan.

"When you know that, you'll know who the murderer is," Oscar told me softly. Suddenly, his gentle voice was no longer soothing. It was annoying.

"Oscar, what are you talking about?" I demanded.

"Your murderer," he told me. "Take care, Cally." And then he hung up.

I slammed the phone back down and glared. I was about to call Oscar back and force him to talk like a regular person instead of an oracle when the phone rang again.

I scooped it up and barked "What?" into the receiver.

No one answered. But someone was there. I could tell. I hung up and wrapped my arms around myself. I was cold, way too cold. I climbed into my bed underneath the covers and burrowed down into their warmth and safety. And then someone knocked on my door. I remembered the warnings we'd received. Should I even answer? Before I'd decided, a voice boomed through my door.

"Lazar, open up for God's sake! It's me, Kapp."

I pulled open my door, and Kapp marched in.

"Well, your boyfriend isn't locked up, but he probably should be," he growled.

"Is he okay?" I asked.

"He's still frothing at the mouth about protecting you, but I got him to come back to the inn." Kapp tapped his cane. "What I don't get is why he isn't here with you if he wants to be so damned protective. What's the matter with him, anyhow?"

"He thinks he puts me in danger by being near me. The darkness that surrounds him is moving my way. So he thinks that everything that goes wrong for me is his fault, too," I tried to explain. "That's why he won't live with me anymore—"

"Well, where'd he get a screwball idea like that? Jesus and the saints, he's nuttier than a walnut grove. And another thing—"

My phone rang once more before he could finish.

It was Officer Yukawa, ordering me to come to the dining hall to be interrogated again. The police had new information. He asked if I knew where any of the other group members were. I told him Kapp was with me. Kapp stuck out his tongue and murmured, "Fink." Obviously he knew who, or at least what, was on the other end of my conversation.

So the two of us made our way to the dining hall. Vick and Oralia were already there, along with Officer Walras and Sergeant Zoffany. And Eddy, Aileen, and Harley arrived a few mutters from Kapp later. Then, Roy and Dee-Dee. Dee-Dee had her hand on Roy's arm and was whispering in his ear. His eyes were wild and his hair was sticking out as if he'd run his hands through it.

"Fer God's sake," Harley said to Aileen. "The whole nuthouse is here."

Chief Dahl was the next to enter, followed by Rhoda and Phyllys.

She paused for a moment, her eyes seeming to take us all in simultaneously. She didn't have to ask for silence. Everyone stopped talking, muttering, and whispering.

"Okay, people," she began. "Our doctor's had an initial look-see at Linda Frey's body. Linda was sedated before she drowned. We're treating this as a potential murder."

"But couldn't she have taken a sedative herself and drowned—" Oralia questioned, her voice subdued and shaking.

"We have other evidence that would seem to dispute that theory," Dahl answered carefully.

She didn't look at me, but I would have bet she meant the cover of the hot tub being pulled over the body. You didn't sedate yourself, go for a nice hot tub, and then pull the cover over your head. Not even if you were Linda Frey, I decided.

"She was murdered?" Eddy parroted as if it was only sinking in now. "I gotta get out of here."

"No one leaves now," Chief Dahl declared emphatically. "And I will interview you each again individually. But as a group, I'll ask one more time. Does any of you know what happened?"

Silence was her only answer.

She turned on her high heel and stalked out of the dining room. Zoffany checked a list in his hand.

"Rhoda Neruda," he called out. Rhoda stepped up to him, and he led her out the same door the chief had exited. The rest of us stood for a moment. Then people began to sit at the tables. I walked toward Dee-Dee and Roy.

"Listen, Roy—" I began.

"No talking," Officer Walras ordered.

I felt a tug on my arm. Kapp. He escorted me to a table for two, and we sat silently. I closed my eyes, searching for the connection I had felt before, searching for the feel of the murderer. I searched for a long time. But for all the lack of talking, there was too much static in the room energetically for me to find anything. Fear, anger, self-pity, sadness, grief, and more were all mushed together in one big mess. I thought of Oscar's blender. What had he said exactly?

I looked at Kapp, longing to talk to him. He looked

back and rolled his eyes. I swiveled my head to see Roy. He sat completely still, his eyes closed. Was he meditating? If he was, the focus of his meditation was probably darkness. I looked around the room. Vick's eyes were closed, too, Oralia's downcast. Then my eyes caught Aileen's. She was surveying the group as avidly as I was. I smiled at her. She smiled back.

"Phyllys Nesbitt," Sergeant Zoffany's voice boomed.

I didn't see Rhoda anywhere, so I assumed she was off the hook for now. Phyllys got up, her cheeks pinkening. She followed Sergeant Zoffany out.

Time seemed to slow down then. I watched Eddy squirm in his chair and Harley cross and uncross his arms. I watched Officer Walras, who shifted from foot to foot, as uncomfortable as the rest of us, but without the benefit of a chair to sit in. Then I looked at Roy again. He hadn't moved since the last time I'd looked. What was he thinking about so motionlessly?

"Cally Lazar," Zoffany called.

As I got up, I hoped the murderer didn't make any assumptions about me being called right after the innkeepers.

Roy's eyes were open and staring as I followed the sergeant out the dining room doors. We went back through the lobby, where Officer Yukawa stood guard over an empty room, to Rhoda's office behind the reception desk.

"Your name," Chief Dahl demanded from behind the desk before the door even closed behind us.

"Cally Lazar," I answered, not sure if she'd forgotten already.

I was halfway into my chair when she barked out the next question.

"You're sure the cover of the hot tub was closed before you touched it?" she demanded.

My seat hit the cushion of the chair, and I nodded.

"Say 'Yes' for the record, please," the chief requested, and then I saw the tape recorder on Rhoda's desk.

"Yes," I said loudly.

"Well, no one else noticed it was open before you opened it, if that makes you feel any better," Chief Dahl told me.

I relaxed a little. She cared how I felt. There *was* good in everyone—

"Can you explain your relationship with Roy Beaumont?" she followed up.

"No," I shot back. Dack, and I had just begun to relax.

"Well, then *try* to explain your relationship," she ordered.

I tried. Fifteen minutes later, the chief didn't look any more enlightened than she had before I'd begun.

"Listen, Roy is functioning just fine. He just sees things a little bit differently—"

"So, did you think Linda was functioning just fine, too?" she demanded. "Is this some kind of psychic thing?"

"No, I didn't think Linda was functioning well," I answered briefly.

But briefly wasn't enough. We went over all the same information we had before, plus some. And then she wanted my impressions of all the members of the group.

I babbled like a brook. I was just analyzing Eddy's writerly ambitions when the chief interrupted me.

"We found a sedative that might have been used on Linda Frey in the kitchen here," she said softly. She was leaning forward, watching my face. Keerups, I was a suspect. She was watching for my reaction.

"In Rhoda's kitchen?" I asked stupidly.

"What about my kitchen?" came a voice from behind me. I turned and saw Rhoda, her usually lovely face pulled taut over her bones. She looked sick with worry.

"Rhoda Neruda!" Chief Dahl shouted, jumping from her chair. "You aren't supposed to be here."

"This is my office, Debby," Rhoda replied, the same tension pulling her voice taut. "Sergeant Zoffany asked me for some information about the guests, so I came to get my files." She paused, then asked again, "What are you saying about my kitchen?"

Chief Dahl sat down again, staring at Rhoda.

"The drug that was probably used to sedate Linda Frey was found in the spice rack in your kitchen in a chili bottle," she announced.

Rhoda's head bounced back.

"In *my* kitchen?" she asked softly.

The chief just nodded. I didn't tell her to say "Yes" for the tape recorder. I just watched the two women square off.

"Was the chili bottle in alphabetical order?" Rhoda asked finally.

"No," the chief admitted. "That's why we noticed it."

"Then it wasn't one of us," Rhoda said triumphantly. "We all know to keep the spices in alphabetical order."

"Does Wiz?" Chief Dahl asked softly.

Rhoda's face reddened from bronze to terra-cotta.

"Of course he does," she hissed. "You just wait right here, Debby Dahl!"

And with that, she whirled out of her office, appearing within minutes with Wiz in tow. The chief hadn't said anything in those minutes. She'd just closed her eyes and breathed deeply.

"Wiz, tell her," Rhoda ordered.

"Allspice, almond extract, anise, arrowroot, basil, bay leaf—" he began.

"Okay, okay," the chief gave in. "He knows them in order."

"But the murderer didn't know they were in order," I put in.

"Maybe," Dahl conceded. "Still, since when is almond extract a spice? Or arrowroot?"

Rhoda seemed to grow six inches as she reared up on her legs.

"Just kidding," Chief Dahl assured her from across the desk. She stuck her hand up, palm out. "Honest."

The chief let me go after that. I headed straight to my room, snuggled under the covers, and fell into an exhausted sleep.

I woke up in the early evening and heard the sound of bagpipes playing. I looked out my window, and though I didn't see Harley, I did see Oralia furiously jogging toward a stand of trees. There was a shadow beyond the trees, but then it was gone.

And then I saw him: Rick Ryan. He stood, staring at the inn. And for the first time, I saw his full smile.

NINETEEN

What was Rick Ryan smiling about? Did he know something about the murders that I didn't know? Something that even Chief Dahl didn't know? Or was he just thinking about something unpleasant? Unpleasant for someone else of course. Dack, he gave me the creeps. I rubbed my arms.

Someone knocked on my door. The knocks were hesitant, tentative. They couldn't be Kapp's. But what if that was Roy knocking?

"Who is it?" I called out.

"It's Vick," the voice came diffidently through the door. "Vick Usher." I stared at the door. The chief had warned us about letting visitors in our rooms. But Vick? Sweet Vick who thought that sharing our feelings in a group session could solve anything?

I opened the door hesitantly.

"Cally, can we talk?" Vick asked.

Mentally, I went through my options: say no; ask him in my room and shut the door; ask him in my room and keep the door open; or go to the lobby to talk. I was the one who'd invited everyone, I reminded myself.

"What did you want to talk about?" I asked.

He looked down and folded his hands over his solar plexus. "About Oralia," he murmured. He sighed. "I just don't know what to do."

Or we could just stand here, me in the doorway and Vick in the hall.

"Oh, come in," I offered finally. "But I'm gonna leave the room door open."

"Thank you," he muttered, though I don't think he actually heard the part about the door. I was tempted to add "and take the goats off their tethers," just to see if he was listening. But that would have been too mean. Vick was obviously troubled. He didn't need an attention test.

Once we were seated, me on the end of my bed, holding my cane, and Vick in the wingback chair next to the open door, Vick started up again.

"Oralia is stressed to the max," he told me, his musical voice strained. "She's not used to everything being out of control. But even that doesn't explain . . . well . . ."

"Explain what?" I prodded.

"She's acting so weird, Cally. Sad sometimes and angry the next. I don't know what's going on. And I want to help her. I . . . I love her—"

"Vick, have you told Oralia that you love her?" I questioned.

Vick looked up, suddenly mentally present with me for the first time since he'd come through my door.

"Well, no," he whispered. "I just thought . . . I mean, she must know . . . I mean, I feel so much—"

"Tell her what you feel, Vick," I advised.

A smile tugged at my lips. I was advising one of the leaders of the "Love Workshop" on one of the less subtle points of intimacy. And I would have bet Oralia was in love with him, too, and didn't have a clue how he felt. But then we're always better with other people's problems than our own.

"You mean, actually tell her I love her?" Vick asked, his voice so low it was barely audible. He sounded frightened.

"That's what I mean," I answered. "Is that so hard?"

"Well." He considered my question. "It shouldn't be. I

mean . . . okay, I will. I'll tell her. Thank you, Cally," he offered, turned his back, and then marched down the hallway.

I let myself smile as I closed the door behind him.

Someone else knocked on the door, rapping hard this time. Dack.

"Who is it?" I tried again.

"It's me, Kapp!" boomed though my door.

I should have known. Anyone else would have broken their knuckles.

Kapp started in on me the minute I let him come through my doorway.

"What the hell do you think you're doing, letting that bozo in your room when you're alone?" he demanded. "Didn't you hear what Chief Debby said?" I was all ready to yell back at him, but when he said "Chief Debby," I snorted with laughter.

"You think it's funny?" he growled. " 'Oh, I'm in love,' " he mimicked, hands on his heart, eyes rolling. "What if he's making it all up?"

"You were listening," I accused him.

"Damn right, I was listening," he replied. "What if he'd attacked you?"

"I had my cane," I reminded him.

"Yeah, well," he said, pondering my cane-fu. Then he made up his mind. "You're impossible," he finished.

"So, why are you here?" I asked.

He smiled. "I've got more information about the suspects," he told me. "I suppose you're not interested though. You're too busy playing Dear Abby to the lovelorn."

"Kapp!"

"Okay, okay," he said easily. He was as anxious to share information as I was to receive it. "Your client Trica, hooboy! She's not all sweetness and light. According to everyone I've talked to, she and Seeger were arguing constantly before he died."

"About what?" I prompted, interested now.

"About everything, but especially about her weight. Seeger wanted her to lose it. The man didn't appreciate the full female figure." Kapp sighed. "Seeger wanted her to diet, but the more she dieted, the more weight she gained."

I nodded. My friend Joan Hussein had the same problem, along with at least half the female population. Each diet she'd been on was responsible for at least a five-pound gain in the long run. She'd given up on dieting a long time ago, and I was glad. She was a lot happier, and she wasn't putting on weight anymore.

"And there's Linda Frey," Kapp went on. "Linda was briefly institutionalized after the death of her mother. And then her sister was killed in a freak weight-lifting accident. Her sister dropped a heavy weight on her own larynx. Crushed it. She was killed instantly—"

"And her spotter wasn't keeping an eye on her like he should have," I interrupted.

"What?" Kapp's brows went up.

"Linda asked me if Seeger had ever been a spotter. If she wasn't dead herself, I'd wonder if she somehow thought Seeger was responsible for her sister's death—"

"When did Linda tell you this?" Kapp demanded.

"Oh, I think it was on Friday. I forgot until Chief—"

"And you didn't tell me?!" Kapp bellowed. "That woman had a motive—"

"But she's a victim, Kapp," I argued. The bellowing didn't bother me as much from Kapp as it might have from someone else. Bellowing was as natural to Kapp as mooing was to cows.

"Yeah, well, anyway," he went on. "Forget about Linda Frey for a moment." Then he smiled again. "I swiped

Eddy's notebook. Writer, huh! All that notebook had was a bunch of little doodles and a few notes. For some reason, he had the word *notice* underlined four times—"

"You swiped his notebook?!" I cried, not able to full out bellow, but getting close.

"Yeah, it was easy," Kapp said proudly. "I talked to him in the lobby, pickpocketed the notebook, read it, and put it back before he even noticed. 'Notice,' huh! What a chump that kid is."

"Kapp, that's stealing,"

"So, sue me," he replied smugly. "Anyway, that kid's no more a writer than you are. He's just a wanna-be."

"What does that have to do with murder?" I asked sweetly.

"Hell if I know," Kapp answered. He shook his head.

"So, the question is: Who had the motive and temperament to kill Seeger Snell and Linda Frey?" I proposed, trying to bring some sense to our discussion. Or at least an outline of sense.

"Could be anyone," Kapp muttered.

"Kapp!"

"Temperament. How the hell can we really tell? Clever murderers can smile as well as anyone else. Let me tell you, I know. I've represented enough of them in court. Most murderers are as dumb as mud, but the clever ones, hooboy. I've had clients who pulled the wool over *my* eyes."

"But there must be some way to tell," I argued. Kapp was depressing me.

"Evidence," he proclaimed. "Evidence is everything. Without it, you can never be sure. Do you know how many innocent people have been put to death in this country?"

I shook my head. I didn't really want to know.

"Chief Debby is good, though," he assured me. "She

may be able to find it. For all that good cop/bad cop act she puts on, she's sharp as a splinter—"

Somebody knocked on the door for the third time in an hour. This time, the knock was polite but confident. I was becoming a connoisseur of knocks.

"It's Rhoda Neruda."

I looked at Kapp. He nodded. I wasn't alone in the room now. And if Rhoda really wanted to attack me, she'd probably use a passkey. That was a troubling thought. But Kapp opened the door before I could consider the implications of passkeys.

"Oh, Cally!" Rhoda cried once the door was open. Rhoda reached out a hand to me. But before I could take her hand, she noticed who'd opened the door. "And Mr. Kapp," she went on, dropping her hand without missing a beat. I thought of Kapp's description of clever murderers and a tingle went up my spine. "You've got to help us. Someone is trying to frame Wiz."

"So it would appear," Kapp conceded. "But whoever is trying to frame Wiz isn't doing a very good job."

It was as if Rhoda hadn't heard him. "They broke into his magic bag, put the finger in the soup, and the spider in the hot tub. And then, they put sedatives in a chili bottle in our kitchen. It's getting really scary. And we have nothing to do with it, believe me—"

"I believe you," I cut in.

"And more important," Kapp added. "Chief Dahl believes you."

Rhoda and I both turned to Kapp.

"How do you know that?" Rhoda asked him before I could.

"She told me," he answered simply. And I believed him. Everyone told Kapp stuff. He cleared his throat. "We were discussing the murders, and the subject of Aileen's doctored soup came up. I told your chief of police that I was morally certain that your son wouldn't put a severed finger in a guest's soup, and your chief replied that Wiz wasn't a suspect as far as she was concerned. She said she'd watched Wiz grow up, and that he didn't have the requisite spite necessary for the murders. Or the strength necessary to dispose of Linda Frey's body."

Rhoda put her hand to her throat.

"Debby actually said that?" she whispered.

Kapp nodded complacently.

Two questions were vying for first place in my mind. "The chief referred to *both* deaths as murders?" won.

"Absolutely, I told you the woman wasn't stupid," Kapp reminded me. Next time, the chief did interviews, I'd remember to compare notes with Kapp. Because it was unlikely that the chief considered any of us who hadn't been there when Seeger died as serious suspects, and that included Roy. I'd probably been worried about him for nothing, at least on that issue. I decided to feel relieved later and went to my second question.

"What is it with you and Chief Dahl, anyway?" I asked Rhoda.

"Oh, we went to high school together." Rhoda blushed. "We both liked this boy, Tommy Lund. Holy Mother, we fought over him. She sprained my wrist once, pushing me on the ground. But I pulled out some of her hair first. I can't tell you which of us was worse. And then Tommy ended up marrying Nancy Corrigan after all."

I just stared at Rhoda. All this bad blood went back to a high school crush?

"I didn't know I preferred women then," she explained, misinterpreting my stare.

"No, no," I sputtered. "I just can't believe you two are still mad over something that happened in high school." And then I remembered that Oralia had dated Seeger Snell in high school. Dack. Could Oralia have borne a grudge—

"I don't think Debby and I are really still mad at each other," Rhoda offered thoughtfully. "I think it's just habit. We always argue when we see each other. But I'd miss her if she was gone."

"And she doesn't suspect your son," Kapp put in, bringing us back to where we'd started.

"Thank God for that," Rhoda murmured. "And thank you, Mr. Kapp, for telling me."

"No problem," Kapp said, preening.

And then Rhoda shifted into her hostess role again.

"I'd better get back to my desk," she told us. "Everyone's going to Marge's for dinner. Debby has Sergeant Zoffany stationed there. But you still have to ask the officer in the lobby for permission." She took a deep breath. "I'm going to try not to get mad at Debby for invading my inn. I know she's just trying to protect us. But this whole bit about the officer in the lobby is so stupid—" Rhoda stopped and shook her head, laughing. "I'm doing it again already, aren't I?"

I smiled her way. If it weren't for the murders, I might have laughed with her, too.

Kapp and I followed Rhoda out of my room and down the hall to the lobby. Despite the day, or maybe because of it, I was hungry enough to eat snake. Well, maybe not snake, but definitely fish.

Rhoda took her place behind the reception desk while Kapp and I approached Officer Walras. Walras stood at attention near the door, arms at her side, hand near her gun. She no longer looked motherly to me.

"Permission to—" Kapp began.

And then the doors to the inn opened and the kitchen help came in, Geneva striding elegantly and Melinda shuffling in her wake.

"Halt!" Officer Walras ordered.

Geneva stopped midstride, but Melinda wasn't so quick

and bumped into Geneva's straight back, nose first.

"Whoa," Melinda said, rubbing her nose.

"State your business!" Walras demanded.

"Oh my, we're simply the kitchen help, dontcha know?" Geneva offered, back to her Noel Coward role. "Any problem, officer?"

Officer Walras stroked the butt of her gun, clearly thinking. She scrunched her eyebrows together. Somehow, I didn't think the chief's officer was as bright as the chief was.

"You're not on my list," Walras accused. "Do you know this is a crime scene?"

"No?!" Geneva cried, rearing back in mock terror. "How very frightening."

"Well, you don't have to be afraid," Walras assured her. "I'm here to protect you."

"That's a comfort," Geneva murmured.

Officer Walras patted her gun. Geneva began walking again.

"Nice ray gun you got there," Melinda commented. Geneva threw her a warning glare over her shoulder. Melinda shut her still open mouth and refrained from further comment.

But Officer Walras was scrunching up her brows again.

"Okay, you two—" she began.

"Officer," Rhoda said amiably, suddenly by our side. "These are just the two women who're working in our kitchen until Dulcie comes back."

Officer Walras wasn't sure though. She looked at Geneva, then at Melinda, and then at me. Would she notice the resemblance no one else had? And then I had a worse thought. What if the officer asked my sisters for ID? If she had a list, she'd be sure to recognize the last name.

So I interrupted.

"Sergeant Walras, permission to go to Marge's Restaurant," I barked, imitating Kapp.

Walras straightened.

"Permission granted," she barked back.

And then Kapp barked out his request, and Officer Walras barked her permission to him. We might have been a dog kennel, for all the barking going on. But by the time we'd finished, Geneva and Melinda had scooted past the officer and were on their way.

I swiveled my head around as we exited, and Rhoda saluted me. If she only knew she'd just conspired to let spies into her own kitchen.

On the one-block walk to Marge's, Kapp kept asking me about my sister Geneva. What did she do for a living? What were her interests? What flowers did she like? I was so preoccupied, it took me a while to see where his questions were leading.

"So is she single or what?" he asked finally.

"Warren Kapp, are you interested in my sister?" I demanded, stopping in my tracks. It was good Melinda wasn't behind me. She would have smashed her nose again.

"Of course I am," he admitted readily. "She's smart, funny, argumentative. A little skinny, but I can put up with that."

I considered poking him with my cane. But then, Geneva could handle Kapp, I told myself.

In fact, by the time we walked into Marge's, I was beginning to think that it might be fun to watch Kapp try to court Geneva. And the truth was that I didn't know if Geneva had a current significant other. Geneva's private life was very private, even from her little sister. Or maybe, especially from her little sister. I let the door to Marge's swing shut behind us and breathed in the smells of fish, grease, onions, and spice. My stomach gurgled appreciatively. Rhoda was right about the police presence. Sergeant Zoffany had a corner table near the door, and he wasn't eating any of Marge's good food. He was watching. Aileen and Harley were there. Eddy sat nearby. And in the far corner, Roy sat with Dee-Dee.

My heart stopped for an instant. Then Roy stood up from his place at their table and walked slowly toward us. Dee-Dee got up a moment later and followed him.

My heart began beating again and accelerated.

By the time Roy reached us, my heart was zipping through its beats like a crazed jazz drummer.

"Cally," Roy murmured when he stopped in front of us. He looked at his feet. Dee-Dee jabbed a tiny elbow in his ribs. He brought his golden eyes up to look into mine.

"Dee-Dee says the darkness may not mean *I'm* dangerous to you. Just that I see the danger around you."

"Oh, Roy," I breathed and stepped up to embrace him.

"She might be right," he added before I had lifted my arms high enough to wrap around him. "But I'm not sure yet," he finished.

I let my arms drop and opened my mouth. But I opened my mouth far too slowly.

"You're not sure *yet?!*" Kapp bellowed. "What the hell does that mean, boy?"

TWENTY

Roy blanched under Kapp's onslaught, his freckles dark against his suddenly pale skin.

I stepped between the two men.

"Kapp," I ordered, my voice low but my cane high. "Stop it . . . right now."

"But Lazar, listen to the boy—" he began.

"No, Cally," Roy interjected. "He's right. I shouldn't have said anything until I was sure."

"Damn right," Kapp muttered.

I whipped around to glare at him.

And Roy drifted away behind me. I heard the door to Marge's open and shut, and Roy was gone.

"So whadda you guys all standing around for?!" came a shout from the swinging doors of the kitchen. Dulcie emerged, carrying a tray. "Take a seat. I'll be with you in a sec."

I surveyed Marge's. It seemed awfully quiet. Aileen and Harley were staring at us. Eddy and Sergeant Zoffany were, too. Not to mention all the strangers in the place. Dack. I remembered just how much carrying power Kapp's bellow packed. And then, just to top off the peak experience, I saw who was in the far corner of the room. It was Rick Ryan. At least his smile was gone now. But I was sure he was smiling internally.

I turned to Kapp, wanting to lash out at him. But I couldn't. He was right about Roy. *Roy* was right about

Roy. Only I remained a true believer in Roy's good heart and relative sanity.

"He's doing his best, Cally," Dee-Dee reminded me, and I added another name to Roy's supporters.

But that didn't erase the sadness I felt. It just increased it. Roy was doing his best. And we still weren't together. What kind of best was that? A whine entered the voice in my head. Why didn't Roy know I needed him after finding Linda Frey's body? No matter what happened from now on, the memory of Linda's body would be engraved on my own body. Keerups, I needed something to get me through this, and Roy wasn't available.

Kapp, Dee-Dee, and I all sat down at a table for four. I stared at the red-checkered tablecloth and tried to imagine light surrounding me, the kind of light I felt at home. And finally, I could imagine the light, and with it, unconditional love and goodness. Whoa! Maybe I could write a book, *Red-Checkered Enlightenment*.

I brought my eyes back up and saw Kapp's eyes dart away as I did. He looked about as close to repentant as I'd ever seen him.

"Kapp—" I began.

"Here're the menus for the day, man," Dulcie announced from my side, slapping them on the table. "Read 'em and weep." Then she twirled on one foot and made her way to another table.

"So, whaddaya want?" I heard her say, and then her voice was lost in the buzz of restaurant sounds.

I opened a menu absentmindedly. The specials of the day included grilled salmon, crab quesadillas, and ahi tuna in a ginger-sesame sauce. Suddenly, I was hungry again.

"So I guess the verdict is out on dating your sister," Kapp said softly.

I looked across the table at him. I would always forgive

Kapp his trespasses since he was trying to be my friend
the best way he knew how, but still . . .

"If you approve of me and Roy, I might be disposed
to approve of you and Geneva," I offered magnanimously.
Then I hid my face in my menu and waited for the explosion. I didn't have to wait long.

"What?!" he bellowed. Dack, now the whole restaurant
was looking at us again. I could feel it. "That is patently
absurd. The two situations are in no way similar. And
furthermore—"

"Maybe I should keep my nose out of your dating, and
you should keep yours out of mine?" I cut in, peeking
over my menu.

Dee-Dee snorted and buried her own face in a menu.

"Lazar, are you trying to drive me crazy?" Kapp demanded.

"Close enough," I told him.

"Heh-heh," he rasped. For a terrible moment I thought
he was choking; then I realized he was laughing. "I'm
going to enjoy dating your sister."

Before I had a chance to answer, Dee-Dee reached over
and tapped my shoulder. "Look who's here," she whispered.

I followed her gaze and saw Trica, Seeger's grieving
widow, talking with Sergeant Zoffany. Only she was
laughing, not grieving. She whispered something in the
sergeant's ear, and he laughed, too. They whispered back
and forth, and Zoffany put his hand on hers. Was this
romance in bloom, or was I just seeing things?

Suddenly, Trica didn't seem the innocent she had
seemed. I squirmed in my chair. Trica was the reason I
was here in Fiebre. Trica was the reason I'd found Linda
Frey's body. Trica—

"Oooh, Cally," Trica called out. "It's so cool that
you're here! Can I sit with you guys?"

"Certainly," Kapp answered for me, his voice daubed with lust.

"Fickle, aren't we?" I whispered in his ear as Trica approached our table. "I won't tell Geneva . . . I guess."

Kapp's face was pink when Trica sat down at our table. Trica wore a silky blue jumpsuit that matched her eyes. The jumpsuit had a plunging neckline that even I couldn't keep my eyes off of. And Seeger had complained about her weight. Go figure.

"Cally, guess what?" she said, her high-pitched voice as excited as a child's. She didn't stop to let me guess. "Chief Dahl came to see me. She said since someone else was killed that they'll be looking more closely at Seeger's death now."

I stared at Trica as she spoke, because in a weird sort of way, she had a motive for Linda Frey's death. I didn't think Chief Dahl had suspected that Seeger Snell's death was anything but an accident or suicide before I'd found Linda Frey in the hot tub. Now the chief would finally take Trica's concerns seriously.

"She said it was Linda," Trica went on. "Linda was so sad, always crying. Seeger said she was a wet blanket. It was a joke, you know, cause she cried so much she was wet all the time."

I nodded. Kapp tried a phony laugh.

"Do you think the same person killed them both, Cally?" Trica asked, as if I could answer.

"I'm not sure," I hedged. "What do you think?"

"Me?" She laughed, as if her thinking anything would be very funny.

"Trica, how well do you know Sergeant Zoffany?" I demanded just because I was nosy.

"Oh, Zoffy's a total sweetie," she replied. "At first, Chief Dahl, you know, she really scared me, but Sergeant Zoffany explained that she has to act tough 'cause women aren't respected in law enforcement." She frowned for a moment. "I think that's what he said. Anyway, Zoffy is really nice to me. He's so cool."

"Did Seeger know Linda?" Dee-Dee asked next.

"Oh, I don't think so," Trica burbled. "Linda, she was so upset all the time it was hard to tell. But she talked to him once, I know that. I saw them out on the beach. I think he was flirting with her. He flirted with everyone. And she was really skinny."

I thought of Linda's skinny body in the hot tub and shivered.

"Well, I'd rather flirt with you," Kapp offered gallantly, making Trica giggle.

"So, whaddaya wanna eat?" Dulcie asked from my side.

"Crab quesadilla," I squeaked. I lowered my voice. "And a salad with your house dressing."

Trica ordered a shrimp salad with the low-fat dressing. I figured she was still dieting. Dee-Dee wanted the rata-touille and the vegan risotto with pumpkin seeds. And Kapp asked for the grilled salmon with an undressed salad.

"No heart attack special tonight?" Dulcie questioned Kapp with a wink.

"Single men have to keep up their strength," he pro-nounced with a significant leer in Trica's direction. At least he didn't aim the leer at her chest.

"Right," Dulcie said, infusing her voice with a sneer. And then she left.

Trica giggled again. I looked at her and tried to remem-ber why I'd gotten in this mess in the first place. Hadn't I felt sorry for Trica? I let out a little breath, not quite a sigh, because I still felt sorry for Trica. Keerups, it was true.

"Did you and Seeger argue?" Dee-Dee prodded. Way

to go, Dee-Dee. It was good that one of us at the table still had their brains in the right place.

"Oh, all the time," Trica admitted easily. "Seeger was always on me about my weight. He didn't like me fat—"

"You aren't fat," Kapp and I both objected simultaneously.

"Are you guys serious?" Trica asked wistfully. "I mean, I'm so big—"

"Yes, we're serious," I told her. "Trica, you're beautiful. Kapp here is slobbering on his napkin over you. And probably half the men in this place are doing the same thing. Just because you're a few sizes over what some Americans think is ideal doesn't mean that there's anything wrong with you."

Kapp quit looking at his napkin for drool and put in his three-hundred-dollars-an-hour's worth.

"Trica, I find you very attractive," he murmured.

Trica giggled some more and added, "Well, you're pretty cool for an older man, yourself."

Kapp's smile wilted at the edges.

"Did Seeger ever spot for Linda?" I put in quickly.

"Oooh, Cally. That's just what the chief asked. But Seeger never did anything athletic. I didn't even know what she was talking about."

"Who did Seeger know at the workshop?" I plodded on.

"Well, let me think," Trica said. She squinted her big blue eyes. "Vick and Oralia. We've done a lot of workshops with them. And Aileen. Seeger and Aileen, you know, worked together at The Sensual Body. Oh, and Rhoda and Phyllys and that kid. What's his name? Magic or Jouster or something—"

"You mean Wiz?"

"Oh yeah, that's his name, Wiz. Seeger hated that kid."

"Seeger hated Wiz?" I repeated, surprised. "Why'd he hate Wiz?"

"I don't know exactly," Trica answered. "Just 'cause he was always around, I guess. Seeger didn't like kids much. He said the kid was a pest. But I thought he was kind of cute. He talked to me sometimes."

Then Aileen and Harley walked up to our table. Harley stood a few feet back. I didn't blame him. He was out of cane range there.

"Hey," Aileen greeted us. Then she zeroed in on Trica. "How's things, partner?" she asked. *Partner?* Then I remembered. Now that Seeger was gone, Aileen and Trica were partners in The Sensual Body.

"Oooh, Aileen," Trica answered. "We have to get together soon. I love being a businesswoman. We'll have lunch and talk about the shop, okay?"

"Sure thing," Aileen promised. She gave Trica a minihug. "Everyone take care," she finished, and she and Harley made their way out of the restaurant.

Finally, Dulcie arrived with our food.

The crab in my crab quesadilla was fresh crab. And it was smothered in onions, chilies, and two kinds of cheese, all wrapped up in a spinach tortilla with jicama and avocado slices. Criminy, it was delicious. It was hard to believe that food still tasted this good after the day's events, but it did. As I savored the flavors, I decided that maybe I'd be okay after all.

"Aileen is really cool," Trica chirped as I chewed. "Even here in Fiebre, she calls in at the shop every day to make sure everything's going okay, you know. She's great." Trica took a bite of her shrimp salad but didn't seem to taste it. "She's gonna let me work there, like behind the counter or something."

"Don't you own half the business anyway?" Dee-Dee asked.

I took another bite of my quesadilla. There was a third cheese mixed in, I realized, cream cheese. Yum.

"I guess I do now," Trica answered Dee-Dee. "But Seeger never wanted me working there. I think it'll be really fun." She speared another forkful of salad and munched thoughtfully. "Zoffy says something good always comes out of something bad. I guess he's right."

Sergeant Zoffany sounded pretty cool at that. He'd probably managed to do more for Trica's spirits than I had.

"So what's the deal with Aileen and Harley?" I prodded, knowing it was none of my business, but wanting to know anyway.

"Oh, Harley!" Trica squealed. "He thinks he's such a tough guy. But with Aileen, she calls the shots. They've been lovers off and on for a long time. She lets him off his leash once in a while and then, well, you know . . ." Trica giggled again.

Actually, I didn't know. Had Trica made love to Harley? That was an awful thought. Could Harley be the mystery man who was in love with Trica, or maybe her money, and was ready to kill for it? Could Kapp be right about Harley?

I looked over at Kapp. He was eating his salmon in silence. He'd been quiet ever since Trica had called him an "older man."

"Did you and Harley, ever um . . ." I tried.

"Me and Harley?!" Trica bleated. "Eeeew! Forget it. I hate bagpipes."

Well, that was that.

"Who do you think might have been angry at Seeger?" Dee-Dee questioned.

Trica stopped a forkful of shrimp salad that had almost reached her mouth. "Gee, I mean, Oralia got mad once in a while 'cause Seeger would joke around at her seminars.

I think she knew him before or something. And Aileen used to get mad that he didn't work harder at The Sensual Body. But she got over it after a while. Seeger just wanted to have fun, you know. And that Phyllys lady got mad at Seeger when he was mean to what's-his-name, Wiz. And Harley always gave him a hard time about flirting with everyone, but I think he was kidding. That new guy, Eddy, didn't like Seeger 'cause he made fun of him, but so do a lot of people—"

"A lot of people what?" I asked, lost.

"Oh, make fun of Eddy. All that writer stuff, you know."

Kapp looked guilty for the second time that evening. I wished I had a camera.

We didn't talk too much more as we finished our meals. And once we were done, Trica got into her new Volkswagen bug and roared off to her lodgings, while Dee-Dee, Kapp, and I made our short way back to The Inn at Fiebre in the evening twilight.

We heard the yelling the minute we opened the lobby doors.

"You just want to blame it on someone at the inn so no one will boycott your so-called love workshops—"

"And you just want to blame us so no one will suspect anyone at the inn!"

I recognized the second voice. That was Oralia. And once my eyes adjusted to the low lighting in the lobby, I recognized the other combatant. It was Phyllys. Both women stood, nose to nose, hands on their hips.

"Well, we never had any trouble here till *you* came!" Phyllys shouted.

"Listen, we run a good workshop. It *is* about love—" Oralia began.

"Huh!" Phyllys snorted. "More like irresponsible sex—"

"Take that back!" Oralia demanded, stepping even closer to Phyllys.

Phyllys's hands balled into fists. "You gonna make me?" she hissed.

Oralia screamed and made a grab for Phyllys.

Officer Walras ran forward, unsnapping her gun. But Vick and Rhoda were faster. Vick had a grip on Oralia's shoulders, and Rhoda was tugging at Phyllys's arms in an instant.

"Okay, everyone, stop where you are!" Chief Walras ordered, leveling her gun in the direction of the fray.

"Wow," a small voice said. "Is that a real gun?"

Walras turned to see Wiz walking into the lobby from the direction of the rooms. Oralia and Phyllys both dropped their hands.

"Um . . . yeah, it's a real gun," Officer Walras answered. She looked at her gun and then slowly lowered it.

"Why's everyone so mad?" Wiz asked.

"We're not really mad," Phyllys lied, with a pleading look at Oralia.

"No, it's okay now." Oralia sighed. "I'm sorry, Phyllys."

"I'm sorry, too," Phyllys murmured. "Really."

"Maybe a hug?" Vick suggested.

Dack, would one of the two women slug Vick? Or would Officer Walras shoot him first? But amazingly, Oralia and Phyllys briefly embraced.

"Okay, folks, now break it up!" Officer Walras ordered. "Everyone back to their rooms."

We broke it up. I nodded to Dee-Dee and Kapp, and I was back in my room minutes later. I sat on the end of my bed and thought. Then I thought some more. And more. It was hard work. After a couple of hours, I still didn't know who the murderer was. And I was tired. I put on my pajamas and crawled under the covers. I dreamed of Linda, crying out from behind a wet blanket. But I couldn't understand her words.

Monday morning, I got up early to lift weights. And then I went to the convenience store to smuggle some breakfast back to my room. Granola and yogurt weren't as good as I might have gotten in the dining room, but the truth was that I wanted to be alone. I didn't want to see Melinda breaking dishes. I didn't want to see a murderer and not know it. And I didn't want to see Roy.

After breakfast, I sat and thought some more. Then I started pacing back and forth across the room. Dack, alone was almost as bad as being with people.

There was a knock on my door. I analyzed the knock. It was heavy enough, but still, it seemed hesitant. Who?

I opened the door. Harley, that was who.

I waggled my cane in his general direction. Harley kept his distance.

"There's gonna be another bloody group session after lunch," he informed me. "Oralia asked me if I'd tell you. I've told you, okay?"

"A group session?" I was a little dazed. Thinking alone can do that to a person.

"To deal with our grief," Harley explained. Then he laughed, a laugh so astringent it could have puckered platinum.

He turned and strode down the hall without a good-bye. I found myself feeling sorry for him. I wouldn't want to live in his skin, but maybe Kapp was right; maybe Harley Isaacs was a murderer.

I went back to thinking. I even drew some charts. One chart covered the relationships between the murder victims and the suspects. The next was my analysis of temperaments. Another covered opportunity. I had run out of paper and was looking in my suitcase for more when there was another knock on the door.

I closed the suitcase and grabbed my cane. But when I opened the door, no one was there.

TWENTY-ONE

I stood in my doorway, confused. And I stood there way too long. By the time I thought to step out into the hallway, there was no one to be seen in either direction. That didn't stop me from loping down that hallway, hoping to see whoever had knocked at my door. And then I realized I'd left my door wide open and loped back, buzzing with adrenaline.

I entered my own room cautiously, my pulse thumping in my ears, cane extended. But there was no one in the room, or in my bathroom, or hiding behind the shower curtain for that matter. My charts and lists looked untouched, sitting on the bed where I'd left them.

I searched the room with my eyes once again, then left, closing the door behind me this time. I hadn't seen the person who'd knocked on my door, but maybe someone else had. I made my way down to Rhoda at the reception desk. When she looked up at me, there was guilt in her eyes.

"Oh, Cally," she murmured. "I'm so sorry about Phyllys last night." She shook her head, eyes downcast. "And Phyllys is sorry, too. I don't know how things got so out of hand—"

"Don't worry," I interjected, impatient to get to my questions. "Everyone knows it's been tense here. Listen, I came down to see if anyone passed through the lobby recently."

"No . . ." she said slowly, unsure why I was asking.

I looked at her and realized that I'd have to explain why I'd asked if I expected any better answer than that. Apparently, there was a kind of guest confidentiality rule operating here.

"Someone knocked on my door, but when I opened it, no one was there."

Rhoda pulled her head back in surprise and squinted. "What do you think they wanted?" she asked.

I felt a chill that raised the hair on the back of my neck. Because I had no idea what "they" wanted. To scare me? To see if I'd open the door against the chief's orders? Just Wiz playing tricks?

"I don't know," I answered finally. "But it was pretty spooky."

"Can I be of help, ma'am?" a voice nearby asked.

I turned and saw Officer Yukawa coming our way. At least he didn't have his hand on his gun. I thought about putting the mystery of the unknown knocker into Officer Yukawa's possibly capable hands. But if Rhoda hadn't seen anyone, what hope did Officer Yukawa have of finding the perpetrator now?

"No, no," I told him, shaking my head.

Let Yukawa stay in the lobby where it was comfortable. "There's no problem, officer. Everything's fine."

I started back to my room, then looked at my watch before I got there. It was almost time for lunch. And suddenly I wanted to be with people, lots of people.

Maybe I wasn't the only one who was afraid to be alone. Early as it was, the dining room was nearly filled when I got there. Eddy, Aileen, Harley, Oralia, Vick, Kapp, and Dee-Dee were all scattered among the tables. And Melinda was lugging a tureen of something that looked incredibly heavy to the buffet. She set it down without a crash. I felt proud.

She turned to go back to the kitchen, but caught sight of me first. She put her hand by the side of her mouth and opened and shut it furiously. Was she imitating a duck? No. Now she brought her hand out from her mouth in a circular motion.

"Talk?" I mouthed.

She put her finger on her nose.

"You want to talk?" I mouthed again.

She shook her head.

Vick walked up next to me. "Is she deaf?" he whispered in my ear. There was a look of mild concern on his face. "I've only heard her talk once," he told me. "But she sounded normal."

"Uh, I'm not sure," I lied. I looked around me. How many other people were observing Melinda and me doing our sister mime act?

"It's kind of you to try to communicate," Vick commented. "Everyone else just treats the poor thing as hired help."

"Well . . . um . . . she is hired help," I reminded him.

"Oh, I guess so," he muttered. Then his face brightened. "Listen, Oralia wants to talk to you before the group. Would that be all right?"

"Of course," I told him, looking out the sides of my eyes for Melinda. But she'd disappeared. Hopefully, she was in the kitchen. I listened carefully and heard a thud and a muffled shout from behind the kitchen doors. That's where she was, all right. I wondered who wanted to talk to me. Or maybe Melinda *had* been imitating a duck.

"Okay, I'll tell Oralia," Vick promised me. He gave me a quick hug and smiled.

"Oh, yeah, right," I said, coming back to earth.

Dee-Dee and Kapp were waving at me from their table. I went to sit with them.

"Is your sister nuts or what?" Kapp whispered in my ear.

"Melinda or Geneva?" I whispered back.

"Lazar!"

I saw Phyllys heading our way and shushed him.

"I want to apologize to all of you for my behavior last night," she announced. "It was totally unacceptable, especially since I'm one of your hosts here at the inn. There is no excuse—"

"Not guilty," Kapp declared. He slammed a soup spoon down like a gavel. "By reason of extreme provocation and temporary insanity."

"What?" Phyllys said, taking a step back nervously.

"He just means we forgive you," Dee-Dee explained. "You've been under a lot of pressure lately. We understand."

"Oh . . . okay," Phyllys murmured. "Well, thank you." Then she turned around and left.

"Hell's bells, doesn't that woman have a sense of humor?" Kapp muttered once Phyllys was out of earshot.

"Everyone has a sense of humor," Dee-Dee informed him. "But not everyone has *your* sense of humor."

"I think it was the word *insanity*," I added. "Not a very funny word with a murderer running around."

"Which brings us back to your nutso sister, Melinda," Kapp threw in.

"Kapp, cut it out," I warned, wondering if the pressure of this place would push Kapp and me into fighting like Oralia and Phyllys had, but with canes. Was it the murders or simply something about the inn that produced the tension that seemed to touch all of us?

I would have asked Dee-Dee for an opinion, but I saw Aileen approaching our table at warp speed.

"Hey, you guys," she greeted us. "How're you doing?"

We muttered, "Okay," "Fine," "All right," and she went on.

"I'm really freaked over all this stuff with Seeger and Linda," she whispered. "I mean, do you really think they were both murders?"

"I, for one—" Kapp began.

"We really don't know," Dee-Dee finished for all of us.

"Seeger was my buddy," Aileen told us, her voice rising from a whisper to a normal tone. "We were business partners, but buddies, too. I thought he just fell or was stoned or something, but now with Linda dead . . ." She shrugged, then her eyes focused on mine. "Are you really investigating for Trica?" she asked.

My brain scrambled to come up with an acceptable answer. I didn't want to admit to agreeing to try to find out who'd killed Seeger. The whole concept seemed impossibly naive now, especially after finding Linda's body. How many days had it taken to age a thousand years? But presumably, Trica had told Aileen all about my reasons for being here.

"I . . . um—" I struggled.

"Cally's a healer, not a private eye," Dee-Dee put in. "She's here to help put things in perspective."

"Yeah, I—" I began.

"It sounds as if you're doing a little investigating, yourself, Ms. Meyer," Kapp threw in.

I just sat back in my chair. My friends were taking good care of me. Aileen was on the defensive now.

"Well, not really investigating," she demurred. "I know that could be dangerous. I just thought I'd ask around a little."

"Of course," Kapp said, using his courtroom eyes on Aileen.

"Well, see you guys," Aileen muttered, turned, and left.

I swiveled in my seat to congratulate Kapp and Dee-

Dee, but saw Oralia on her way to our table before I could. I wondered what questions Oralia had for us. But Oralia had all statements, no questions.

"First off, let me apologize," she offered once we'd exchanged the usual greetings. Her voice seemed lighter than usual, less solemn. "I can't believe the way Phyllys and I got into it last night. Still, we understand each other better now. We had a really good talk. Phyllys and Rhoda are even going to join our grief group this afternoon."

"Amazing," Kapp muttered. "Women—"

"It was good of you to invite them," Dee-Dee put in before Kapp could expand on his theme.

Oralia waved her hand dismissively, then turned her gaze on me.

"Cally, I can't thank you enough," she announced.

"Uh, right," I murmured, trying to remember what I had done to make Oralia thank me.

"I'm just so happy that you convinced Vick to tell me he loved me," she explained, her square face growing pink. "I had no idea. I thought only I had feelings for him. I mean, Vick is so sweet and handsome, he could have any woman he wanted. I would have never guessed that he was in love with me." She giggled, a strange sound, coming from Oralia. "I guess I could do to learn a little more about intimacy."

"I'm just glad for you," I put in diplomatically. How could I have forgotten my conversation with Vick?

"Vick doesn't even care about the cancer diagnosis," she continued.

"Cancer?" I repeated. The very word sent a shock wave through me.

"Yes, cancer," she pronounced firmly. "Breast cancer. Now that I've told Vick, I feel like I can tell everyone. I was so ashamed before. I'm a nutritional counselor, you know. All day long, I tell people what to do to keep healthy. And *I* have cancer. Vick convinced me that my condition doesn't make my work any less valid, that I'm still a good counselor. Who knows what other factors might enter in?"

"Of course," I offered. Now that she'd said it, I saw the discontinuity in the aura surrounding her left breast. That might have explained her erratic behavior with Vick. Dack, I didn't want Oralia to have cancer. This was a bad reaction for a healer, but one I'd had before. I wanted to cry for her, to rail against the injustice of it, but I kept my features as neutral as possible. Still, she must have seen something in my face.

"Oh, Cally," she assured me, taking my hand. "At least my heart is full now, don't you see?"

"There is always light," I heard myself say.

"Yes!" Oralia exclaimed. "That's it, exactly."

And then I remembered what my words meant. Oralia might have had cancer, but she had Vick and whatever else brightened her life. I let my sadness and anger go and imagined Oralia healing, imagined the discontinuity in her aura untangling and filling in with normal, healthy energy. It wasn't much, but I hoped it would help. And I also hoped Oralia wasn't a murderer. Was there any way her diagnosis could have led to a homicidal hatred of See-ger and Linda?

Before I could really wrap my mind around the possibility, Vick walked up and put his arms around Oralia from behind. She leaned back into his embrace.

"Did Oralia thank you from me, too?" he asked softly.

"Don't worry," I told him, trying to smile. "She thanked me enough for both of you."

And then I hoped that Vick wasn't a murderer either. What would Oralia do if he was?

Criminy, I had to get out of this place soon. Everyone looked like a potential murderer to me. And the fact that everyone *was* a potential murderer didn't make me feel any better.

When I saw Eddy getting up from his table and making a beeline toward ours, I jumped out of my chair to get some food. This was supposed to be lunch, and I still hadn't eaten.

I thought about Oralia at the buffet as I filled my plate with an Indonesian noodle and vegetable salad, mini-quiches, and herbed biscuits. I added a bowl of gazpacho and carried everything back to my table on a tray. Dee-Dee was obviously thinking about Oralia, too.

"Should I offer Oralia a free session?" she asked when I returned.

"You know one session won't do it," I reminded her gently. "It would have to be an ongoing commitment. I've worked with cancer before. It's not simple to get at the root causes, much less to change them." As I spoke, I remembered a woman I hadn't been able to help, whose cancer had spread beyond my capacities. My leg throbbed. I wanted to cry. My brand of healing couldn't cure everyone. I'd failed enough times to know.

Dee-Dee sighed. "Right," she said, as if answering my thoughts as well as my words.

"But we can help," I added. "Even if all we do is nurture the spirit."

The three of us ended our meal on a somber note. Though Kapp still had the spirit to tweak me.

"I've got more information," he whispered in my ear.

"What information?" I asked urgently.

He looked around the crowded room. "Later," he told me.

Then he got up and left the dining room. Dee-Dee left not long after. I snagged some gingerbread with lemon sauce and bit into it with more frustration than hunger, barely noticing its tangy flavor until I was swallowing the last bite. I didn't know if I'd ever have a chance to do energy work with Oralia, and I hadn't begun to figure out who killed Seeger Snell, much less Linda Frey. I needed some fresh air.

So I stopped in the lobby and asked Officer Yukawa for permission to go outside and walk.

He nodded, then added, "Be careful," as I went through the inn's double doors.

The first thing I noticed once I'd exited the inn was how good the cool ocean breeze felt on my face. The second thing I noticed was Wiz talking to Harley in the parking lot. Wiz and Harley? I rushed their way, my mind buzzing with scenarios from every sensational news publication I'd ever read. Was Harley going to abduct Wiz, molest him, bludgeon him?

As I got closer, I heard snatches of their conversation.

"What you really need is a magic spell to protect your motorcycle," Wiz told Harley.

"And you'd be the one to cast the spell?" Harley asked, his rough voice gentle.

Then some of their words were lost in the breeze.

". . . a good magician," Wiz was saying when I was within a few yards of them. I slowed my pace.

"I'm no magician," Harley put in, sadness softening his words.

"You know what would be really cool?" Wiz asked tentatively.

"No, what?" Harley answered.

"Well, I could ride with you on your motorcycle, see, and then maybe I'd be able to do a really good magic spell."

"Could be," Harley allowed. "But only if your mom tells me it's all right."

I turned and reversed course just as Wiz told Harley to wait for him and went running toward the inn.

I could feel Harley's eyes on me as I walked in the direction of the beach. He hadn't missed my eavesdropping. I was almost out of range, when I heard his voice.

"Hey, energy worker!" he called out. "Don't worry. I wouldn't hurt a kid."

I waved my acknowledgment over my shoulder, embarrassed. I didn't really think Harley would hurt Wiz. But would he hurt an adult?

The third thing I noticed was Dulcie, former kitchen help turned waitress, alone under a cypress tree. I walked toward her, wondering what she was doing here at the inn.

"Dulcie!" I greeted her.

Maybe I should have walked around in front of her first, because Dulcie jumped and twirled to face me, her face startled and childlike, notwithstanding the diamond stud in her nose.

"Damn," she greeted me back. "What are you doing here?"

I took a second to regroup. "I'm staying here at the inn," I reminded her. "How about you?"

"Me?" she squeaked. "Me, oh, I'm like visiting, you know, man, for . . . uh . . . old times' sake."

"You mean Rhoda and Phyllys?" I asked. I couldn't help interrogating her, she was acting so guilty.

"Yeah," she muttered sullenly. "Yeah, Rhoda and Phyllys. You know, to see how they are and stuff."

"Well, I'll see you later." I turned to go, as Dulcie was clearly not enjoying my company.

"Whoa, man!" she shouted out after I'd taken a few steps away. "Don't tell my Aunt Debby, okay?" she whined.

"Why would your Aunt Debby mind?" I asked.

"Oh, man," she muttered, almost inaudibly. "You don't

know my aunt. She spies on me, man. I might as well be in jail."

That didn't really answer my question, but I hadn't answered her request either. Maybe there was a reason I *should* tell her aunt where she was. I shivered a little in the breeze. Just because Dulcie was young didn't mean she couldn't be a murderer. I felt her presence behind me as I walked away, and it wasn't comfortable.

I kept walking until I was back to the lobby. I wanted to ask Rhoda if she knew Dulcie was on the premises.

But I was stopped by Vick and Oralia as I walked in the lobby doors. They beamed at me, holding hands.

"A half hour," Oralia told me.

I didn't respond. *A half hour for what?*

"The grief group, Cally," Vick reminded me calmly. "We'll see you there, won't we?"

"Oh, sure thing," I told him. Short-term memory loss was becoming a habit with me. But then again, my brain was full. I took another step toward the reception desk, hoping to ask Rhoda about Dulcie.

But Eddy popped up in front of me before I could make it two steps.

"Are you going to the grief group?" he asked.

I nodded cautiously.

"Well, I'm not sure whether I'm going," he announced. He paused pensively. "I know it might be meaningful, but I'm sensitive. All that despair. I don't know if I can handle it. . . ."

Twenty minutes later, I was nearly comatose under the barrage of Eddy's angst.

I looked at my watch and jumped in place.

"Almost time for the group," I announced cheerily. "See you there."

Then I got permission from Officer Yukawa and headed

back outside for one short breath of air before the group.

I walked quickly and looked out toward the ocean.

Dulcie was still under the cypress tree, but she wasn't alone anymore. She was with Rick Ryan.

TWENTY-TWO

I didn't even think. I just ran across the sand toward
Dulcie and Rick. It wasn't an easy run. Running is never
easy with my trick leg, and the sand was sucking me
down. But my body told me to run, so I did.

By the time I got to the cypress tree, gulping the ocean
air, only Dulcie remained under the tree's sheltering
branches. Rick had run the other way. Maybe he'd seen
my manic rush, or maybe it was my cane, but he certainly
didn't want to share quality time with me. Dulcie stared
at me, slack-jawed with confusion.

"Dulcie, do you know that Rick Ryan is a reporter?" I
demanded.

"He said he was some kind of writer, like freelance or
something, but—"

"Have you ever read what he's written?" I interrupted.

"No, man," she answered, putting up a hand as if to
fend off a blow. "But he said he'd write something that
would help Rhoda and Phyllys if I like gave him the scoop
on all the guests at the inn."

"He lied," I told her.

"No way!" she objected. "He's cool. He even asked me
out. He just wants to know what's happening, man."

"Dulcie, he's—" I stopped myself. I'd almost used the
word, "evil," a concept I didn't believe in.

"He's malicious," I corrected myself. "Anything you
tell him will be used to trash Rhoda, Phyllys, the guests

at the inn, you, me. That's his shtick. His writing is filled with hatred. He especially hates the New Age. Can you imagine what he'd do to Vick and Oralia in his column?"

"He wanted to know about the workshops," Dulcie said, her voice small now. Then, in an even smaller voice, she added, "I thought he liked me, you know, that way."

"Oh, Dulcie," I murmured and reached out to put my hand on her arm. I wanted to hug her but sensed that a hug wouldn't be appreciated. Beneath that nose piercing was a young, too-thin face filled with longing to be accepted as a cool, hip, and with-it adult.

She straightened her shoulders after a moment. I took my hand away from her arm.

"That dude is history, man," she growled. "Trying to con me. Like I can't take care of myself. Wait till he scarfs down his next fish plate at Marge's." Her whole face curved into a smile. "Whoa, he'll get a surprise then! Sand, red pepper, dishwash soap. Yee-haw! The choices are like endless."

"Don't get yourself in trouble," I warned.

"Moi?" Dulcie replied. Then her face got serious again. "Hey, don't tell my aunt anything about this guy conning me, okay?"

"It's between us," I assured her, reaching out my hand to shake hers.

"Cool," she muttered and slapped my palm. *"Très* cool. Catch ya later, man."

As Dulcie walked off, I looked at my watch. It was exactly time for the grief workshop. And I was standing outside. I started running across the sand again.

The workshop was already in progress when I barged through the ballroom doors. I took a moment to adjust to the darkness, letting the silk hangings and candlelight come into focus. And the people. Everyone was there, even Roy.

"You will each work with a partner—" Oralia was explaining. I sniffed, smelling something burning, then realized it was incense.

"And each of you will take turns expressing yourselves—" Vick took over the flow of words.

"You may wish to talk about your feelings concerning the two deaths—" Oralia fielded smoothly.

"Or any other feelings that may come up—"

"You may feel grief—"

"Or you may feel other things: fear, anger—"

"Whatever you feel, it's all right to let it out."

They were doing it again. I felt the hypnotic pull of Oralia's and Vick's back and forth. I wondered if Dee-Dee felt as hypnotized as I did. Or did her own practice of hypnotherapy keep her immune?

"You may feel the need to be touched in a loving way—" Vick went on. I glanced at Roy. He lowered his eyes.

"Ask your partner for what you need in a respectful manner—"

"All the time, each of you remembering your boundaries."

"Now," Oralia said more vigorously. "Each of you find a partner."

And suddenly, everyone in the room was moving. I looked at Roy hopefully. He looked back at me and began to walk my way. But Aileen intercepted him, holding out her hand. Dack. Roy was far too polite to refuse her.

I turned my head and saw Eddy walking toward me. I panicked. I swiveled around, looking for *anyone* else to pair up with. And I came face-to-face with Harley.

"Okay with you, energy worker?" he asked brusquely.

Eddy or Harley? I nodded my consent.

"Not gonna hit me with your bloody cane?" he added.

"Not as long as you remember your boundaries," I answered.

He laughed, his laughter as morose as another person's sigh.

Harley and I walked to the wall with the silk-curtained windows. I looked past him, curious about the final pairings. Rhoda and Phyllys were together, Roy and Aileen, Kapp and Dee-Dee, and Vick and Oralia were tripled up with Eddy.

"Now, decide which of you wants to speak first," Vick instructed us.

I looked at Harley.

"Ladies first," he said, then paused for a beat. "But I guess you can go first anyway."

I tapped my cane and tried to look menacing. Actually, that was pretty cute . . . for Harley.

"Joke," he assured me, putting a hand over his groin. "Joke."

"Ho, ho," I growled, listening to the voices around me.

"A little anger there?" he enquired in mock innocence.

And then I did laugh. I couldn't help it. Criminy, I was beginning to like Harley.

"I guess we might as well do the bloody exercise," he suggested finally. "So how do you feel about the two deaths?"

"Frustrated and sad," I answered after a moment's thought. "And afraid."

"Afraid of what?" he prodded. He wasn't bad at this.

"Afraid that there is someone walking around who is so—" I stopped myself. That *evil* word had popped into my mind again. I really did have to get away from The Inn at Fiebre. I didn't believe in evil. Murder or not, people weren't evil—

"Someone so . . . what?" Harley broke into my thoughts.

"Someone so . . . disturbed," I answered slowly. "People die. I know and accept that. But someone so disturbed that they could kill, that's . . . I don't know, unnatural. It frightens me because it doesn't fit my worldview. I can't understand it. What could drive someone so crazy?"

"Ach, you really are an innocent, aren't you?" Harley muttered.

"I'm not an innocent!" I flared. "Is it innocent to be unable to understand the inner workings of someone who would purposely kill another person?"

"Will you keep your cane down if I tell you the truth as I see it?" Harley asked cautiously.

Dack, he was right. I had lifted my cane into ready position without even knowing it. I thumped it back on the floor.

"I'm sorry," I muttered and then answered his question. "Yes, I'll keep the cane down."

"You think you can control the world," he accused. "You think other people are like you. Well, some are decent enough, but some aren't. There are people in this world who would think no more of killing someone than you would of . . . of eating fish."

I flushed. He'd watched me at Marge's, I supposed. And there was something of the truth in what he was saying. If we were supposed to be in touch with our inner upset, this group was working well.

"How can there be people like that?" I challenged. I could hear the anger in my own voice.

"Chemicals, brain damage?" Harley shrugged. "But I've met them."

I looked into his eyes and saw that he was perfectly serious. I wondered if Harley was one of them.

"All right," I conceded, trying to calm down. "Actually, I believe you. I read newspapers occasionally. But I've never met a person like the kind you're describing—"

"Of course you have," he reminded me. "How else do we have two murders here? You just don't *know* you've met one."

My mind had a collision then. I wanted to argue with Harley, but I remembered feeling someone's energy, someone who fit the model Harley was describing all too well. And suddenly, I was sure that that someone was right here in this room. The breath jolted out of me. A blast of cold calculation froze my consciousness. I felt, rather than heard, a mind weighing the benefits and risks involved with killing one more time. Urgently, I tried to locate the source of the calculation. But the instant I tried, it was gone.

"What?" Harley asked, his head tilted in curiosity.

"I felt—" I began.

And then the sound of Eddy's crying interrupted my confession.

"I'm so sorry!" he yelped, his voice thick with tears. "I'm just so sorry."

I turned and saw Eddy slumped in Oralia's arms, her own eyes moist.

When I turned back, Harley raised an eyebrow.

"Is he the one, do ya think?" he asked quietly.

"Not by your definition," I answered. "Your murderer wouldn't care, wouldn't be sorry."

"Good girl," he commented. I might have been a dog rewarded with a biscuit.

Maybe I raised my cane again, because Harley added very quickly, "Not that you're a girl, mind you. Definitely a woman. I just meant that you understand what I'm trying to tell you."

"Yeah," I murmured, deflating now. I didn't just understand it, I had felt it.

"Still," I rallied. "These people aren't evil, they're just different, like an animal is different. A cat doesn't think about a mouse's feelings, and they're not evil."

"Never said they were evil," Harley objected. "That's something you thought up. They just don't have consciences."

The skin all over my body tightened. There was no "just" to not having a conscience. But I didn't argue with Harley. I simply wondered how I could ever expect to find a murderer without shedding my worldview. And I didn't want to shed my worldview.

"Are you all right?" Harley asked, a chord of concern in his brusque voice.

I nodded my head, though I wasn't really all right.

"You look a bit green about the gills, is all."

Before I could assure him that I wasn't going to throw up, Oralia's voice rang through the room.

"Okay, that's it for partner one," she announced. "Wind it down, and go to partner two."

"Need to wind anything down?" Harley asked.

"Nope," I answered. I just needed to leave Fiebre, get a memory wipe, and go home to my goats and cat.

I calmed myself by closing my eyes and breathing for a few seconds. Then I opened my eyes and looked at Harley. He'd done a good job for me as my partner. I owed him my centered focus.

"So how do you feel about the two deaths here at the inn?" I asked.

Harley paused, frowning.

I was surprised to see the shape and color of sadness in his aura. I couldn't see anything of the anger he habitually displayed. Was the anger a cover for his sadness?

"I'll not be flip about these deaths," he answered finally. "They sadden me and frighten me. But I didn't truly know Seeger or Linda."

He paused again, and his silence ticked away the minutes in a room noisy with other voices.

"But you're still sad," I prodded finally. "Very sad."

"Ach, I remember, you're the one with the gift of second sight," he murmured, sounding so Scottish that I almost asked if that was where he'd been born. But he was still talking. "You know I had a wife once," he continued softly. "She died a long time ago, cruelly. No murderer could have done worse than God did."

"And you do penance by your grief," I guessed. Only it wasn't really a guess.

"I suppose I do," was all he said.

I heard more sobbing behind us, Rhoda this time, and more softly, Vick and Oralia. But I don't think Harley heard the sobs at all, he was so lost in memory.

"And do you think your wife would have wanted you to be sad so long?" I pressed gently.

Harley put a hand to his temple, shading his eyes. He shook his head. "No, she was a sweet woman. Too sweet."

I resisted taking his hand. I resisted pulling the sadness out of him. It was his core, his identity all these years. But still . . . if I could get his consent.

"Do you think you could let go of a little of that sadness, just a little?" I prompted, part of me willing him to do exactly that. "You know your wife—"

"No!" Harley cried. He lowered his voice, but it still vibrated with pain. "I see where you're going with this. You're a good woman and want to help. But it won't work. My wife would have wanted me to be happy. She even made me promise . . ." He shook his head violently. "But I can't, I just can't." Harley gripped my hand for a moment, and then he was gone before I had time to think what to do or what I had done.

I stood miserably alone, having broken my own rule against attempting energy work on someone who hadn't asked for it. Not only had Harley not asked for any work verbally, he'd emotionally resisted. And I'd still pushed him toward my own goals. I hung my head. My actions had been both ethically shaky and ineffective. And I knew better.

I was quiet when it came time for everyone to share. But Eddy wasn't.

As he went on about how sad he felt over Linda's death, I looked around the room, trying to spot the source of the cold energy I'd felt earlier. Nothing jumped out at me. The person with this energy must have learned to keep it well hidden.

And then I wondered, what if that cold energy had been the energy of the person no longer in the room? What if it had been Harley's own energy that he'd explained so well? Could his wife's death have left him unfeeling to all others as human beings? I told myself it wasn't possible. He carried too much sadness. But could he shield his anger?

I felt a gentle hand on my shoulder. Any thoughts about Harley dissolved once I recognized the touch. I reached up to squeeze Roy's hand. I closed my eyes and let myself sink into the moment, no longer listening to the voices talking around us. I would think about murder later.

"Well, that's it for this exercise," Vick announced much too soon. My eyes popped open. "I hope that it's helped some of you."

"Thank you so much," a voice said. Another voice said, "It was wonderful." And then all the voices blended together into crowd noise.

Roy patted my hand and walked away. I let him go. Right now, I had a murderer to find. I sat quietly, watching each person as they left, searching for that cold energy. I never found it. I was the last to leave the ballroom.

When I got to the lobby, I asked Officer Yukawa for permission to go outside and stepped out into the salty air.

I was walking past a bank of California lilacs, each shrub the size of a small tree, when I heard a hissing sound. I stopped, then started walking again. "Psst!" the sound came once more, louder this time.

The lilacs rustled and two faces peered out, Kapp's and Geneva's.

"What—" I began, but Geneva reached out and pulled me behind the shrub before I could object. Actually, it was a pretty good hiding place, invisible to passersby . . . just as long as no one talked and attracted attention.

"Tell her, Kapp," Geneva ordered in a whisper.

"Can we go to my room for this?" I tried, but Kapp ignored my request.

"Eddy tried to commit suicide when a woman left him some years back," he informed me. "He was in the loony bin for a while, till his parents bailed him out."

And I had laughed at Eddy. My heart contracted with pity.

"I think Eddy's our murderer," Geneva announced.

I shook my head. "Suicide is different than murder," I objected.

"Then what's Eddy 'so sorry' about?" Geneva demanded.

"How'd you hear that?" I demanded back.

"Oh, it was easy," Geneva explained. "I left Melinda in charge of the kitchen, snuck out, and listened at the ballroom windows. They're open behind those repulsive silk hangings, you know."

"You left *Melinda* in charge of the kitchen?"

Geneva had the decency to blush.

"Forget Melinda, forget Eddy," Kapp hissed impatiently. "It's Harley."

I shook my head. "No, he's not the right temperament. This murderer is unemotional." I rubbed my arms for warmth. "Cold, calculating, and without conscience."

Kapp and Geneva looked at me intently.

"Do you know something we don't know?" Kapp asked. "Haven't you ever heard of a crime of passion? Murderers have all kinds of temperaments. Why are you picking out a sociopath?"

"I . . ." I began. Kapp and Geneva peered at me. I didn't want to explain what I'd felt yet. So I didn't. "I don't know, I just think that's the kind of murderer that would have committed these particular murders," I theorized instead.

Kapp looked thoughtful. "You may be right, but that certainly doesn't rule out Harley—"

"Or Eddy," Geneva interrupted. "He could be putting on the whole 'I'm sorry' routine."

"Oh, I doubt it," Kapp pronounced, and they were off and arguing again.

I tried to tune them out, which was not easy, closeted with them behind a giant shrub.

Finally, Geneva announced that it was time for her to get back to the kitchen. But she didn't crawl out from behind the lilac fast enough.

Kapp grinned like a shark, slicked back what was left of his hair, and focused his gaze on my big sister. "So, do you have a current significant other?" he asked.

"No," Geneva answered, astoundingly smiling back at him. "Do you?"

I propelled myself through a break between a couple of the California lilacs and started my way back to my room before I could hear Geneva or Kapp say anything that would make me sick. Dack! I didn't want to be around people anymore. I wanted to be alone.

TWENTY-THREE

I stomped back through the lobby and down the hall to my room, fuming. It was true that Geneva was fifty, old enough to make up her own mind what man or beast she dated, but Kapp was eighty. Criminy, that was a thirty-year difference! I unlocked my door, stepped inside my room, and slammed the door behind me. Then I propped my cane against the nightstand, sat on the end of the bed, and asked myself why I was so angry. Was I jealous? Geneva was my sister, and I didn't want to share? Was that it? Or was it Kapp as a friend that I didn't want to share? Or both?

A knock on the door jostled the questions from my mind.

"Who is it?" I called out.

"Open up!" the voice on the other side of the door ordered urgently. "It's Aileen. Kapp's been hurt."

I had the door open in seconds, my blood pumping so hard I could barely breathe.

"What happened?" I demanded as Aileen stepped into the room, closing the door behind her.

"The police found Kapp unconscious on the beach. Someone hit him on the head. Chief Dahl radioed in. Said for you to stay in your room until she came."

A wave of dizziness washed over me. Kapp? Kapp hurt because of me? Aileen stepped forward. "You don't look

so good," she murmured. Something about her felt cold.
I took an involuntary step backward.

"When did this happen?" I managed.

"About ten or fifteen minutes ago," Aileen answered.
"You know, you're really pale, honey. I've got an herbal
relaxant that might help. Why don't you just lie down?"
she suggested, her voice quiet, almost gentle.

But Aileen had to be lying. Because it hadn't *been* ten
or fifteen minutes since I'd last seen Kapp. It'd been more
like three.

Kapp wasn't really hurt! My surge of relief was interrupted by a new surge of panic. If Kapp was all right,
then why was Aileen here, lying to me? To get into my
room so that she could kill me? No, not Aileen—

"It's just a little herbal remedy," she whispered, opening her hand. A gelatin capsule rested in her palm. It
might as well have been labeled Poison. I pulled my gaze
up from Aileen's palm and really looked at her. I'd never
noticed her aura before. Or had I? There was a red-tinged
halo around her body now. I recognized it as the aura I'd
seen outlining the intruder who'd entered my room days
before.

She stepped even closer. I wanted to yell, "Boundaries!"

And then I felt that peculiar coldness that I'd searched
for in the ballroom. Here was the source, having calculated that the benefits outweighed the risks when it came
to another murder. My murder.

"Is Kapp going to be all right?" I asked, keeping up
the pretense. I locked my eyes on Aileen while I mentally
located my cane too far behind me, leaning against the
nightstand.

I thought about my chances of shoving Aileen aside
and making a break for the now-closed door. Armed with
my cane, I would have had a good chance, but without

it . . . Dack, Aileen was tall. Not to mention muscular. I reminded myself I still had my mind as a weapon.

"I even brought water," Aileen told me, pulling out a clear plastic bottle from her jacket pocket. "Kapp will be fine. You'll feel much better if you lie down and relax. Here, take the relaxant, honey."

I put out my hand. She put the gelatin capsule in my palm and opened the bottle of water. As she handed me the water, I turned my head to the window.

"Isn't that Kapp?" I asked.

Aileen turned her head, too, but a lot faster. I dropped the capsule down the front of my turtleneck and took a long swig from the water bottle.

Aileen jerked her head back to look at me. "Kapp's not out there," she hissed.

"Oh, I . . . I must be in shock," I muttered truthfully. "Maybe I *should* lie down."

"Did you take the pill?" Aileen asked sharply.

I nodded, lying down on my back as close to the nightstand and my cane as possible.

"Oh, that's fine then," Aileen purred. "You'll feel sleepy in a little while."

I lay with my eyes half closed for what felt like forever, wondering how soon I should act drowsy. Would Aileen just leave me to die then? And I tried to figure how long it would take me to stand, grab the cane, and strike.

"Are you feeling tired?" Aileen finally asked.

"Oh . . . yes," I mumbled thickly. "So sleepy."

"Do you want to hear a bedtime story?" she offered.

"Yes, please," I whispered faintly.

"It all began when Linda killed Seeger," Aileen said. I had to resist the urge to object. *Linda?* "Really, it began before that, but Linda's doing the deed was the best part."

I burbled a little sleepy sigh. Aileen didn't need any more prompting than that.

"You know, Seeger and me, we started out as lovers," she told me, her voiced relaxed, almost nostalgic. "We still had sex once in a while. Trica never knew."

I thought about grabbing my cane now, while Aileen was off guard, but I wanted to hear her story. She obliged before I could decide to do any grabbing.

"See, I used to be an anesthetist at a plastic surgeon's, CRNA, certified registered nurse anesthetist. It was cool till those bastards kicked me out for stealing drugs. They fixed it so I couldn't ever work in the field again. I was totally screwed. I had some of my stash left, a few barbs and the conscious sedation stuff, but that was it."

A sociopath, wasn't that the word Kapp had used?

"So I took a job in a head shop. That's where I met Seeger. And with the help of a few cool drugs, I got him to go into partnership with me on The Sensual Body. It was my idea. He just had the money, Trica's money. The creep had me sign this agreement when we started. If either of us quit, the other one could do a buyout or be left with almost nothing. Man, I sweated for that business. And sure enough, once it's up and successful, Seeger decides he wants to dump The Sensual Body and open a winery. I would have gotten half the money the inventory and fixtures were worth. That's all! And I didn't have the money to buy *him* out."

She paused, and my hand twitched toward my cane. But she just seemed to be thinking. She went on.

"See, it was Trica's money. So, I figured that with Seeger dead, Trica might keep the shop. And she did. We're partners now."

Aileen smiled. I felt cold again, remembering how I'd liked that smile.

"I was smart. When I heard about the workshop, I packed all my goodies: barbiturates in capsules that looked like herbal remedies, the conscious sedation drug they'd used where I'd worked, and needles."

So she wasn't trying to kill me with the "herbal relax-ant," just to knock me out. I thought of Linda's sodden body. Criminy, was that what Aileen had in mind for me?

"I thought I might get him to shoot up the conscious sedation stuff. It's a hypnotic, you know. One shot, and they'll do what they're told and not remember afterward. You get the dose right, and they're completely suggestible but still mobile. Perfect!"

She smiled again. I eased my hand closer to my cane.

"Then I met Linda. I couldn't believe my luck. Linda's sister had been killed in a weight-lifting accident because some fool named Seeger something-or-other hadn't been doing his job. She asked me if our Seeger was the guy. We never use our last names in those stupid exercises. So she believed me when I said it was him, and that he'd even joked about the accident. Linda went nuts. She said she wanted to kill him. I told her I'd help her. God, it was so perfect, I couldn't believe it."

Suddenly, I understood Oscar's dream. Linda was the blender. And Aileen had known exactly what button to push.

"I told Linda the plan. All she had to do was go up to Seeger's room, located on the third floor since I made the reservation. Then she could tell him all about this cool new drug she had. She gives it to him. He shoots up. She tells him there's a pool beneath his balcony, to climb up on the railing, wave to Trica, and then dive in. Simple. And if it didn't work, he wouldn't remember, 'cause those conscious sedation drugs make you lose your memory."

I remembered the motion that Linda had mimed. Had it been Seeger shooting the drug into his vein?

"At first, I was afraid Linda was too wussy to do it. But she agreed. So I sat down on the patio with Trica and watched when Seeger climbed on the railing and dived off. Splat! A dream come true.

"Shoulda been the end of the story, right?"

I almost said something then, but remembered I was unconscious.

"When the police came, Linda heard Seeger's last name and realized she'd killed the wrong guy. I mean, Jeez, how many parents named their kids for Pete Seeger, right? But Linda was all freaked out. She shoulda just kept quiet. The cops called it a suicide, and Trica cremated him. There was no way anyone would ever find out. But Linda!" Aileen rolled her eyes. "Crying, asking if she should confess, what a mess!"

Oh, poor Linda. But this wasn't the time to mourn for her.

"The wuss even came to the workshop again to talk to me. She was completely gonzo. And she kept going on about confessing. So I waited till the middle of the night, then went to her room, and gave her one of my self-packaged barbiturates." Aileen's voice went falsetto. "Oooh, I mean, an herbal relaxant," she cooed. "I told her it'd help her sleep.

"And then, when Linda was unconscious, I put her on a luggage cart, wheeled her out, and lugged her into the hot tub, facedown. I pulled the cover over so no one would see her too soon. My only mistake." Aileen shook her head and frowned.

I feigned a little snore, reached out my arm, and touched my fingertips to my cane.

"Then you had to come around!"

I froze on the bed.

"You found Linda's body! I thought the police would assume Linda was the killer and had committed suicide 'cause she was sorry. But you had to object. The damn cover. It never occurred to me that it would make her

death look suspicious. And on top of that, you were working for Trica to find the murderer. I got in your room
once before. I wasn't sure what I was going to do. But
you chased me out with that stupid cane of yours. Well,
your cane can't help you if you're unconscious. I even
knocked on your door to see if you would answer, and
you did. But you didn't know I was there. I ran down the
hall and went back in my own room. Betcha you didn't
know I was just a couple doors down from you.

"But you don't know anything, do you? Barbiturates
are wonderful things. Hope you're enjoying yourself. You
just had to keep asking questions, didn't you? And Harley
just told me you have real psychic powers. You're bound
to figure it out. At least you *were*."

Aileen cackled.

"So this is what I'm going to do," she told me. "You're
going to drown in your own bathtub, and then one of your
weirdo friends will find you. It'll be easy—"

There was a knock on the door.

I gripped my cane firmly.

"It's Wiz, Cally!" the voice came.

I sprang up with my cane in both hands. Aileen ran
toward me. I swung the cane and hit her in the chest. She
gasped, but her hands were still reaching for me. I slashed
her across the knees. She went down, falling on the bed.
She howled and pushed herself up. I begged whatever
divine presence existed that I wouldn't kill her and delivered a blow to her temple. Finally, Aileen lay immobile
on my bed.

She was still breathing, so I sat on her while I called
911. I had faked unconsciousness. She might try it, too.

And then Wiz burst in the room with a passkey and a
hank of rope.

"Is that rope real?" I asked him.

"Hey, of course it is," he told me indignantly. "I

wouldn't use my Houdini rope on her. She stole all my cool magic stuff."

By the time we heard the sirens, Aileen was tied in sixteen varieties of knots and returning to consciousness. And I held the gelatin capsule in my hand.

TWENTY-FOUR

"It was really cool," Wiz was saying a few days later. "I saw that witchy lady in the room with Cally, so I got a passkey and a rope. See, I knew we'd have to tie the lady up."

"Wiz!" Rhoda's voice came from somewhere, and Wiz went running, waving good-bye as he did.

It was early Thursday evening, and Dee-Dee, Kapp, and I were still there at The Inn at Fiebre, enjoying our last day of vacation. Once the murderer was safely in Chief Dahl's custody, I'd decided to enjoy the place instead of running away. And oddly enough, Roy was still here, too. We all sat on the patio, talking, remembering, and re-hashing what we should have noticed one last time.

"Aileen was never as upset as she should have been over the deaths," Dee-Dee reminded us.

"And Aileen had the motive," Kapp pronounced, shaking his finger. "If Seeger was dead, she had a good chance of keeping her partnership in The Sensual Body." He shook his head and growled, "I'll bet Harley knew all the time."

"He never knew, but he wondered," Roy threw in unexpectedly. "I talked to him before he left."

There was a brief silence, then Dee-Dee jumped back in with more of what we all knew but couldn't help repeating.

"Aileen was always there, consoling Linda—" she began.

"And Linda asked me if Seeger was a spotter," I cut in. I could kick myself just as hard as anyone else. "And every time Linda wanted to talk to me, there was Aileen, whisking her away."

"What could Linda do but turn herself in?" Dee-Dee asked for the fortieth time. "And Aileen wouldn't even let her do that."

"Suicide by hot tub!" Kapp snapped. "Pah!"

Then suddenly, the subject changed.

Dee-Dee said, "Listen, Cally. Kapp's coming back with me in my car."

Kapp looked at his feet. Dee-Dee looked at me. I looked at Roy. Roy looked into the air.

Well, we're packed," Dee-Dee announced and rose. Kapp stood with her and raised his cane once more. I blocked his strike and tapped him gently on the wrist with my own cane.

"Counselor," he said, bowing.

In minutes, they were gone, speeding away in Dee-Dee's old Maverick.

I turned to Roy. He smiled at me, his golden eyes like sunshine.

"Ride with me?" I offered tentatively, my limbs weak with confused feelings. "I've still gotta pack."

"Me, too," he murmured. "I'll be back down here faster than a cat's whisker."

We both hurried to our rooms, and I packed like a lawyer bills, quickly but missing nothing. I didn't want Roy to disappear on me again.

When I made it back out to the patio, Roy was waiting for me. My heart opened. And then I saw who he was talking to. It was Rick Ryan.

"You simply can't write the column," Roy told Rick firmly.

Rick smirked. "Why not?" he asked.

"Because I know who you are," Roy answered quietly. "I remember you from high school. And my mama knows your mama. If you do this evil thing to these nice people, my mama will tell yours, and your mama will bedevil the life right out of you."

Rick Ryan seemed to shrink. He wasn't sneering anymore.

"You know she will," Roy pressed.

"Okay," Rick mumbled. "You win, Kentucky boy." He laughed, his laughter a harsh, coughing sound. Finally, he turned and left, his bowlegs even more bowed than ever.

I ran toward Roy and wrapped my arms around him, chortling. Criminy, when he was good, he was good.

We were climbing in my Honda, when I saw Melinda in my rearview mirror, dragging out the garbage in a black plastic bag. The bag split, but Melinda continued to drag it, leaving a trail of food remains behind her.

"Maybe you can do something about my sisters, too," I told Roy.

"Don't believe I'll have to," he declared and pointed at Dulcie, driving her old Volkswagen into the circular driveway. Kitchen help to the rescue! I waved good-bye to Melinda and drove away from The Inn at Fiebre.

We rode in silence up the coast highway for an hour. It was good to just feel Roy with me in the car. But words were irresistible.

"I told you no dark forces were involved in these murders," I finally burst out. "Only two mixed-up human beings."

"What makes you so sure the dark forces weren't at work?" Roy challenged. My stomach tightened. He turned his head my way. "What do you think made those women do those things?"

I buttoned my lip and pulled off the road. The sun was shining its last rays of the day on the gray blue satin sea. Then I just kissed Roy. He didn't struggle. He didn't even look over my shoulder. And once the sun went down, there were still stars and moonlight.

There is always light.

JAQUELINE GIRDNER'S
Kate Jasper Mystery Series

Meet mystery's most offbeat sleuth, vegetarian-entrepreneur-amateur detective Kate Jasper, in these irresistible tales...

"A sly send-up of series protagonists...an outlandish, droll sense of humor." —*Publishers Weekly*

Available wherever books are sold or
to help yourself, call 1-800-788-6262

PENGUIN PUTNAM INC.
Online

Your Internet gateway to a virtual environment with
hundreds of entertaining and enlightening books
from Penguin Putnam Inc.

*While you're there, get the latest buzz on
the best authors and books around—*

Tom Clancy, Patricia Cornwell, W.E.B. Griffin,
Nora Roberts, William Gibson, Robin Cook,
Brian Jacques, Catherine Coulter, Stephen King,
Ken Follett, Terry McMillan, and many more!

**Penguin Putnam Online is located at
http://www.penguinputnam.com**

PENGUIN PUTNAM NEWS

Every month you'll get an inside look at our upcoming books and new features on our site. This is an
ongoing effort to provide you with the most
up-to-date information about
our books and authors.

**Subscribe to Penguin Putnam News at
http://www.penguinputnam.com/newsletters**